The
LAST
WITCH
of
SCOTLAND

The
LAST
WITCH
of
SCOTLAND

PHILIP PARIS

BLACK & WHITE PUBLISHING

First published in the UK in 2023 by
Black & White Publishing Ltd
Nautical House, 104 Commercial Street, Edinburgh, EH6 6NF

A division of Bonnier Books UK
4th Floor, Victoria House, Bloomsbury Square, London, WC1B 4DA
Owned by Bonnier Books
Sveavägen 56, Stockholm, Sweden

A CIP catalogue record for this book is available from the British Library.

ISBN: 978 1 78530 450 7

3 5 7 9 10 8 6 4

Typeset by Data Connection
Printed and bound in Great Britain by Clays Ltd, Elcograf S.p.A.

www.blackandwhitepublishing.com

Historical Note

During the sixteenth, seventeenth and eighteenth centuries the 'enemies of God' were sought throughout Europe in every sector of society; men and women, the old and young, as well as the rich and poor. People watched out for signs of witchcraft amongst their neighbours, friends and families, while an accusation spread fear faster than an outbreak of smallpox.

In Scotland the church was particularly diligent. The Bible was clear *'thou shalt not suffer a witch to live'* and in 1563 the Witchcraft Act became law in Scotland, making witchcraft a capital offence.

The last person in Britain to be executed for witchcraft, known as Janet Horne, was arrested with her daughter in 1727 in the Sutherland parish of Loth in the Scottish Highlands.

*Dedicated to all those who suffer
persecution because of their appearance.*

1

Inverness, 7 July 1723

'IMAGINE YOU'RE AN APPLE.'

I loved the way my father used words. He could paint a picture in such detail that I'd been known to wipe the salt spray from my skin after listening to a story about his life as a ship's captain. My father craved new words like some men desired coin, women or power. He was an anomaly in the world in which we lived. Of course, I interrupted him, as expected, and he gave a theatrical sigh of exasperation, which was also expected.

'What sort of apple, Father?'

'Sweet . . . tender . . . a Grey Leadington,' he added, anticipating that I would ask the variety. 'And the apple is cut into two halves.'

'Both equal then,' I said.

'Yes, exactly like the characteristics you've received from your mother and me.'

This was what lay behind the analogy. While we had been setting up our ale stall at the weekly market in the nearby Highland town of Inverness, we had started discussing how people became what they were. Like most of our conversations we were soon so engrossed and carried away by our enthusiasm that we forgot where we were and what we were meant to be doing, often to the annoyance of those around us.

'So, what did I get from Mother?'

'Well, your beauty didn't come from me.'

'Am I beautiful?'

I was sixteen, yet this question did not stem from a search for praise, rather it was a quest for a greater understanding of the reasons for attraction. I was tall compared to other girls of a similar age and my hair was as black as jet stone. My skin was smooth and, according to Father, my eyes were emerald green, although Mother felt they were blue. Whatever the reality, I had become increasingly aware in recent years of men watching me as we went about our day-to-day business of brewing and selling ale. But was this anything to do with *beauty*?

'Leave that question for another day.'

'What else then?'

'You have her determination and strong sense of right and wrong ... Her love of the land and nature ... Of wanting to understand different cultures.'

'What did I get from you?'

'The most obvious are your height and strength ... A thirst for knowledge, and an interest in the sea.'

'My love of language?'

'You get that from both of us, along with your intelligence.'

My father was not a vain man. To him his intelligence was simply a gift from God. There was no reason either to hide it or brag about it. The sin would be in not using the gift. He was also forthright, treating everyone as an equal and describing a situation as he believed it to be, whether he was speaking to a beggar on the street or a laird on his estate. This earned him respect from all but the meanest of souls.

It didn't hurt that he overflowed with humour and cheerfulness or, indeed, that he was so big and prodigiously powerful. I once saw him beat off three men who were attacking a poor woman upon the road we were travelling then he insisted on taking her to our home so that Mother could nurse the woman back to health, which she did with a tenderness that made me weep, at least in the privacy of my box-bed. This example of how well my parents were suited often came into my mind. It did again that clear, bright summer morning.

'A man could die of thirst while you two blether your nonsense!'

I had rarely met a man more unpleasant and certainly never one more like the produce he made than Inkster. He was repulsively smelly, sweaty whatever the weather and had something so unwholesome about him that you were always left with a nasty taste in your mouth. He had obviously waddled along from his cheese stall and been listening to our conversation without us realising.

'Mister Inkster! I apologise. How could we possibly have missed such a presence?'

When he wanted to, Father could charm bees into bringing out their honey, spreading it on your bread and then enquiring if it was thick enough.

'I should be able to sample that before I spend my money.'

This was a huge insult as our ale was renowned for its quality, yet we would never let someone unsettle us with such a comment and instead usually set out to make great fun of the person without them realising. It was a game my father and I played all too regularly and there had been occasions when I wanted to laugh so much that I had had to quickly excuse myself.

'You've always struck me as a man of unusual wisdom, Mister Inkster,' said my father, handing over a pewter cup.

Inkster looked suspicious, but my father met his gaze with an expression of total innocence. The cheese maker sniffed the liquid as if he suspected it contained arsenic then he swilled it around his mouth for an unseemly amount of time before swallowing. The idea of arsenic had its appeal.

'It'll do. A mutchkin of strong.'

'Let me get this for you, Mister Inkster,' I said, forcing my way into the conversation. 'I expect you'll enjoy it almost as much as the free sample you enjoy every week at the market.'

As I handed over the cup, filled to the measure of a mutchkin, he appeared to be trying to work out if my attitude was disrespectful. Although the cogs of his mind moved at the speed of maturing cheese, I had managed to irritate him, which, I should confess, was my intention.

'Isn't it about time your daughter was married? It seems to me that the firm hand of a strict husband wouldn't go amiss. Women need to know their place and we men have a responsibility to show them what it is.'

I smiled, imagining my fist slamming into his fat, squat nose and putting him on the ground on his fat, squat arse. God, I would have enjoyed that so much.

'It's always interesting to hear the opinion of an educated person, Mister Inkster, but I've never believed that a man owns his daughter or his wife as though they were merely property to do with as he wishes.'

How I loved my father.

'That's where you've gone wrong! You can see it in her manner and hear it by the unnatural words she speaks,' said Inkster, pointing as if he couldn't bear to acknowledge me by speaking directly to my face, although I hadn't missed his earlier sly glances. 'And I thought you were meant to be clever,' he added with a sneer.

There was a brief pause in the conversation then one of Father's enormous hands shot out with such speed that Inkster yelped in fright, too slow to otherwise react. But Father, as I knew, was playing with him and had opened his hand flat, while his expression of innocence never faltered.

'That will be tuppence if you please, Mister Inkster.'

We would normally never rush a customer but Inkster gulped the ale as if his innards were on fire then he hurriedly put the cup down on the table before handing over the coins. For a moment he appeared unsure what to do.

'It's always a memorable experience to converse with you, Mister Inkster,' I said with gushing respect. Father made a little noise that he turned into a convincing cough. 'We look forward to your business again next week.'

The cheese maker glared at our smiling faces, muttered something under his breath and waddled away.

'What a despicable toad,' said my father quietly, just as the man turned to stare back at us. We waved enthusiastically and he continued on his way.

'I think you're being unfair to toads.'

'Ah Aila, I believe you are correct.' Suddenly, he broke out in a booming voice that made several people glance in our direction. 'If there are any toads within earshot, I offer my humblest apologies.'

My father and I looked at each other and moments later we were bent over double, the world around us blurring through our tears. We were still laughing when Mother appeared a short while later. As was her habit, she had walked around the market while stalls were being set up to see who was present that week and what bargains might be had.

'I'm not even going to ask what the pair of you have been up to. Goodness me, I can't leave you alone for a moment without some mischief or other.'

Father walked around to the other side of the table and enveloped her in an enormous hug then lifted her off the ground as if she was a child. One of his many unusual traits was a willingness to show affection in public, even though this was frowned upon by many elders of the kirk. Mother always loved it, while always pretending that she didn't.

'William, put me down this instant! What will people think?'

'Janet Horne, if you believe that I'm going to be influenced by what other people think then you don't know me at all.'

'That's all very well, but it's hardly dignified to be on view to every passer-by, dangling in the air like . . . like . . .'

'A marionette?'

She slapped his arm, which had no effect whatsoever, but he gently put her down and kissed her forehead. Mother straightened her clothes and her dignity with a great deal of huffing and puffing, although I could see she was struggling not to smile.

'Have you even sold any ale?'

'Only to Mister Inkster,' I said.

'Oh, I'm sure that was pleasant. Well Aila, there's some good material on a couple of stalls but not much, so we had better make haste.'

'I'm ready,' I said eagerly.

'I thought you might be.'

Mother was skilled at making clothes and had promised me a new coat plus other garments for the winter depending upon what cloth she could obtain.

'I shall see you ladies later,' said Father. 'Try not to spend today's profits.'

'Well at the moment we've enough from your sales for a small piece of ribbon, so it's a good job I brought money with me from home.'

The market thrilled me. Its conflicting smells, sights and sounds jostled for your attention with such force that your senses were shaken up with every step. Sometimes I wanted to shout out with the sheer excitement of it all. The assortment of goods on display was always staggering: live chickens and ducks flapped in cages alongside their already departed cousins hanging on an array of bloody hooks, while another few yards took you to a stall selling vegetables, fruit or preserves, or better still a craftsman like a leather worker or basket weaver. A queue was forming at the baker's stall but I knew that Mother's regular order would already have been set aside for her. Like most Highland people we didn't have an oven, and used our girdle to make bannocks. Any chance to buy fresh bread was always grabbed at.

By noon, our stall and the one selling whisky would be busy with groups of boisterous men, although they were generally good humoured. For all its apparent chaos the market was well ordered and organised, with stallholders paying for their pitches at the nearby tolbooth and sheriff officers walking around throughout the day to ensure there was no trouble. There were also officials whose job it was to check the quality of goods on sale as well as confirming that quantities and measurements were accurate. I could never understand how Inkster got away with selling his cheese.

We spent a long while with the cloth merchant, buying several rolls of material and striking a deal that pleased everyone involved. Mother was a respected merchant in her own right, successfully brewing and selling ale long before meeting my father. It was a skill she had learned from my grandmother, who had learned from her own mother, an era when brewers were often females.

When she was a young woman, Mother had travelled around Europe accompanying a wealthy lady from a powerful Highland family. Her position had always seemed vague to me, much more than a servant yet not exactly a companion, although by the end of the journey there had apparently been as good a friendship as two people could have from such totally different backgrounds.

I loved her stories of these far-off places with their strange languages and buildings, their exotic foods and colourful clothes, their customs, religions and traditions, so different to what we knew in Scotland. As a young girl I dreamed often about the great Highland lady and imagined her to be a fragile, romantic heroine with a long line of handsome suitors. Yet to make her more real she needed a name and I pleaded constantly to know her identity. That was until the day when I was seven and Mother sat me down for a 'serious' discussion.

'Aila,' she had said, 'do you understand the meaning of honour?'

'Yes,' I had replied, although both of us knew I really didn't.

'I only tell you these stories because I have not revealed who this lady is. To do so would break the great trust there had been between us. It would not be an honourable act and if I told you then I would never again speak of my adventures. It's your choice.'

I had sat for some while before answering. My desire to know the true identity had existed for as long as Mother had tucked me up in bed with her captivating stories. However, not to hear them again or the untold ones that I knew were yet to come would be more than I could bear.

'Father says that honour cannot be bought or in . . .'

'Inherited.'

'Inherited . . . and that we can only achieve honour by the way we live. To break the lady's trust would be shameful. I will not ask again.'

Mother had hugged me so tightly that I almost couldn't breathe, but I could tell she was pleased. I had given my word and never did enquire further, although over the years I still wondered at times about the woman whose journey helped to make my mother into the woman she was. In turn, of course, this lady had also influenced the person I had become.

One of the results of travelling so widely was that Mother had a vast knowledge about a wide variety of subjects and she knew quality when she saw it. She could also spot a liar or a charlatan with the precision of an owl falling upon a mouse.

'Ladies!' a voice called out from a stall ahead. 'I can see you are women who appreciate an object of beauty and my wares have been produced by one of the most skilled artists in Italy.'

I had never before seen this stallholder, who was dressed in such a strange mixture of clashing items that I assumed it was an attempt to create an image of mystique or at least something foreign. He looked so foolish I wanted to laugh. Mother adopted her 'disarming' expression as we walked over to inspect his goods. If the young man was false he could hardly have chosen a worse country of origin for his produce, as Mother had stayed there for many months.

'Italy you say?' said Mother, carefully examining the highly painted vases and bowls on display. 'And is that where you're from?'

The man was so obviously Scottish that he hesitated in replying, probably wondering if the person facing him was a bit simple in the head and how far he could push his luck.

'No mistress, but I worked there for years and although I'm not a craftsman I can appreciate the skill and time ... That piece you're holding, for example.' He tipped his chin at an impressive-looking bowl Mother had just picked up. 'You'll not see anything so fine in the whole of Scotland. It's a bargain,' he said, quoting a figure that had probably changed second by second while he tried to guess how wealthy we were, and how gullible.

'Quindi parlate Italiano.' Mother's face remained as unchanged as the bowl, but in contrast the man's expression went through so many transformations that I couldn't prevent the laughter that burst from me. 'I doubt that you could even find Italy on the map.'

'Mistress—'

'Never ever lie to your customers! Apart from anything else you'll end up in serious trouble with the authorities. There are some nice pieces. Sell them for what they are and at a fair price. By the end of the day you'll have made more money than you would have pretending they're something they're not and trying to charge fees that people won't pay. And for goodness' sake remove that ridiculous-looking cloth around your neck!'

With the stallholder sorted we turned to walk away and were immediately aware of people pointing towards thick black smoke rising in the air from an area of the town where the poorest lived so close together it was said no sunlight ever reached the ground. With so many densely packed, wooden buildings, fire was everyone's greatest fear. Although we weren't in any danger, I was gripped by a sudden apprehension that I couldn't explain.

'Mother, let's get back.'

Our stall was unoccupied, which increased my anxiety tenfold, so we hurried over to the man next to us, who was often a neighbour at the market.

'Mister Sinclair, where's my father?'

'There's a rumour going around that a baby is trapped in the building on fire. Your father rushed off, shouting at me to watch his stall, but it's not easy keeping an eye on both. Now you're back you can mind your own.'

'Mother stay here.'

'No wait—'

But I was already running, darting into gaps in the crowds and pushing my way through when there wasn't. Large numbers of people were moving in the same direction, drawn towards the drama as though they were compelled to witness whatever tragedy was about to unfold. When I finally emerged into the relevant street I was surrounded by total confusion, with shouts of warning and cries of panic competing with the crackle of flames. You could almost smell the panic in the air as sharply as the acrid smoke.

A line of men passed buckets that had been filled in the nearby river Ness and threw them, not onto the burning building, which was regarded as already lost, but onto those either side. It was quickly apparent that my father wasn't in sight and the only face I recognised was that of Inkster. I had to yank his arm to gain his attention.

'Have you seen my father?' I shouted. He stared at me with such a vacant expression that no one would have believed he had been to our stall only a short while earlier. 'My father, Mister Inkster! Have you seen him?'

Slowly, he turned his head towards the burning building and for a moment I thought that such wits that he possessed had completely left him – then he raised his hand towards the doorway.

'Oh God, no!'

Before I could react further, a huge cry arose from the crowd. I looked up to see my dear, sweet father stretching as best he could out of a small window on the second floor, desperately trying to hold the baby in his hands as far from the billowing smoke as possible.

'Save my baby!' screamed a young woman standing a few yards away from me. There was a moment of horrible indecision, with no one appearing to know what to do. Even the men with buckets stood as motionless as if Medusa's head had been unveiled before us. Then the woman spoke again and if our hearts had been turned to stone her pleading would have shattered them.

'*Please.*'

Suddenly a figure forced its way towards the front, calling to others as he did so.

'Help me hold this! For God's sake be quick!'

Several men dashed forward, grabbing the edges of a large blanket and positioning themselves under the window. I swear every person in sight held their breath as that bundle fell, tiny fists angrily punching the air as if proclaiming its right to life. My father never left the window until he saw that the baby was safe. At the very moment he disappeared back inside there was a sickening sound of cracking timbers as a section of the roof collapsed.

'FATHER!'

I made to run, but discovered Inkster's meaty fingers around my wrist.

'Let go!'

'You can't enter that!'

I had no time for this and lashed out wildly, catching him on the nose with sufficient force to make him raise both hands. It was enough. I ran for the door before anyone else could try to prevent me.

The gloomy inside was made worse by smoke, although I glimpsed a rickety stairway straight ahead and began my ascent immediately. With every step the entire building seemed to sway more and more beneath my bare feet. It became increasingly difficult to see and breathe, and when I reached the first landing I had to grope my way along trying to find the next set of stairs.

I blundered around for so long I was despairing, to the point where I almost wanted to sit down and give up, for my father must surely be dead or he would have descended by now. He screamed just as my toe hit the bottom step.

I flew up them, driven by fear, possessed by a spirit, guided by God ... who knows. To my surprise it was actually easier to see and breathe on the next floor because the large section of open roof provided an escape for the smoke and heat. I was greeted by a scene that belonged to a description of hell: in the middle of it all lay my poor father, face down and trapped under a pile of heavy timbers.

'Father!'

'Aila, get out!'

'Not without you.'

We had to shout above the roaring of the flames and the cries of the dying building, which moaned, creaked and cracked as if in agony. The timbers seemed to be alive, shimmering before my eyes. I reached down, placed both hands under the end of the nearest one, and heaved. I don't know where the strength came from, but I lifted it off him.

'Go, Aila.'

'I can't leave you.'

'Please.'

I shifted the second timber in the same way. However, the beam across his back was colossal.

'Father, you must help me.'

'It's too late.'

'NO! I won't let you go.'

Somehow, he got his terribly blistered arms underneath his body while I went to one end. He nodded. All sense and reason deserted me. I became a wild thing, a creature from a tale of sea monsters and dragons. His huge muscles bulged and I thought my heart would burst, but I knew we would do it. God would not let such a noble man die in this hideous way.

Our love for each other could move a mountain. Our combined strength would shift the obstacle and I would save him. Of everything I believed in my life, I knew this to be true.

The beam . . . It didn't budge an inch.

'Aila, I love you with all my heart, but for God's sake get out now. GO!'

I wailed in response and he was about to speak again when another part of the roof collapsed, creating so many sparks that the air itself appeared to be a living flame. I staggered away, knowing that the image of my father would stay with me until my dying day. I don't remember how I got outside. The crowd had moved further back and a couple of men ran forward, half carrying me to safety while an unnatural hush descended upon those nearby.

I didn't understand why so many people stared at me and not the burning building. Not me as such . . . my feet. I looked down, but my mind initially refused to comprehend what my eyes were seeing. Finally, when it did, I raised my hands in shock.

Dear God, my hands.

That was when I started to scream.

2

Edinburgh, 4 March 1727

THE CROWD GASPED AS THE flames leaped higher, Sim's hands moving faster and faster until flesh and fire merged into a single living entity; a seemingly impossible display of precision, dexterity and daring. People held their breath. Children buried faces in mothers' aprons. A woman stifled a scream and men whispered bets on the outcome.

Jack studied the surrounding expressions of awe. He had seen the demonstration on hundreds of occasions and it always gathered an audience. Sim, he knew, was building up to a climax of speed before deftly catching the burning torches. Jack had to admit it was an impressive sight. Before the end of the performance his eyes were always drawn to the slightly built figure of his friend, even though the scene sometimes forced into his mind another image of flesh and fire ... One that haunted his nights. One at which people also cheered and clapped.

Sim broke the spell by catching the torches as if this was so easy anyone could have done it then he casually extinguished each in the tub of water that had been placed nearby. He smiled. He bowed. The crowd exploded into applause. He bowed again. Jack could have written the script. It was the same reaction wherever they went.

Bess and Ellen walked around with buckets and in their enthusiasm onlookers threw in coins. Jack kept a careful watch but he suspected there was little danger from this gathering other than someone trying to run away with a handful of coins. It wouldn't be the first time a lad, assuming Bess too old and plump to react quickly, had ended up flat on his back with an ear stinging from a backhand. Jack waited until he judged the women had collected as much as they could, while not leaving it so long that folk moved away.

'Ladies and gentlemen!' Jack had a voice that commanded attention and a countenance that drew admiring and jealous gazes from both sexes. 'I can see that you appreciate great skill and courage. And I promise much more – acts that will entertain you … acts that will mystify you … acts that will delight you.'

'I can't remember the last time my husband delighted me!' The voice came from a bundle of dirty rags near the front, the figure so swaddled that only a part of an ancient face was visible. Jack imagined he could smell her unwashed body above all the many other unpleasant odours, but he smiled nonetheless and those within earshot laughed. This was exactly the sort of ribaldry they loved. 'When will you be free, my lovely?'

'Alas, if I was not so busy your door would be, without doubt, the first that I would knock on.' Jack could play an audience as well as he played the clàrsach, an instrument on which he was proficient.

'I'll keep my entrance open for you!'

The crowd roared at this and the bundle of rags bent over in a fit of hysterical cackling. A short while later Jack spotted Ellen gently take hold of one of the old woman's withered hands and slip a few coins into it. Once Jack had the current takings safely in a thick leather purse that he tucked inside his tunic, the group split up.

Sim sat at a small folding table upon which he had three upside down tumblers. It was a popular game. He would take a bet from someone then cover a stone with one of the tumblers and move them around at great speed across the table's surface. When he stopped, the person had to pick the relevant vessel, which they invariably got wrong.

Jack strolled away to check that the others were alright. Bess had already gathered a large circle of wide-eyed children, who sat in front of a tiny theatre where she enthralled them with an array of different hand puppets and voices. Bess was born to be on the stage and although this turn resulted in few coins she loved doing it and there was little enough pleasure in their lives to forbid such a thing.

Anyway, could he forbid it? At twenty-five he was the youngest of the troupe yet the others looked to him for leadership because he was naturally good at it. However, he had no right or desire to prevent one of them doing something they liked.

Jack went to find Hector, a blacksmith by trade and the strongman in the troupe. He found the huge man casually holding a rope, at the other end of which three men were arguing about their plan of action. It was obvious they had little experience of tug-of-war and certainly had no coordinated approach to the task.

Ellen wandered around, taking bets. In her early thirties, she was still a striking woman and knew exactly how to manipulate men, particularly when they had been in their cups for the last few hours. She swung her hips and teased them to be manly enough to place money on what must surely be a win for the locals.

Jack knew that Hector would have already studied his opponents, who were so completely mismatched that they could have come straight out of a comedy scene in a play. The heaviest man was at the front, yet his weight came from fat not muscle, while the man at the back was so tall and lean he looked vulnerable to a strong wind. It was the one in the middle who posed the biggest threat, a stocky farmer by his appearance. He also seemed to be the most drunk, shouting orders at his companions, neither of whom were taking any notice. Ellen caught Hector's eye and when he nodded she strode into the open.

'Ladies and gentlemen of the great city of Edinburgh, hear me now. On my left stands a man so strong that as a baby he lifted the midwife in the air while the cord was still attached to his mother and he was rightly named after that most famous of Trojan warriors . . . Hector!'

Jack had always suspected that this was not his real name, yet despite being a close friend for six years he had never queried this. God knows, they all had their secrets, parts of their past that they never spoke of and no one ever asked about. The five of them were a family now, whatever had happened in their previous lives or wherever they had come from. If someone didn't want to reveal something then that was up to them.

'And on my right we have . . .' Ellen deliberately paused to let onlookers enjoy some good-humoured mocking and ridicule. '. . . three athletes who could each of them be mistaken for Achilles himself!'

This comparison resulted in a huge cheer and she had to wait for the hoots of derision and laughter to die down before continuing.

'Take the strain!'

She raised a cloth into the air, hesitated for dramatic effect, then let it fall. The square was immediately filled with a cacophony of sound as men screamed encouragement to those representing Edinburgh. This was a matter of pride and honour.

Hector was a mass of hardened muscle which he combined with technique based on years of experience, as well as stout, nail-studded boots that gave solid purchase on the potentially slippery ground. He held his position for several moments. It was not just a matter of strength, but of giving the audience value for money without tiring himself out. This would not be his last trial of strength that day.

Jack waited for what he knew would come: Hector took two quick steps before digging in his heels, every sinew straining against the shock of the sudden extra force. As the fat man fell backwards he knocked the others off balance so that only the one in the middle held on. Hector smiled and his opponent glared back in anger at the trick. The competition was now completely uneven and the farmer fell flat on his face as he tripped over the prone figure in front before being dragged ignominiously through the dirt.

'The winner!' cried Ellen.

Jack moved nearer in case anyone thought they should have their bet returned, but nothing occurred other than a few men staggering forward to help up their companions. Hector was the first to the farmer and stretched down his hand. The man stared for a while without taking it then he smiled and reached up.

'You're a devious bastard,' he said, dusting off his clothes.

'Aye, that's been claimed before,' replied Hector, wiping mud from the man's jacket. 'You did well. I admire someone who hangs on until the end. If you're in the White Horse tonight I'll stand you a drink after our performance.'

'What performance?'

Hector turned to Jack and Ellen, who had moved close enough to be involved in the conversation.

'What is it again?' asked Hector.

'For heaven's sake, I hope you don't forget your lines as easily as the play,' said Ellen.

'It's *To Live, Lust or Love*,' said Jack.

'You'll be in a play?' asked the farmer in disbelief.

'Aye,' replied Hector.

'Dressed up and prancing around?'

'Something like that.'

'Hell, that was worth ending up in the dirt for. I'll be there . . . right at the front.'

* * *

Their stage could be erected and dismantled quickly and they had set this up in the large yard at the back of the inn. Jack was a natural performer rather than actor, but what he excelled at most was writing dramas for the troupe, which struggled to put on some of the well-known plays that required more than five people; imagination and rapid changes of costume only went so far when those watching had parted with hard-earned money. He instinctively understood how to entertain with tales of corruption and lust, comedy, tragedy and reconciliation.

The play that evening was a version of a familiar theme and when Sim walked on he was the epitome of an evil-looking wealthy man, ignoring his loyal wife because he believes himself in love with a much younger and prettier woman. The audience went wild upon seeing him, shouting and throwing objects, hating and loving him within minutes ... exactly as Jack intended.

Throughout the entire performance the audience was increasingly loud, drunk and abusive while constantly moving around and talking. The play was a huge success. As they took their bows Jack marvelled at the connections that actors could make with strangers in such circumstances. Afterwards, once they had cleared away their props and changed into ordinary clothes, the troupe squeezed together at a table in the inn and ordered venison pies and ale.

'That was quite a crowd,' said Ellen, who was counting out coins with Bess, neat piles of different denominations gradually spreading across the surface.

'It's a good venue,' agreed Hector. 'Excellent food.'

'With an honest, fair owner,' said Jack.

'And that's as difficult to find as a virgin in a brothel,' said Sim. 'Not that I've ever been in such a place.'

'Of course you haven't,' chided Bess.

'It's only what I've heard,' said Sim, suddenly reverting into the character he had just been portraying, which made everyone laugh. He excelled at playing the comedian both on and off stage.

Like most travelling groups they often performed at venues such as inns and taverns, and the previous year they had played for a month at the White Horse Inn. The owner was so pleased at the extra business that this time he had given them a room to themselves, a significant luxury in such an establishment. Bess and Ellen shared the one bed while the men slept on the floor, which was considerably more comfortable than many of the nights they spent when travelling.

If they weren't making their living acting or entertaining, the five of them would do whatever work they could find. Hector was particularly successful at this as he was an imaginative blacksmith, and when he wasn't repairing broken objects he made small items for Ellen or Bess to sell. Whatever they had done during the day, they would always gather in the evenings to sit, eat and talk.

Their dinner was over and yet another round of ale ordered when Sim stood up. Even with an ordinary movement like this his body seemed to flow with an unusual subtleness and grace, an impression almost of elegance but which was tarnished as soon as he opened his mouth.

'I'm off for a piss.'

'You can excuse yourself without being crude about it,' chastised Bess.

'Especially when there are ladies present,' added Ellen.

The two women had grown as close as sisters. Ellen was kind and practical and although she would flirt with men it never went beyond a certain point ... while Bess? Jack studied her across the table, a small smile on his face that he hid behind his tankard.

He guessed she was around fifty but was one of those timeless people who made estimating an age almost impossible. It would be a foolish person indeed who actually enquired. Now as round as an oatcake, Bess was a mixture of hardness, tenderness, coarseness, finesse ... It was often difficult to know what side you were going to get. Jack wondered how much of the real person they ever saw, although he knew such a question could be levelled at any of them.

There were occasions when you could believe Bess was a lady from a wealthy family yet he knew that, hidden amongst the vast array of clothes she normally wore, Bess carried a neat but highly effective wooden cudgel and was not afraid to use it. He remembered once having to drag her off a man she had beaten almost unconscious because he had threatened Ellen. Yes, a complex character. However, she had a fondness for Sim, and they smiled at each other before he left.

*   *   *

Sim was heading back inside, glad to leave behind the obnoxious smell of the privy, when he heard a young woman shout out. The sound was followed by a slap and a cry of pain. It was somewhere close. It was none of his business. The streets were full of danger and people needed to look out for themselves if they risked walking alone at night. Besides, Sim really didn't want to get involved in anything that might attract the attention of the local authorities. He started to walk again when he heard pleading ... A girl, not even a woman.

He set off towards the source, entering a gloomy alleyway. In that instant Sim was transformed into the person he used to be – the one he tried so hard to run from, a highly trained killer whose name had once instilled respect in even the most feared Glasgow gangs. With a throwing knife already in his hand, he became a shadow, moving so quietly that he came upon the men without them noticing his presence. He watched. There were three, one of them on the ground with their helpless captive.

'I think it's time you let her go.'

The two standing spun around and Sim deliberately moved into what light there was, keeping an arm behind his back as if it was merely the affected posture assumed by some gentry. There was a moment of stunned silence before the men made the common mistake of assuming the slightly built figure wasn't a threat.

'You can wait your turn or you can fuck off,' said the larger of the two, revealing by his comment to be in charge.

'No, there won't be any fucking here tonight. Let her go.'

Sim spoke calmly. His experience had allowed him to quickly sum up his opponents; drunks who had taken the opportunity of attacking someone defenceless. The rogue who spoke was big and brutish, but there was a way in which a professional fighter holds himself and he was not in that class. Despite the fact that the third one was now on his feet, Sim reckoned the greatest danger came from having to hurt someone more than necessary because they simply wouldn't back down. The last thing he wanted was to end up standing over a dead body.

The leader pulled out a dagger.

'If you don't scarper, I'll carve you up like the scrawny chicken you are.'

Sim's arm was a blur in the gloom and seconds later the man's weapon clattered on the ground as he cried out, reaching for the hilt of the blade now sticking out of his shoulder.

'The bastard's stuck me!'

Sim walked forward as if merely on a Sunday stroll and it was this absolute confidence, the utter certainty flowing from him that he could kill all three if he wanted, that made two of them take several steps away while the third backed up against a wall.

'I'll take that,' said Sim, yanking out the blade, then, in a display that demonstrated his utter contempt, he slowly wiped the blood on the man's tunic. 'If I ever come across your ugly face again this knife will end up sticking in your neck. Now piss off.'

The rogue stared, but did no more than slide along the wall until clear enough to join his friends, not even bothering to retrieve his dagger. Sim watched them disappear into the darkness of the alley towards the exit at the far end. The figure on the ground whimpered piteously, so tightly huddled into a ball it was as though the girl was trying to make herself invisible. Sim bent down and gently laid a hand on her head. She flinched and he quickly made to reassure her.

'Shh ... You have no need to fear me. No one will hurt you. I promise. What's your name?' There was no answer and Sim shook his head at the scrap of humanity trembling uncontrollable beneath his touch. 'Well lass, what on earth am I supposed to do with you?'

*   *   *

Jack and the others had been joined at their table by the farmer who had been dragged through the mud earlier that day. Alastair was a solid, straight-talking man who had quickly demonstrated a good sense of humour. They had all taken to him and were enjoying his company.

'So, what's your real name?' he asked, taking a sip of the free ale that had been put in front of him.

'You don't believe it's Hector?'

'As much as I believe you lifted the midwife off her feet when you were a baby.'

'It's probably more plausible than the idea that you and your companions could be mistaken for Achilles,' said Ellen with a well-practised disarming smile that let her get away with comments which might otherwise be too risky.

The farmer was silent for a moment before he burst out laughing. 'You have a fair point, mistress.'

The door to the inn opened and Jack saw Sim carrying what appeared to be a child wrapped in a large bundle of clothing. A few drinkers glanced over but such a sight didn't warrant their interest and no one made to intervene.

'Trouble,' said Jack.

The others followed his gaze and they all stood as Sim reached the table.

'I had to save her from three rogues, down a dark alley.'

He didn't have to say more. They all knew what happened to women and girls down dark alleys.

'Anyone hurt?' asked Jack, expressing their unspoken concern that Sim might have been forced to do something that brought them to the attention of the city officials.

'A scratch, that's all. As for the girl, I can't see enough of her to tell.'

Bess was already tenderly peeling away the rags of a shawl in order to get a better idea of what or who Sim actually held in his arms.

'We can't do anything down here. Bring her up to our room,' she said, immediately setting off in the knowledge that no one would disagree with the suggestion.

'Hector, stay here and watch the table,' said Jack as the others headed for the stairway. 'And keep an eye open for any strange-looking characters that may have followed Sim.'

'Christ, most of the people in here are strange looking.'

As Jack entered their room he saw Sim lighting another lantern. The girl had already been laid on the bed and stared at them with huge brown eyes. Bess sat down and gently stroked the girl's filthy hair.

'My name's Bess, and whatever has happened to you in the past, I swear that you are safe with us.'

From the little Jack could see beyond the multiple layers of clothes and the multiple layers of dirt, he thought she looked about eleven or twelve, but she could easily have been a few years older. It was the all-too-common malnutrition that often made guessing a child's age difficult.

'What's your name?' asked Ellen, who had taken hold of one of her hands. Both women were sitting either side of the figure while the men stood at the foot of the bed.

'Malie,' said a tiny voice, as if it didn't get used often.

'Well, Malie, I think you need hot food and hot water,' said Bess. 'Sim, go down and get a pie and small ale. Make sure the pie is steaming.'

'We'll wait forever for water,' said Ellen. 'I'll get that myself.'

Once the two of them had left, Malie stared at Jack as if transfixed. He smiled. On stage he could hold an audience in the palm of his hand and make them experience whatever emotion he wanted, but what could he say to this girl?

'Malie is a lovely name. I'm Jack. The man who rescued you is called Sim. He looks fierce but there's no reason to be frightened of him. And there's a big fellow called Hector. He's also a friend. No one here will make you do anything you don't want to.' He stopped, wondering what horrors Malie had already experienced in her young life and whether he had said as much as he should for now. 'Bess and Ellen will take good care of you.'

With that he went to join Hector and the farmer who seemed to have discovered a lot in common. Shortly afterwards Sim arrived at the table. His expression was unusually grim and the others waited in silence as he drained his tankard then they listened intently while he relayed the details of what had happened in the alleyway.

3

Kintradwell, 4 March 1727

THE PART OF THE DAY I liked best was evening, when I was alone in the barn with our horse, Abel: everything was quiet and still, and I could gently brush his coat and talk. He was the only one I could confide in, for it wasn't fair to burden Mother with everything. I knew he understood my heartbreak and fears, if not the actual words, while Mother ... Something in her broke that market day in Inverness. Of course, neither of us were ever the same.

The year that followed passed in a nightmare of pain and grief. We were so overwhelmed by despair that we drowned in it like a doomed ship at sea, although in reality I didn't remember that much, unlike the morning itself where every minute detail was etched into my memory, as if a painting of the event was always hanging just to the side of my face and I only had to turn my head to see it.

Mother's life was completely taken over by her grief and caring for me. No thought could possibly be given to brewing and it didn't take long for all our hard-earned business to be stolen by a couple of local men.

We emerged from our dark hole to find we were alone, with no income and no heart to continue in the house that had been such a happy home since I had been a baby. And so, two years ago we had bought a croft in Kintradwell, in the Sutherland parish of Loth, because Peggy on the adjoining land was one of Mother's few living relatives and we thought that starting a new life could only be achieved far from Inverness. There was one more benefit: I loved the sea and even at my slow pace the beach was only ten minutes away. It seemed the right decision.

The land was fertile and we still had money enough to have sufficient stone brought in to build a much more substantial house than the usual low sod-and-turf constructions, where people and animals lived almost side by side during the winter months. We also had a stone barn built adjoining the house. Whether our coin had been spent wisely was perhaps debatable, for it enforced in the minds of local people that we were different. However, my mother has a refinement about her and a determination not to drop below a certain standard. For better or worse, this was one of the characteristics I'd inherited from her half of the Grey Leadington.

I looked around to check the lantern, although I knew it was hanging safely on a stout hook and that there was nothing to catch fire even if I fumbled and dropped it. I checked just the same. Abel snorted and moved his head because I'd stopped brushing him.

'Sorry, my darling.' I started again and he settled immediately. 'You're the only one who doesn't judge, who sees beyond my disfigurement. What chance is there that I will meet a handsome young man with the foresight and understanding of a horse? No . . . you're right . . . it's not likely. Perhaps I'm better off with just you and Mother.' As if listening, a loud 'moo' came from the next stall. 'And our valiant cow, of course. Without her we would have no milk, butter or cheese.'

I enjoyed the moment, although it was all too brief. The reality of the life I lived now was always there in front of my face. Two of the fingers on my left hand had fused together and they'd all contracted so much that the hand was almost useless. When we left the croft I kept it hidden in a specially made leather glove. I could use my right, although it tired easily and work demanding fine manipulation such as knitting or spinning fell entirely upon Mother.

I didn't run anymore. I could walk for a few miles as long as I was wearing my boots. Through her contacts as a merchant, Mother knew a skilled shoemaker and trusted the man enough to invite him to our house. His visit was the one time someone else had seen my feet. However, he was kind, examining me with great tenderness, and I could see he did this so that he could create something suitable and not because of any unpleasant curiosity.

He produced two pairs of cleverly cut boots, thicker than normal, and designed so that sheep's wool could be laid along the inside to provide an extra cushion against stones and sharp objects. At times my soles could be so sensitive that I couldn't bear to put weight on them and I always had to be careful to keep them clean.

I stopped what I was doing, unable to hold the brush any longer, and Abel looked at me, sensing my loneliness. I put my arms around his neck and held tightly to him for so long that my muscles ached, as if in a desperate attempt to forget the ache in my heart. Although I was loath to let go, eventually I simply had to.

'Ah, time for bed. Maybe I'll wake tomorrow and find it was all a bad dream.'

In the floor between the stalls was a narrow gulley which ran through a hole in the wall and into a ditch outside. I squatted down to relieve myself then checked that the sturdy wooden bar was fitted securely across the large barn doors. We had heard that reivers were active in the area and knew of more than one neighbour who had lost their cattle over the last few weeks. Having collected the lantern, I returned to the house through the connecting door, just beyond Mother's box-bed. One glance around was enough to confirm she was not there.

'Oh no, where have you gone?'

Twice during the last couple of months my mother had wandered off into the night, and by the time I'd found her I'd been in a state of near panic. Her coat still hung from the peg, so I grabbed this and set off with the lantern. This was really for her to see me, as there was a full moon and light enough to negotiate the familiar ground.

There was no sign of her from the house so with nothing else to guide me I headed towards the place I had last found her, a low hill that bordered with land belonging to Butcher. Surely she hadn't strayed that far? The thought worried me because I didn't trust Peggy's husband. We were forced to hire him for jobs like cutting peat, but I was always uncomfortable when he was around our property and it was quite obvious that he was envious of everything we had. However, the worst thing was that Peggy stumbled and bruised her face too many times, even now when she was heavy with child.

I hurried as much as I could, knowing that if I was heading in the wrong direction my mother was getting farther away from me with every step. It was a struggle, and once I nearly fell, until finally I saw a small figure at the top of the hill, arms outstretched to the sky as if beseeching God.

'MOTHER!'

She either didn't hear or didn't want to acknowledge my calls, so I was forced to continue. When I reached the crest I was too out of breath to speak, and therefore stood watching and listening, hoping to glean some sort of clue as to what was happening to the only person in the world I loved.

'Bonny moon tonight. Shining like a pretty silver coin. Will you come to me, moon? I can almost reach you. If you were a little closer, I could take you home and hang you above my bed.'

She stretched up her arms even more as if believing the moon really was almost near enough to take hold of. An owl flew close by, attracting her attention.

'Hoot ... Hoot!'

This was too much for me and I moved forward. 'Mother, what on earth are you doing?' Fear made my words sound harsher than I intended. I helped her into the coat.

'There's a bonny wee moon.'

'Never mind the moon! It's night and you've got on no more than your shift.'

'You're angry.'

She was suddenly almost childlike in her manner. I'd never seen her like this and for some reason it terrified me, although I did my best to be reassuring. 'When do I ever have reason to be angry? Come on, let's get you safely home and settled in front of the hearth.'

'The moon—'

'Is very bonny and will still be there tomorrow night, exactly where you left it.'

We made our way cautiously back down the hill, my heart pounding and full of unexplained dread while I could feel my mother's body trembling next to me. Eventually, we got back inside and she obediently sat by the fire, which I added another peat to before swinging over the cast iron pot to reheat a pease broth made earlier.

I slid the front door's heavy bolt in place and closed the curtains across the windows. As I moved about performing the other small tasks carried out each night, we settled a bit more. Mother's coat hung back on its peg as I'd wrapped her in a thick woollen blanket. While I stirred the broth she stared in silence at the thin twists of smoke swirling up the chimney. I wondered if this was what she was really seeing.

When it was hot, I ladled the food into a bowl and knelt by Mother's feet. I'd never fed her before, yet she appeared to expect it, and as I put the first spoonful to her lips she behaved as if this was a normal activity. The significance of this reversal of roles was not lost upon me.

'At least you've stopped shaking like a leaf in the wind. Mother, I've said before, you mustn't go out like that. It's dangerous to wander around in the dark. Also, we've made few friends since coming to the area and I don't trust some of the neighbours.'

I didn't specifically mention Butcher and, in truth, he was not the only local I felt uncomfortable being around. I assumed it was because we were newcomers and that people were frightened by my appearance. When we first arrived we couldn't believe the level of superstition that still prevailed in the area.

Some of the wild stories and myths people told, portrayed as undisputable facts, had left us speechless. However, we'd always been careful not to challenge these beliefs.

'Why don't you trust them?'

'It's just the way they look at us. Best that we don't give anyone a reason to cause trouble.'

She seemed to accept this, although I doubted that she really understood what I meant by not giving anyone a reason to cause trouble. I was not sure I understood it myself. Rather, the words revealed an unease that had settled upon my soul and which I found impossible to explain.

'Your poor hands.' She said this as if never having noticed them before.

'They're no different than they've been for the past four years.'

'Is it that long?' I nodded. I was still trying to get broth into her. 'I miss your father.'

'We both do.'

'He was a good man.'

'There was no one better.' I succeeded with a few more spoonfuls then decided that was probably enough, so I laid down the bowl. 'Sometimes ...'

'What is it, daughter?'

'Even now, I can't prevent the events of that morning going around in my head ... The flames ... The image of Father trapped.'

'God was nowhere to be seen that day.'

'Be careful what you say.'

'I can speak my mind in my own home.'

'Yes, you can if it's only to me. But never say anything about God in front of others that could be taken as a criticism. People can be quick to judge and slow to forget. Promise me.'

'I promise.'

There was a time when my mother's word was an unbreakable bond but tonight, kneeling at her feet, I was surprised by the extent of my doubts.

'You were so brave that day, Aila, attempting to save poor William when those men, cowards all of them, stood around watching.'

'They weren't cowards. It was only me who couldn't see the hopelessness of trying. Even Inkster realised. I achieved nothing, except to end up like this.'

I held up my hands. She took them in hers and laid them in her lap, stroking the fingers with the gentleness of a butterfly's wing, like mothers the world over, not seeing their hideous appearance.

'And now I'm becoming a burden,' she said, almost to herself.

This was a line of thinking that I had never heard before and I was shocked. 'You're no burden to anyone. I couldn't manage by myself. You still do the work of ... of ten giants!'

Mother laughed. It was good to hear. Neither of us laughed much these days. 'But I won't be around forever. You need to find yourself a husband.'

'No man would look in my direction unless he had such a squint that he never saw me.'

'A man worth his salt would see you, beyond your injuries to the inspirational woman that you are ... brave and beautiful.'

'There's little chance that anyone would ever call me that, perhaps foolish and ugly.'

'I watch you every day and I know what is before me.'

'Well, I can't imagine how I'll ever meet such a man even if he should exist. You and I ... our lives are bound to each other as surely as if we were trees growing side by side, each needing the other to stay upright.'

She gave me a smile that I couldn't quite interpret. 'You remind me so much of your father. One day there'll be a man who is right for you. God will show you the path to find him.'

'It better not be long or my feet will hurt too much before I reach him.'

I laid my head on her lap and she stroked my hair. I felt she had come back to me after the bizarre scene on the hill and so we remained silent for a while, simply enjoying the closeness.

'You're a good daughter, Aila. Never forget.'

'And you're a good mother . . . when you don't go wandering.'

4

Edinburgh, 8 March 1727

THE TROUPE WAS SUCCESSFUL IN Edinburgh, putting on individual performances for crowds in the nearby streets during the day, then in the evenings entertaining even more appreciative audiences with a variety of plays that drew people from throughout the city.

Malie barely spoke and rarely left the room, yet she would watch the dramas from the window as if something magical was taking place in the yard below. Each night she nestled down in bed between Bess and Ellen. Jack imagined she was like a fragile, rare book that had never been opened, protected by two fierce bookends. She continued to appear wary of the three men who slept on the floor, the huge figure of Hector across the doorway. This was for all their safety as there was no lock and it wasn't unknown for other guests to try to enter, either by accident or for mischief.

'I love this place,' said Hector tucking into his second plate of porridge that Saturday morning. He had a ferocious appetite yet he often made the most money, and so no one felt aggrieved at his food bill.

'What do we do with the girl?' asked Sim.

'I've been wondering about that,' said Jack. 'She can't stay in the room forever.'

Although it was clear Sim had also been considering the situation, he hesitated at revealing his thoughts. 'You can walk through Edinburgh any day of the week and see scores of children in a similar position.'

'But you feel responsible for this one because you saved her?' said Jack.

'It's a strange sensation. The idea of just turning her out onto the street again . . .'

'That doesn't sit well with any of us,' said Hector in between mouthfuls. 'Can she act, do you think?'

'Impossible to say,' said Jack. 'I haven't heard her speak more than a handful of words.'

'I think she's frightened of me,' said Hector, suddenly appearing rather sad.

'Big man, even I'm frightened of you,' said Sim.

A short while later Jack stood just inside the doorway of the room. He had brought up a steaming bowl of porridge, which Bess had placed on the small table where Malie was sitting, before going with Ellen to join Hector and Sim downstairs.

'It's quite tasty,' said Jack. 'Best to eat it while it's still hot.'

'What are you going to do with me?' said Malie, ignoring the food.

'Well, you're not ours to do anything with. You can leave whenever you want, no one will stop you, but what sort of life will you go back to?'

'Why do you care?'

Jack could see that a lifetime of mistrusting people, almost certainly with good reason, had left the girl wary of anyone showing kindness. He sat down on a nearby stool. Trying to make some sort of connection was going to be difficult.

'Is there nobody to look after you?'

Malie shook her head. Two huge tears trickled down her cheeks and fell into the bowl.

'I think all of us ... Sim, Hector, Ellen and Bess ... we would be the same if we didn't have each other. We've become family over the last few years, at least as much of one as we'll ever know.'

'You pretend to be someone you're not.'

Jack was momentarily stunned, fearing Malie had seen inside him and discovered his terrible secret until he realised what she meant.

'Do you like our plays?' Malie nodded but made no comment. 'Will you do something for me?'

'What?' she said, immediately suspicious.

'Will you eat your breakfast? If it's still there when the others come up I'll get into terrible trouble, and just between the two of us Bess can be really scary.'

And there it was, a fleeting smile that transformed her face almost beyond recognition. The moment was gone as quickly as it came, but Malie picked up the spoon and began to eat.

*   *   *

After their performance that evening, the troupe gathered to eat and drink as usual in the busy inn. Ellen and Bess had already counted out the money and the older woman had this tucked securely away in a leather purse. It was as safe with her as with any of the men.

'We're doing well,' she said. 'Another few weeks of this and we'll have enough to see us through several lean months.'

'Aye, there are always lean months,' agreed Hector, finishing off a bowl of hotchpotch with a hunk of bread.

'It's the nature of the business,' said Ellen.

'You know, we do need to discuss Malie,' said Jack.

There was an unusual silence around the table and it became clear to him that nobody wanted to be the one to say she should leave. Sim stood up.

'Well I can't make any decisions until I've had a—'

'Sim!' said Bess warningly.

'Until I've stretched my legs,' he said, grinning. 'These days my bladder doesn't last so long.'

'Perhaps it would help if you didn't drink so much?' suggested Bess innocently.

'That can't possibly have anything to do with it.'

'Yes, well, I'm going upstairs to check on Malie,' she said.

With that they went their separate ways, effectively preventing any further conversation about the strange girl who inhabited their room, their minds and the fringes of their hearts.

*   *   *

Sim was just about to return inside when three figures came towards him out of the gloom. They were the men he had saved Malie from. His hand was already moving towards a knife when a voice spoke behind him.

'I wouldn't do that.'

Sim spun around to see two men casually leaning against a wall. He recognised a hired killer when he saw one. These would be a different kind of opponent altogether and Sim knew he was in deep trouble.

*   *   *

44

Ellen was about to order more ale for the table when their new friend the farmer approached. He was often in the White Horse Inn and they had noticed him earlier in the far corner with a group of men.

'Alastair, you'll join us?' said Hector.

'Perhaps later.'

'What's up?' asked Jack.

'I spotted two men that I've not seen in here before. They're known by reputation and are the worst sort, the type people pay to kill someone.'

'There's a lot of bad folk about,' agreed Hector.

'Yes, but this is the bit that worries me . . . They appeared to follow Sim when he went outside.'

* * *

When Jack and Hector reached their friend, he was backed up against a wall facing a semi-circle of five men who were either hesitating to attack, despite their superior numbers, or were merely in no hurry to do so. 'What's the idea of having a party and not inviting us?'

Heads snapped around at Jack's comment as men sought urgently to understand who had suddenly arrived amongst them. The dynamics had changed completely and the two hired killers moved away from the group, eyeing up the new threat.

'Happy for you to join,' said Sim. He held a knife in each hand and turned to face the original three who didn't look so cocky anymore, although they were too close now for anything other than hand-to-hand fighting.

Most men carried a knife, as a working tool if nothing else, and everyone in the alleyway had one drawn. Jack could look after himself in a fight, but he could see that the man closing in on him was expertly weighing him up. His companion was doing the same with Hector, and Jack worried about the blacksmith. Pit him against someone with bare knuckles and he had never been known to lose, but he had little skill with weapons and only his greater reach and strength would give him any chance of surviving tonight. This was going to be a close encounter for all of them.

'You're a pretty boy, aren't you?'

Jack's opponent was shorter but well built. Violence seemed to emanate from every part of him; his eyes, his voice, the very pores of his pockmarked skin. Both of them were crouching, ready to strike if given the slightest chance.

'I doubt that's ever been said of you, even by your mother.' Jack wondered if he could sufficiently anger the man to make him rash and careless, but his instinct told him he was far too professional to fall for any goading.

'Well, you won't be so pretty by the time I've finished with you. I think I'll start by gouging out your eyes.'

'It'll be a relief not to see your mangled face. Did someone sit on you as a baby?'

It wasn't working. The killer chuckled; a chilling sound. Jack was no coward, yet he couldn't help being gripped by a level of fear he hadn't known since boyhood. The man moved forward and Jack stepped back, searching desperately for something, anything that would give him more of an advantage. He was vaguely aware of grunts and scuffles, the metallic sound of blades glancing off each other, a shouted voice giving a warning. Then his entire world shrank even more until there was nothing other than the face and dagger coming towards him.

46

'Stop moving away, pretty boy. I tell you what, I'll make it quick. I can't say fairer than that.'

If Jack turned and ran, he would condemn his friends to death for certain, yet he could see his own death advancing towards him as surely as morning followed night. Slowly and very deliberately he straightened up, lowered his arm and in his most commanding Shakespearean voice addressed his opponent.

'Fates, we will know your pleasures. That we shall die, we know, 'tis but the time, and drawing days out, that men stand upon.'

The killer was so utterly astonished that he stood frozen in disbelief, and in that one brief moment of opportunity Jack kicked out as hard as he could. His boot hit the man's knee with a satisfying crack then Jack threw himself upon him and the fight was suddenly no longer about skill, it was just a brutal contest of headbutts, bites and kicks as they rolled around, both trying to obtain the advantage of being on top.

Each of them had grabbed the other's knife hand and they were locked together . . . the desire to kill and the desire to live creating a grotesque intimacy between them as they rolled around in the filth. Then Jack became trapped underneath. The man's stale sweat and breath filled his lungs with revulsion, while their arms shook with effort as the knife crept towards his face. It got closer still and Jack realised with horror that he couldn't match his opponent's brutal strength.

'Pretty boy . . . pretty boy.'

The man seemed quite mad, repeating the phrase over and over as the tip of the blade crept closer. Jack twisted his head away and felt the cold metal cut a fine line across his cheek as it moved steadily onwards, an unstoppable evil force that was about to take away his sight.

'Pretty boy ... pretty—'

There was a sudden movement above them, a dull thud, a grunt and then a heavy weight collapsed on top of him. Jack was aware of hands pushing the body away, and when he could focus properly Bess was standing above him with her cudgel as though she was an eighteenth-century avenging Boadicea.

'Are you hurt?'

The question came from Ellen kneeling by his side. Jack was too winded to answer so shook his head while struggling to his knees, desperate to find out what was happening around him. His first sight was of Hector, who had disarmed his assailant and, with uncharacteristic brutality, was beating the man senseless.

'SIM!' cried Bess, before charging down the alleyway with no apparent concern for her own safety.

'Shit! Ellen, help me up.'

The brute that Sim had so humiliated days earlier turned to face this potential new threat and bellowed a challenge at the approaching woman before running at her with his arm raised.

'NO! Bess!'

Sim threw a knife and moments later the blade entered the back of the man's neck. He took two more steps and stopped just as Bess neared. The cudgel smashed into the side of his head with such force that he was likely dead before hitting the ground. With his attention on Bess, Sim had made himself vulnerable to the remaining attackers, but Jack could see that when his friend faced them again they turned and ran.

Hector had sunk into a frenzy of violence and when Jack reached him he had to shout to make him cease. 'Stop Hector! Stop! For Christ's sake, you're killing him.'

It was Ellen who calmed down the blacksmith, forcing her way in front of him and putting her hands on his face to make him focus on her.

'Hector my love, come away from him. He can't hurt you anymore. Let me check that you're unharmed. Come now, it's over.'

The big man seemed almost unaware of where he was, yet let himself be led away while Jack bent down to examine the man who had slumped onto the ground. Even in the poor light he thought that the killer would never recover fully from the beating. Eventually, the five of them gathered around the dead body, ignoring the two unconscious figures a few yards away. Sim retrieved his knife and for the second time wiped blood on the man's tunic.

'We'll swing for this,' he said straightening up.

They all stared at the gruesome sight for several moments in silence.

'Sim's right,' said Hector, who had regained some of his composure. 'Strangers like us will find no justice here, regardless of the facts.'

'What are we going to do?' asked Ellen.

'I'm not dancing the hangman's jig for dirt like this,' said Sim.

Everyone turned to Jack. He had never come so close to being killed and his mind seemed frozen in shock, but they needed a quick decision and he would not let them down.

'We'll dump the body in the river. That should hopefully give us a bit more time before the hue and cry is raised. Then we need to leave Edinburgh, fast and far.'

'But where to?' said Bess.

They fell silent again. In the end it was Sim who provided the answer.

'Well, if no one else has any suggestions ... I've always fancied visiting the Highlands.'

5

Parish of Loth, 9 March 1727

OUR CROFT WAS AROUND FIVE miles from the kirk in Lothmore and we travelled to the mid-morning service that Sunday as usual, Mother walking by the side of Abel while I rode him. Most people thought it was extravagant to keep such a fine animal when a sturdy Highland pony would do the work required for considerably less cost, but Abel was Father's horse and neither of us could bear to part with a living connection to him, something with eyes that once looked upon his face and ears that once listened to his voice.

Despite the fierceness of our normal winters the one now coming to an end had been unusually mild, and from my elevated position I could see the occasional splash of yellow where patches of gorse flowers were announcing their early arrival. The seasons dominated everyone's life.

This particular morning was bright and crisp, Abel's breath making small clouds that disappeared into the air every few seconds. I was glad of the heat rising up into my body as I felt the cold more since the accident. In bad weather Mother rode behind me as neither of us was heavy and I suspected Abel preferred this as he could go faster. He tossed his head and snorted, as if reading my thoughts and confirming his current frustration at our slow pace.

'I think we'll miss our dear Reverend MacDonald,' said Mother.

We had heard that our minister had had to make an urgent visit near to the town of Tain where his twin sister was seriously ill. Nobody we'd spoken to knew anything about the temporary replacement other than his name was McNeil, but I shared my mother's misgivings. Our small, rotund minister was loved by his congregation and respected even by those who risked the wrath of kirk elders by missing a service.

'I hope we can speak to Peggy without her husband getting in the way,' she added, the welfare of her cousin having become a constant concern recently.

I walked the last half mile, partly because I didn't want to appear haughty, and, if I was honest, I didn't want to admit how crippled I really was. This close to the kirk we started to meet others on their way to the service and we greeted familiar faces; nearby tenants and landless cottars, tradesmen we'd employed such as the local blacksmith and carpenter. Few craftsmen made a living solely from their particular skill and, like us, they generally worked a croft as well.

We encountered the farmer who sold us our pregnant cow and he was so interested to know how it was doing that we had to give him a detailed account of the animal's health. Gaelic rolled easily off Mother's tongue. She was born in Caithness, so grew up with the language, and she taught me even though it was much less dominant in the Inverness area by the time I was born.

Inside the kirk's entrance Mother added some coins to the collection plate, which was already filling up with farthings, halfpennies and pennies. This money, and that made by the mandatory hire of the mortcloth for burials, formed part of the alms that were handed out most weeks by the minister to the poor of the parish. Reverend MacDonald was particularly active in providing practical and spiritual help to the elderly, sick and those who had fallen on hard times.

Mother and I made our way slowly to the pew near the front where we always sat. Those who could afford it pledged a subscription so that they could sit at each service in what was essentially their pew or seat, while at the same time contributing money towards the kirk. Many wealthy people believed that being nearer to the front meant they were closer to God, and although neither Mother nor I agreed with this line of thought we did appreciate being farther away from the draughty entrance.

I liked the kirk in Lothmore. There was a beauty in its simplicity and when we sat in the pew, the thick oak planks worn smooth by the years of worshipping that had gone before us, I felt a connection to those people from the past. Mother believed Presbyterian kirks were too austere, too bare of anything to interest the eye. There wasn't even a figure of Christ because of the association with the Roman Catholic faith and its use of icons. Since we'd moved to the area, Mother had never spoken openly of her time in Italy as she feared this might be unwise.

We greeted Mistress MacGregor, who always sat next to Mother, her husband and two sons spread along the pew and their dog on the floor by the boys' feet. A few men tied up dogs outside, but there was no rule against bringing them into the kirk and there could easily be more than a dozen, snapping and snarling at each other so often that a kirk elder with a large stick was always on hand to beat the offenders.

Directly ahead of us, and immediately below the pulpit, sat Murdo, the precentor. He was also the gravedigger, session clerk and part-time schoolmaster. As there was no school nearby he visited people's houses to instruct children, parents paying a set amount each quarter depending upon the subject. A large, dour man, Murdo was chosen mainly for this role because he had a loud voice. The sound he produced always reminded me of the occasion when I watched a cow give birth, although that event was slightly less noisy and significantly more melodious.

'Almost full,' said Mother. 'I think the singing is about to start.'

This was a little joke between us. The problem lay not merely with the precentor's lack of musical talent but in the method of lining-out used in Scottish kirks. Because books were expensive and many folk couldn't read, the precentor would sing two lines of a psalm or hymn then stop in order to let the congregation repeat the words. However, people sometimes sang a different melody if they preferred it and unfortunately Agnes Munro, who always sat behind us, appeared to know only one tune. It felt like a minor miracle when this matched the words actually being sung.

'The Lord's my shepherd I'll not want ...'

Murdo stopped. As was the custom the congregation remained seated and a few moments later a sound erupted from the kirk floor that must have made the angels in heaven weep. I think every dog joined in apart from the MacGregors' on the floor near us. As ever, he had buried his head under both paws as if in great distress.

54

I loved singing and had to force myself to ignore my surroundings. Mother tapped my thigh with a finger when Agnes enjoyed a brief solo because her phrase finished a little after everyone else and I had to clench my teeth in order to stop myself from laughing. This torment continued for many agonising minutes as lining-out was tedious beyond belief, but any humour in the situation died when the temporary minister walked into view and slowly climbed the stairs. His appearance had a powerful and immediate effect, with many voices simply trailing away.

It wasn't his clothes, for they were similar to most Presbyterian ministers – black breeches and leggings on top of black shoes and with a long black gown. The only white items were his cravat and preaching tabs. Nor could you really say it was his physique, even though his extreme thinness was the opposite of what we were used to. Rather, the huge impact came from an aura of hostility, which made me think, although I didn't know why, of a reptile. When he stepped into the pulpit the minister looked down upon us with an expression that seemed ... angry.

There was a rigid format to a Sunday service and when the psalm was over we all stood for the first prayer, men removing their bonnets if they hadn't already done so. The prayer normally formed a significant part of the morning but it was surprisingly brief. As we sat and Reverend McNeil stared upon us, I felt a strange unease creep over me. He gently laid down the Bible in his hand. As expected, he had no papers; ministers who relied on notes were viewed with suspicion.

'Evil walks among you! It works beside you in the field. It eats at your table and sleeps in your bed! Look around. Yes, examine closely those sitting nearby because evil can enter even a house of God.'

Mother and I glanced at each other. This was not the type of sermon we were used to. Heads turned this way and that, people looking at family, friends and neighbours as if expecting to see someone different to the person who had sat there every Sunday month after month. I wondered if the minister was leading up to an attack on the Catholic faith or perhaps those who secretly held Jacobite sympathies. The last Jacobite rising had occurred only eight years earlier.

I couldn't have been more wrong.

'Witches! There are witches among you!'

This caused a huge stir, with murmured comments flowing throughout the kirk. It was a sign of how shocked people were that they made any noise at all, as speaking during a service was severely frowned upon. The minister waited patiently before continuing.

'You think that Reverend MacDonald has had to leave because his sister is sick. I say to you no! He has gone because it is God's will that I should come here to root out the evil that has been left to spread like the pox. Remember the words of Peter: be sober, be vigilant; because your adversary the Devil, as a roaring lion, walketh about, seeking whom he may devour.'

No one felt comfortable at such talk of witches, while many feared mentioning smallpox so openly would tempt yet another wave of cases. The country had been battered by the disease, an unstoppable tide coming back again and again. Within only a few minutes the minister had created significant unrest. Mother tapped my thigh and I leaned in slightly towards her.

'Sowing mistrust is a dangerous seed to plant. It's a crop that can so easily lead to violence.'

There was enough noise for there to be no risk of her whispered comment being overheard. I straightened up as people quietened down.

'I tell you that in doing God's good work I have come across women who have renounced their God-given baptism . . . Who have stood with a hand on the crown of their head and another on the sole of their foot and offered everything in between to the Devil!'

He paused, scanning the faces below as if seeking out a guilty expression. Many of the congregation found something of interest by their feet. The minister could certainly play an audience, his dark eyes blazing with such passion and zeal to do God's work. Then they alighted on me and I felt a physical jolt throughout my body that left me unable to break his gaze, as if he was indeed a snake hypnotising its prey before striking.

'I have seen women who have willingly given their naked bodies to the Devil in vile lust and depravity! I have seen the marks on women who have let the Devil's imps feed at their breast!'

Mother gently laid a hand on one of mine, breaking the spell by her touch. She gave me a tiny nod of reassurance. After that, I didn't let myself be controlled again regardless of how much the minister focused his attentions on me.

When we finally emerged from the kirk I thought that the fresh air had never felt so welcome. A breeze was blowing in from the sea and it carried the salty tang of seaweed from the nearby shore. Mother and I moved away from the rest of the congregation, who were babbling as noisily as excited children.

'I didn't like his apparent interest in me.'

'No,' agreed Mother, 'that was unfortunate.'

'For some reason I can't explain there is something about this man that scares me.'

'I know what you mean. He'll believe he's doing God's work when the dead body of some poor soul is burning at the stake.'

'Some poor woman,' I added.

'Yes. I've come across this type of zealot before, although not for many years. He'll seek out witches amongst women.'

'Because he hates them?'

'Perhaps not in the way you mean. The words of John Knox and his like continue to echo down the generations. I suspect he hates what he sees as the enemies of God and thinks he is more likely to find them amongst women.'

'Seek and you shall find.'

'Mmm, well he needn't go searching in our direction.'

We paused in our analysis to study those around us. No one appeared to want to leave and potentially miss an exciting incident that would no doubt be talked about for weeks to come. I sighed, wishing my father was here. I did every day. Even a man of the cloth would hesitate to threaten us if Father had been present.

'Look, Aila, there's Peggy by herself. Let's take our chance.'

Even before reaching her it was clear that Mother's cousin had a new bruise on one cheek. We embraced. She looked so fragile that I was frightened to hold her too tightly. Peggy was big with child.

'Not long.'

'No, Janet. April for sure.'

'If you have no one else then you must send Butcher to us at the time.'

'Thank you.' Peggy lowered her voice. 'I don't think my husband will want to pay for a midwife.'

'Perhaps we can pay her without him knowing,' I offered.

'I wouldn't want to upset him.'

She said this as though merely being thoughtful of his sensitive feelings, rather than that she didn't want him to have an excuse to beat her – not that he usually needed one.

'Let me speak quietly to midwife Jenkins,' said Mother. 'I can slip her the birthing fee and when the time comes she can appear to offer her services for free.'

'You're very kind,' said Peggy. A single tear ran down her face and she hurriedly wiped it away as if it was something to be guilty about. 'Mister Butcher, he would like some work if you have any?'

What she meant was that the brute wanted money and free ale for as little work as he could get away with. However, Mother and I were forced to hire someone for tasks like cutting and transporting peat, and Butcher was the only man nearby who was readily available. Before Mother could answer, Peggy's expression suddenly changed and I thought that Butcher had approached without us realising. When we turned around, I found myself face to face with Reverend McNeil. Mother was quicker to recover her composure.

'Reverend McNeil, I am Mistress Horne, the merchant, and this is my daughter, Aila.'

Like my father used to be, Mother wasn't subservient towards those in authority beyond the necessary acknowledgement of their rank or social standing. She gazed steadily at the minister, waiting for a suitable response, but his eyes were fixed upon me as though I was the only other person present.

'Reverend McNeil,' I said, with the minimum amount of respect necessary. I met his stare and deliberately said no more so that he would be forced to set the tone of the conversation. It seemed clear that, with the entire congregation around us, he had specifically hunted me out.

'Do you attend the kirk regularly?'

'We do, Reverend.'

The question was put to me, yet I let Mother answer as was fitting to her status as head of our household. It angered me that he was ignoring her.

'We attend every Sunday as Reverend MacDonald will confirm when he returns,' added Mother.

'But we do not know when that will be. Until then I am the minister in Loth and therefore your minister.'

I hadn't thought such a comment could possibly sound like a threat, yet it certainly did coming from the lips of this man, who was now standing uncomfortably close. I was a similar height and refused to back down one single inch. This meant I was forced to endure the unpleasant experience of us both gazing into each other's eyes. It felt painfully intimate.

'And this is our good neighbour and my cousin, Peggy Butcher,' said Mother, forcing him to move away from me.

The minister looked at Peggy for several moments. She curtsied, then we stood in an increasingly awkward silence waiting for him to speak. His expression was curious and I was still puzzling on this when Butcher arrived.

'Reverend McNeil. I was greatly moved by your sermon. I hope my wife has been suitably respectful?'

'I can see that your wife is a good and God-fearing woman and I expect you to be looking after her properly in her current condition.'

This concern for Peggy's welfare was a surprise to me, and I suspected also Mother. It certainly was to Butcher, who seemed so taken aback at the comment that he was momentarily lost for words.

'Yes, yes, of course, Reverend. My dear wife means everything to me. If you wish, I could show you around the area.'

The encounter was becoming stranger by the minute. I had never heard our neighbour refer to his wife with affection, nor offer to help anyone. The minister nodded and when he spoke again he was once more looking at me, as though his next comment was directed at no one else. His previous expression had returned, and the idea of a reptile once more came into my mind.

'Yes, perhaps tomorrow you can show me where people live,' he said.

I shivered. It wasn't because of the cold.

6

North-west of Edinburgh, 13 March 1727

JACK PUSHED THE LITTLE GROUP hard and by the morning of the fifth day even Hector was tiring. The blacksmith was also worried about one of their three ponies, each of which pulled a sledge that was loaded with their portable stage, props and every other item they owned or needed to survive.

There was one addition. Malie lay cocooned amongst a pile of clothes, too weak to match the forced pace that they were making. No one had discussed whether the girl should come, even with her, and during the early morning after that terrible fight she had simply been bundled up with everything else in their frantic bid to get away.

'We need a proper rest,' said Hector, having caught up with Jack, who was at the front. 'The grey is beginning to go lame and I don't think Bess can keep going much longer.'

They were far enough ahead for none of the others to hear. Jack already had concerns about Bess, although nobody would dare suggest to her that she was struggling, while Hector's experience with animals meant that his comment had to be taken seriously. There had been occasions before when they had had to drag a sledge by hand and it was a desperate task.

'I guess if the authorities were pursuing us we would have been caught by now,' said Jack. 'Let's keep our eyes open for somewhere suitable.'

They were lucky and only a few miles farther on Jack led them off the track. They soon found an ideal spot to spend a couple of nights, near a river and a large wood. Malie emerged from the sledge and looked around with eyes as wide as those that had gazed upon Jack from the bed at the inn. He wondered if the girl had ever been outside Edinburgh.

'Christ, it's good to get the stink of that city out of my nostrils,' said Sim, stretching his arms and cracking his knuckles.

'Yes, well, speaking of stink I suggest we all take this opportunity to carry out some serious washing of bodies and clothes,' said Ellen. 'Jack, I dread to think what you rolled around in the other night but you smell like an overflowing privy.'

'Sorry,' he said, 'I was aware of not maintaining my usual standards of cleanliness.'

'Well there's the other bar of soap,' continued Ellen. 'We three ladies are taking ours to a secluded spot downriver.'

The two women had spent what little spare time they could find during the previous few days altering some clothing so that they would fit Malie, who, they had quietly agreed, was going to be scrubbed head to toe at the first chance whether she wanted it or not. Lovely as the young girl was, they doubted that Malie understood the meaning of a good wash.

'I'm off to set traps,' said Sim.

'Then you can wash,' said Bess, 'and Hector can wash after he's seen to the ponies. That means Jack, you can go first.'

Later on Jack changed into a clean set of clothes while the offending items, having been thoroughly beaten against a rock and repeatedly dunked and rubbed in the icy cold water, dried from various branches. Hector had laid a fire and had this burning brightly by the time his friend walked up from the river.

'I'll ride back to that last farm for supplies,' said Jack.

'I thought you might. Take the bay.'

It had long been an unspoken agreement that when they needed to purchase food from a remote dwelling Jack would be the one to do it. The other men were too intimidating and likely to initiate a negative response while it was potentially risky for Bess or Ellen to approach a property alone. At the very least the owner was likely to try and charge more because he was dealing with a woman.

It was nearly an hour later when Jack led the pony back into their camp, the pack harness bulging with an assortment of vegetables, as well as oatmeal, cheese, eggs and other items, while a large bundle of hay had been tied securely across the animal's back. Jack cradled a stoneware jug that he rested carefully on the ground.

'Am I glad to put that down.'

'Is that what I think it is?' asked Sim, picking it up and removing the stopper. 'Ahh, smells good.'

'It took all my powers of persuasion to get the farmer to believe that I would return the jug. I promised that we would buy more food, so he eventually agreed to let me take it.'

Hector and Ellen were quick to unload the items then he led the tired animal away to be tethered with the others. They all knew the blacksmith would be quite some while, fussing about the pony as though it was a child. Jack sat wearily by the fire and took a ladle of clean water out of the nearby bucket.

Bess was gutting the trout that had been caught and Sim was equally occupied skinning the second of three rabbits. His ability to set traps and catch prey was unrivalled.

'Where's Malie?' asked Jack after finishing a second ladle.

Sim smiled but said nothing, so, puzzled, Jack turned to Bess for an answer. She returned his gaze with a strange expression of amusement then indicated with her head that he should turn around. Malie was walking towards them from the river.

'That can't be her.'

Jack couldn't believe it was the same filthy, terrified girl they had rescued less than a week ago.

He had never seen such striking ginger hair, which cascaded in delightful ringlets like the swirl of an artist's brush on canvas. She stopped a few yards away and smiled. He thought there was something more to this transformation than soap, water and clean clothes.

'I found another fish in the net, Bess,' she said.

'Just put it with the others I've yet to gut,' said the older woman, not breaking off from her task.

Then Jack realised what it was. Malie no longer seemed afraid. The real change was the lack of fear that had clung more steadfastly, more intimately, than any dirt on her skin. Now she radiated such innocent joy at being out in the countryside, of simply bringing a freshly caught fish for their meal, that her pleasure washed over him more refreshingly than the river had earlier. Jack knew how fear could eat away at a person's spirit and he wondered if Malie had ever been free of it.

'You've got some more food?' she asked, having deposited the latest catch.

'I have,' said Jack, knowing instinctively that a lifetime of hunger meant there was more behind this question than merely conversation. 'Tonight, we shall have a feast and tomorrow we will rest and eat until we are all as round as the grey.'

'Well I won't need much,' said Bess.

Malie laughed and it was like listening to music from a great harper; a sound you felt rather than heard. She sat beside him, which he considered was probably a huge endorsement of trust.

'Hector showed me his bad foot.'

'I didn't know Hector had a bad foot,' said Jack, pretending to misunderstand.

'Not his, the pony's!'

And there it was again. Despite all of the occasions Jack had watched Bess entertaining children from her miniature theatre, this was the first time he had been so enthralled by the noise of innocent laughter.

* * *

As they sat around the fire that evening their meal felt as though it was indeed a feast. They cooked the trout on the large, round girdle that Hector had specially made years earlier when he had access to a forge. The flat surface was held up by three sturdy legs so that it could easily be positioned over an open fire. Above this a heavy cast iron pot hung from a chain that was fixed to three much taller legs. As soon as Ellen had transferred the fish onto plates, Jack removed the girdle and Hector lowered the pot.

'Fresh trout and oatcakes,' said Ellen, sitting back to eat.

'Rather better than nettle soup,' said Bess.

'You can't beat eating something you've caught yourself,' said Hector. 'In this case, what Sim's caught,' he added, in response to a polite cough from his friend.

The meal continued with a pottage that included the meat from several rabbits, plus carrots, onions, pease and kail.

'That was excellent,' said Hector. 'I'm full.'

'I think my hearing's gone strange,' said Sim. 'I thought I'd just heard the big man say he was full.'

'It must be a sign,' said Ellen.

'A sign to have some music,' said Hector, 'to ease the digestion.'

Smiling, Jack went over to a sledge and returned with a triangular, stout leather case from which he retrieved an ancient and intricately carved clàrsach.

'A harp!' said Malie with delight. 'I once heard a man play one in the street.'

'You'll not hear many that are more skilled than the person opposite you now,' said Bess.

The instrument had belonged to Jack's mother, who had begun instructing him when he was five years old. It was made by a master of his craft, yet it was more than an object of beauty; the clàrsach represented strength and a sense of permanence with a connection to players and composers of long ago, but at the same time it seemed extremely fragile.

Everyone remained silent as Jack concentrated on tuning the instrument, altering the tension on the shiny brass strings using a small wooden key. He played a few bars of a tune then made some finer adjustments until he was satisfied. He paused. Even the ponies tethered nearby were silent, as if anticipating a great event.

Jack began with a slow air, the strings reflecting the light from the flames so that they appeared to dance to the notes. He had performed before many audiences over the years, yet sitting by the fire with the people who were closest to him he felt as happy as he believed it was possible to be, despite the horror in Edinburgh only a few days earlier.

Jack thought the music had awoken a fairy in the woods when he imagined he heard beautiful singing. Without stopping, he glanced around. The others were also looking about them. Then the sound became more defined and there was suddenly no doubt that he was really hearing it.

It was Malie.

Jack was no longer the centre of everyone's attention, merely the accompaniment to a voice that was so pure he didn't believe he had known its equal. It was a tragic love song about a man and woman who loved each other yet never revealed their feelings until they were old and he lay dying in her arms. When they finished, no one applauded. There are some experiences which go far beyond a performance that can be adequately praised with clapping or cheering. Such events touch the soul and there is no sound that can be made to mark their occurrence. The only response is silence, and they were silent for a long while.

Finally, without speaking, Malie stood and walked slowly around the fire to face Hector, sitting on the ground with his back against one of the sledges. Everyone watched as the two figures studied each other, one so large and strong and the other so small and delicate. Then Malie took a couple of steps forward, sat down on Hector's knee and cuddled into him, while he put his huge arms around her as if she was his young daughter and this was the most natural thing in the world. Jack thought it was one of the most unexpected sights he had ever seen. He looked about; Sim raised an eyebrow, Bess nodded and Ellen was grinning widely. The only people who appeared to think there was nothing unusual about the situation were the two figures at the centre of everyone's attention.

The evening wore on with songs, music and storytelling, until the jug was empty and Malie was asleep in Hector's arms. Bess got up and headed to a cluster of nearby trees that provided some privacy.

'I'm for my bed,' she said upon returning.

As usual one of the sledges had been emptied and placed on its side to provide a solid backing for the heavy canvas that had been fixed via ropes and stout wooden poles to create a shelter for the women. Only the side facing the fire was left open. Bess got down and moved farther under cover.

Hector stood up, Malie appearing to weigh nothing in his arms. Jack studied the scene and he knew that Sim and Ellen were doing the same. The blacksmith knelt down and gently laid the girl next to Bess, who immediately wrapped a blanket around her.

'It's been a long day. I think I'll join them. Good night,' said Ellen, although she was held up by Hector still fussing.

'He'll be tucking you up in a minute,' said Sim.

Ellen replied with a rude hand gesture that made the two men watching smile.

'Thank you, Hector,' said Ellen. 'I'll see to her now.'

'If you're sure.'

'Yes. Go and keep those two out of trouble.'

Ellen was eventually able to get under the blankets and Jack realised that since Sim had rescued Malie she had slept every night between those fierce bookends. He marvelled at how quickly she had become an integral part of their tightly knit group. Perhaps what they had been missing all these years was to have a child amongst them.

* * *

The three men sat next to each other, leaning against a sledge, which allowed them to talk without disturbing the others and more easily pass around the flask of whisky that had been brought out. Jack was concerned that no one had discussed the fight and the death of the man, a horror that he was sure preyed on everyone's mind.

'How are you both?' he said, once they had been watching the flames in silence for a while.

After a long pause, Sim replied, 'I had hoped that when I joined the troupe I would never have to kill again. There've been too many already. During these last six years I haven't thought of them, haven't seen their faces when I close my eyes, but since the other night they've come back to haunt me like a plague of bloody locusts. Strange that it's not the face of the one I knifed in Edinburgh. I can't remember what he looked like at all.'

They were silent again, passing around the flask. Despite the closeness of their lives, the constant being together day after day, there were still conversations that had never taken place, subjects never broached.

'What about you, Jack?' asked Sim. 'Have you ever killed a man?'

Jack had never spoken to anyone of this terrible secret in this life, but his recent near-death experience had changed something within him and now that he had been asked the question he realised that he wanted to speak of it.

'Once,' he said. 'I wasn't much more than a boy.'

'Do you regret it?'

'Regret? Yes and no, I suppose. It's a terrible thing to do, yet I guess at the time I felt it was the only thing to do. It's odd, I don't recall anything of actually stabbing him.'

'Is it his face you see in your nightmares?'

'No.'

'You cry out at times, you know, in your sleep.'

'Do I?'

'Something haunts you. Over the years, we've all of us gently stroked your head on occasions, speaking soft words of comfort to ease your troubles until you've settled again.'

Jack couldn't speak for several minutes. That the others had been doing this for him, a grown man, and he hadn't even been aware touched him more deeply than he could express.

'I didn't know. It's not the image of the man I killed that haunts my dreams. It's another one altogether.'

It was easier to speak sitting side by side in the dark, not having to make eye contact. They had the flames to watch and it was almost as if each of them spoke to the fire. So far Hector hadn't joined in.

'You're quiet, big man,' said Sim, patting his friend on the thigh.

'Aye. The truth is, I didn't believe I had such violence within me. If Ellen hadn't stopped me, I would have carried on until I had sent that man to his grave.'

'It was fear, a reaction to the threat of someone trying to knife you and nothing to be ashamed of,' said Sim. 'I've seen people do far worse things because of their terror.'

'Even so,' said Hector, 'it troubles me to find that I could have committed such an act, that I didn't stop once he wasn't a danger anymore.'

'Well, he would have been no loss to the world, that's for certain. And the one who attacked you Jack was a mad bastard. The five of them had been confident and not in any hurry to finish me off. Before you two arrived I had time enough to get an impression of him and there was something wrong in his head.'

'Maggots,' said Hector.

'Maggots would have been the least of it,' replied Sim.

'I couldn't beat him,' admitted Jack.

'I'm not surprised, he was a hired killer,' said Sim. 'You did well. How's the cheek?'

Jack instinctively reached up, although there was little of the injury to feel. Fortunately, the cut hadn't been deep and Ellen had insisted on rubbing whisky onto it once they had returned to their room.

'Healing fine, thanks. Bess saved my life.'

'And possibly mine, drawing away the one she did.'

'I think,' said Hector, 'she's secretly punishing herself at the thought that she killed that man.'

'She didn't. He was already dead from my blade. He just hadn't realised.'

'Yes, but you need to speak to her and explain that,' said Hector. 'It's an awful thing for a woman to believe she's taken a person's life. It preys on their conscience more than us.'

'I do need to speak to her.'

Hector, who was between the other two, passed Sim the flask and they had a few moments of silence while the whisky did another round. The affection Sim and Bess had for each other had been suddenly thrust into the open down that dim alley. No one had spoken of it since, yet at some point the situation would have to be acknowledged.

'That song of Malie's,' said Sim, 'Christ, it could have been about Bess and me ... Two people in love, neither telling the other until they're old. What a pair of fools we are.'

'Perhaps we should stay here for a while,' said Hector, 'and make sure the grey is fully recovered. That would give people the chance to find some privacy for conversations that need to be had. What do you think, Jack?'

'It's fine with me if that's what everyone wants. I'd be happy to rest here for longer. There's plenty of fish and game and the farmer will sell us other supplies. Maybe Hector, you should speak to Ellen about your feelings and thank her for what she did ... Make sure she's alright.'

'Aye, I'll do that. There's one more thing about that night in Edinburgh.'

'What is it?' asked Sim.

'Malie must never know about the killing.'

7

Kintradwell, 14 March 1727

LTHOUGH WE HAD OUR OWN box-beds, Mother and I slept in the same one during the winter months and I woke that Friday morning to find myself wrapped in her arms. I felt safe and had no desire to endure the cold air any earlier than necessary. I snuggled in even more closely, remembering how she would often say when I did this that I was like a wee shrew hiding from a storm.

Other than her I had never touched another person since the accident. People didn't want any physical contact; children were frightened and adults either wary or repulsed. Women no longer let me hold their babies. Although I was reconciled to living a life without a husband or children, I cried inside at times for the all-consuming want of simply being held by someone. Of course, such a thing wasn't simple.

A box-bed was designed to protect the user from draughts yet they also felt to me that they were somehow separate to the rest of the world. Whatever happened outside, this was our little sanctuary, a place no one else ventured and where there was nobody to put us down. Sometimes, in my dreams, I was still whole and could run and dance and do a hundred complex tasks. Even after waking there was a part of me that would cling to the illusion for as long as possible. While we remained in our sanctuary, it was easier to pretend.

Mother stroked my hair. 'Another day calls, and we must answer.'

'Good morning, Mother. I'm quite happy here.'

'Yes, but my bladder is not going to let me lie much longer, so make the most of the next few minutes because then we're getting up.'

Every night, when we undressed, we laid our clothes carefully on two nearby chairs so that they were in the right order to put back on over our shifts, the only garment we wore apart from our bedtime linen caps. We often had to find everything in complete darkness. Reluctantly, I got up and took two steps to the right to reach my chair and began dressing as quickly as I could. Mother had gone in the other direction.

I quickly pulled up woollen stockings and once I had secured these with garters I put on my boots before adding the first of my petticoats. The stays were the most difficult item for me as I sometimes fumbled with the cords, particularly if my fingers were cold, but I managed that morning, the stomacher held securely but not too tightly or it restricted movement.

I then fitted the two pocket bags around my hips and my second petticoat, this one quilted for warmth. I tucked a linen kerchief around my shoulders and added my outer petticoat, followed by an apron around my waist and finished by replacing the cap with the one worn during the day. Sometimes Mother and I raced each other and we could end up sitting on our chairs part-dressed, tears streaming down our faces, laughing at our own foolishness.

There was little that could be done until we had some light. Unless we were away we strove never to let our peat fire go out completely and the previous night I had banked it up with extra turfs and ash so that it could be coaxed quickly back to life. There was soon enough flame to ignite a candle, which Mother put inside a glass lantern before she went off to milk our cow while I lit more candles and set the kettle to boil.

We preferred to start each day with a wash and a cup of tea, avoiding the usual habit people had of drinking ale first thing, despite being brewers. Maybe it was because of it. For breakfast we normally ate brose, and when the water was boiled I poured it onto some oatmeal and stirred this together with a little salt and butter. By the time Mother returned with a pail of warm milk, the tea and our meal were ready.

'How are the animals?'

'What you really mean is "how is Abel". He's fine. You can let him out after we've eaten.'

When the cottage was warm we ate meals at the table but in the mornings we sat either side of the fire. Once the breakfast items had been cleared away, we sorted out the bedding. Mother and I worked well as a team. We folded the thick woollen blankets and laid them aside then removed the linen sheet, which would be thrown over the line for a few hours to freshen it. The material was about thirteen feet long, covering the mattress and then being folded at the bottom to come back up to form the top sheet.

Heather was plentiful locally, so we dried large quantities and used this as the filling rather than straw. It was less inclined to go hard and lumpy, though we still had to shake the mattress every morning. We drew the heavy curtain across the opening to the box-bed during the daytime; on the coldest nights, we slept with it drawn too, cocooned in our sanctuary.

We had our routines. As it was a Friday I wound up Father's longcase clock. The London maker had created an object of intricate beauty; sometimes the coloured floral marquetery within the walnut case appeared to dance in the light of our fire. Father once spent half a day explaining how the mechanism operated, drawing numerous diagrams and removing the hood so that we could more easily study the workings.

Now I carefully wound it once a week, just as he demonstrated all those years ago. Father's career as a ship's captain meant that his strict sense of order and precision had influenced us to the point where we often joked our cottage would pass inspection by an admiral in the Royal Navy.

I went into the barn to let Abel and the cow outside. They were followed by more than a dozen hens, some more reluctant to leave than others. These were brought inside each night. It was difficult to keep them safe from the fox, which had recently become more daring. We had lost two over the last month. With the barn to myself I started hunting for eggs, finding them in the usual hiding places and a few new ones.

Our main task was to brew ale. Like other local brewers and whisky distillers we bought malted barley from a maltster near the Sutherland town of Brora. Following the harvest, the maltster allowed his barley to germinate for a few days before drying it, which stopped the process and meant that it could be stored until ready for use.

Over the winter months we only made sufficient ale for ourselves and to sell to people nearby who didn't make their own. However, we would start attending the Dornoch market the following month and this meant we had to increase our output significantly. We kept our malted barley on a high shelf in the barn and the previous afternoon my mother had crushed the amount needed and spread this in the bottom of our large oak tub, which we had scalded out earlier on.

The copper vessel that was used for washing laundry had been thoroughly cleaned and we hung this just above the fire before filling it with fifteen gallons of water, which required several trips to the Kintradwell burn. In the autumn we added heather blossom, but at this time of year we included seaweed as this was so readily available and it gave our ale a distinct flavour that helped to set us apart from most other merchants.

'It's at this stage that I wish my ancestors had been skilled at a more elegant craft, like embroidery.'

'Mother, you say that every time.'

She smiled, but there was some truth in her comment as I knew that each year she found the task a little more physically challenging, particularly as her rheumatism became worse with every winter. Fortunately, although I could hardly grip with my left hand, my arms were strong and also, when our house was built, Mother paid the blacksmith to incorporate a system of pulleys and chains which he had to make specially to her design. These allowed us to gently swing the copper vessel out from the fire.

We still had to tip the boiling water into the oak tub and this part of the process required coordination, care and a significant amount of effort. Mother had made thick gloves to protect our hands from splashes, and as we slowly lifted one side of the copper we were surrounded by even more steam, tinged with the growing scents of the craft.

Despite the door and windows being open our clothes felt damp by the time we had finished and both of us took a moment to remove our quilted petticoats. We had been stirring the mixture in the tub for about twenty minutes when we heard a voice outside and moments later a dishevelled figure stood in the doorway.

'Goodness me, Peggy, you look half frozen.'

'I'm alright, Janet. Mister Butcher has sent me for some ale.'

Neither of us commented as to why he hadn't come himself. He was likely doing very little. Mother insisted the three of us fortified ourselves, so we put the copper out of the way and moved an armchair back to its usual place near the fire, then I set the kettle to boil while Mother fetched oatmeal scones, butter and cheese.

'I mustn't stay long.'

Peggy was so pale that the black and blue on her face stood out even more hideously than normal. Mother and I made no mention of the injuries and tried to make light conversation. It was obvious that Peggy was not in a good way. Her clothes were dirty and her bulging stomach only emphasised how terribly thin she was.

'If I take the ale over on Abel you don't need to rush back,' I said.

'That's an excellent idea,' agreed Mother.

'Well ...'

Peggy wasn't a quick thinker, so we always felt that we had to work out what was best for her without taking away her right to make her own decisions, as much as any woman had such a right.

'And I'll walk back with you, so there's plenty of time to eat something,' said Mother, handing over a plate along with a clean linen napkin, her cousin almost hesitating to touch the latter.

Later on Mother helped me load two stoneware jugs into Abel's pack harness. We had left our guest by the fire.

'At least she's stopped shaking,' I said.

'I'll bring some food when we come over, but you'll be with him by yourself, so be careful.'

I nodded. Nothing else needed to be said. Mother knew that I hated these encounters, yet what else could we do? On horseback the journey was only about ten minutes, and I arrived to find Butcher cursing his cow, which appeared not to be giving much milk.

'What do you want? Oh, my ale. About time. A hard-working man needs a drink to sustain him.'

I didn't like him being so close, but it was a lot easier to let him remove the jugs while I remained on the horse. However, when he unnecessarily touched my leg with his hand, I pressed my knee to make Abel move towards him so that he was forced to jump backwards. Abel didn't like him either.

'Can't you control that horse!'

'I don't think he's fond of being touched without good reason, rather like me!'

He glowered yet said nothing and retrieved the second jug without incident. There was no suggestion of him paying. Mother and I had long ago decided that providing ale was worth the cost if it meant a reduction in violence towards Peggy. There were so many times in my life when I wished I was a man the size of my father and could thrash men such as Butcher for their cruelty.

'Where's my wife?' he said, almost as if he'd just remembered he had one.

'In case you hadn't noticed she's heavily pregnant and needed to eat and rest before returning. My mother will come with her shortly, so you can enjoy your free ale in peace.'

I turned the horse and left without another word. On the way home I met Mother and Peggy, and I sensed that their slow speed was due to a reluctance to arrive at their destination rather than because of Peggy's condition. Unfortunately, it was never an option to offer her a ride on Abel as she was frightened of him, even though he was the gentlest of horses.

'Ale successfully delivered?' asked Mother, who was carrying a large cloth tied up in a bundle.

'Yes, the only problem seemed to be with the cow.'

'We've lately been getting a poor amount of milk from her,' said Peggy.

'It looks underfed,' I said, although Mother's expression warned me not to comment further. In truth the beast seemed even more starved than Peggy. Considering the hardiness of Highland cattle, I could never understand how Butcher managed to keep an animal in such poor condition throughout the entire year.

We said our farewells without further comment. When I arrived home I hung the pack harness in the barn and let Abel loose in the small, enclosed area we had. I was still thinking about our poor neighbour and what else we might do to help as I walked into the cottage and the next moment found myself having to stifle a cry of alarm.

Reverend McNeil sat in Mother's chair by the fire as if he owned it. The front door of a house was rarely fitted with a lock and key because Highlanders believed they had an obligation to welcome friends and strangers into their home. Even so, I was so shocked at finding the minister that I merely stared at him from the doorway. He didn't stand or comment and returned the gaze as if enjoying my discomfort.

I realised that I hadn't seen his horse, which meant that he must have hidden it once he discovered we weren't there. Very deliberately I let my eyes look slowly about the room and although everything appeared to be in its usual place, I couldn't help feeling that he had taken the opportunity of our absence to search through our possessions. The thought made me crawl inside.

'Reverend McNeil,' I said eventually.

'You've been visiting?'

'Peggy came here requesting ale for her husband. I took it over on our horse while my mother walked back with Peggy. She'll be here soon.'

I shut the door. He wasn't going to intimidate me in our own home.

'So, you were alone with her husband?'

'A few moments only and I remained on the horse.' He would get nowhere implying there was something going on between Butcher and me.

'You're brewing ale,' he said, peering at the contents of the oak tub near his feet. 'What happens next?'

'We draw off the liquid, leaving behind the malted barley and seaweed, and put it in the copper to be brought to the boil again, then when it's cooled a second time we add barm – that's the foam from the previous brewing.'

'Then God does the rest. How many times will you use the same mixture?'

The conversation felt unreal. I didn't trust this man, not one bit, yet he seemed genuinely interested in how we made ale and it was a subject that I was always willing to talk about.

'We normally use the first two worts, sometimes the third, but then the ale becomes too weak to keep for long. It's better for us to make it strong and let customers dilute it at home if that's what they want.'

'How soon after adding the barm can you put it in the oak casks?'

This certainly is odd.

'We'll leave the copper near the fire and the mixture should start bubbling and foaming within a few hours. When it stops, my mother and I will strain it into oak casks but then we have to leave it for at least four days to clear before the ale can be sold.'

'I hear it's pleasant to taste.' In the pulpit the minister's eyes were ablaze with zeal and passion, yet now I saw the calculating intelligence behind them as he studied me. 'I would be pleased to try some.'

I went over to the nearby jug and poured a small amount. He remained completely still so that I was forced to stand in front of him, holding out the cup. He studied my hand with a curiosity that went well beyond rudeness. Finally, he took the vessel, making no comment at how little it contained.

'Sit down. It's good that we have this chance to talk.'

He indicated my armchair on the other side of the fire, but I sat at the table which provided a bit more distance and made me higher.

'I understand your feet are similarly injured?'

'The result of a tragic fire.'

'In which your father died.'

He obviously knew the story. 'My father lost his life saving a baby that was trapped in a burning building.'

'You have no other marks?'

'Marks?'

'About your body.'

I hesitated at the strange question. 'Nothing that would not be considered normal on a person.'

'You've seen many naked bodies, Aila?'

I used to debate endlessly with my father on any topic that came into our heads and was not frightened to hold a strong belief that was different to someone else's, but this slithering about was not a conversation; it was unnatural, unwholesome and, I sensed, dangerous. I was wary of speaking in case my answer was twisted into something that had an entirely different shape to my meaning. However, I needed to respond somehow.

'I suspect no more or less than you, Reverend McNeil.'

A tiny smile played at his lips which he tried to hide by taking a sip of the ale. The minister was enjoying this game of trying to catch me out, although to what purpose I couldn't fathom.

'I've heard that you and your mother are known in the area for being quarrelsome.'

'Then you've heard wrong.'

'You deny holding opinions that go against the natural order and that you announce them forcibly to others, even your betters?'

'There is no law against a woman holding an opinion, although there are some misguided people who would make out there is. Perhaps if you could give me an example of what you mean by quarrelsome, I could more easily set your mind at rest.'

Any glimmer of humour faded from his face. It felt as if a large cloud had just blocked out the sun and reduced the light and heat in the room. He glared at me, and his eyes seemed to hold as much humanity as the piece of jet stone on the shelf behind him. It was unnerving how suddenly and dramatically his eyes could change.

'Your obvious disrespect towards a minister of the kirk is not healthy!'

'I am never disrespectful to a respectable man of the cloth, but my father taught me to use my intelligence and not to be cowered into letting the truth be drowned in falsehood.'

'The truth?' He paused as if considering something, then appeared to change his mind. 'Your father must have been an unusual man.'

'He was, and I wish he was here.'

You wouldn't be slithering about with him, you obnoxious snake.

'And you're an unusual woman.'

I couldn't see how to answer this without creating an opportunity for him to twist my words, so I remained silent.

'I'll be spending my time as the minister for Loth visiting as many families in the parish as I can,' he said. 'I trust I'm not going to hear things that will disturb me.'

'About what, Reverend McNeil?'

'Why ... about you, Aila.'

8

Dornoch, 2 April 1727

MOTHER AND I DIDN'T ATTEND the weekly market at the royal burgh of Dornoch during the winter months, so this Wednesday would be our first stall since last year. Even though we had been successful on our own, the absence of Father's huge frame and spirit was still keenly felt. Of course, everything was on a smaller scale as we couldn't produce, transport or sell the quantity of ale that we used to. However, the quality remained as good and we had gained a reputation as a reliable supplier.

The twenty-mile distance from Kintradwell forced us to travel the day before and return home the day after, which meant we could only attend every fortnight, otherwise the croft would be impossible to manage. The journey was made more challenging because many parts of the Highlands weren't suitable for a wheeled vehicle, so we had to use a sledge.

Fortunately, Mother had become friendly with a wealthy widow who owned a large house on the outskirts of the town and was happy to provide us with accommodation. The formidable Mistress Hamilton enjoyed our company and our ale, so the agreement worked well for everyone.

Early in the morning we led Abel through the usual confusion of bodies, animals, products and sledges. Part of the market was held within the shadow of the great thirteenth-century cathedral, now largely a ruin apart from a section of the nave and the bell tower. Some stallholders set themselves up amongst the graves in the cemetery, which appalled Mother and me, although the authorities allowed it, so there was little point in complaining. We quickly set out our bench and were about to move a few barrels when one of the officers walked by.

'Good morning Mistress Horne, Aila. May I help?'

'Good morning, Duncan,' said Mother. 'That would be kind of you.'

The town employed a handful of officers who performed a range of tasks on behalf of the sheriff, and we had met Duncan several times during previous visits. He had always been pleasant and willingly lifted a few of the barrels onto the bench before positioning some others so that they were more convenient for us to swap later on. Once this was completed, he went on his way and I took Abel back to Mistress Hamilton's property. On my return I called at the tolbooth and joined a small line of stallholders waiting to pay their fee.

I hadn't lost my love of the markets, and since attending this one we had got to know several of the other merchants, craftsmen and sellers, at least enough to enjoy a pleasant blether. There were also other 'regulars'. Between the queue and the town's stocks, which were currently unoccupied, an old man with a missing leg sat on the ground. He wore his pewter 'Beggar's Badge' that had been given to him by the local authority to show that he was permitted to beg legally within the parish boundaries. I dropped some pennies into his bowl.

'God bless you, Mistress Aila,' he said, looking up at me and smiling.

'And God bless you, sir. My pennies are poor payment for such a lovely smile.'

'And my smile is poor payment to be looked upon by such beautiful eyes.'

This was a common exchange between us, yet it lost none of its joy for all that. During our conversations I had learned that he had once been a strong and proud soldier in the king's army. A musket ball fired during the Jacobite rising of 1715 had taken away his leg and misfortune had done the rest to reduce him to the poor state he was in now. Yet he retained a dignity that I admired and he deserved respect more than some of the so-called dignitaries in the area.

Father had instilled into me the need to treat everyone as an equal and that I should be treated with the same courtesy, although we had both acknowledged that the latter was unrealistic. I heard his words in my head so often and with such clarity that it often felt as if he was standing by my shoulder.

'Don't lose your place,' said the old soldier, noticing that the queue had moved forward.

'I'll be back.'

'And I'll be waiting for you right here, mistress,' he said, winking, which made me laugh.

Later on I walked along the main streets, passing the weaver and shoemaker, the blacksmith's forge and the Wolf's Head, where men stood around the doorway drinking. I often attracted attention in public. When I was in the open I liked to have my hair uncovered, which was unusual, but the thing that was almost unheard of was for a young woman to wear boots. My appearance normally resulted in a few unpleasant comments.

Having endured the unwelcome opinions of several of those near the tavern, I decided to head back to the much safer environment of the stalls. Although the market didn't provide the variety of what could be found in Inverness, it still attracted people from a wide area as well as from every section of society. You could almost as easily end up standing next to a wealthy laird as a farm labourer.

I hadn't gone far, having passed the usual assortment of dead and live birds and animals, when I came across the cloth merchant in his normal place next to the burgh's stone ell. I stared at the many rolls of bright material standing out vividly on the merchant's table. In an instant the world around me faded as my mind was flooded with memories of that morning ... Of the flames and heat, Father's body trapped under the burning timber, his face, his voice pleading with me to leave, his agony. There was never any warning as to when I would suddenly be transported back to that bright June day four years earlier ... Father and I had been making fun of Inkster and laughing so much that we were crying, and he had lifted Mother off the ground and—

Make it go away. Make it go away.

I closed my eyes and concentrated with every part of my being to force these terrible visions back into the dark cave where they lived like something evil, watching and waiting ... always watching and waiting. My heart was racing so much I felt as though I was pushing a boulder up a hill, and while my mouth was dry my body was drenched in sweat. I was dizzy, standing as motionless as possible while the battle for control continued.

'Can I interest you in some material, Mistress Aila?' asked the stallholder.

I opened my eyes to find the cloth merchant watching me with a concerned expression. I merely stared at him, unable to reply immediately.

The rolls of material purchased that fateful morning had never been made into the intended clothes. Taking care of me, moving to Kintradwell and setting up our new home and business had taken all of Mother's time and energy. Also, I think she had lost the will to work on it. How could I lie in bed wearing a shift or go outside in a coat that would remind us of what happened every time I put them on?

'No, thank you. Not today.' I walked away slowly, aware that he was still watching.

The surrounding sights, smells and noise gradually settled my mind, although a fragment of the horror lingered ... That evil watching from the cave's entrance. I came across a candle maker and as I knew we needed more I hoped that the distraction of a conversation, albeit on a very basic level, might help. We used to make our own, but the government introduced a tax on chandlers and a law stating that anyone else needed a special licence, which was too costly. Most people made do with rushes dipped in animal fat. Candles were sold in bundles by weight and I chose thick, pale, creamy ones that would smell less and last longer.

Nearby, a man had a litter of piglets to sell, shouting out what good value they were. I smiled and moved on, thinking of the damage an adult pig can do. They often roamed the streets, even rooting around in the graveyard and exposing recently buried bodies. The area around the cemetery was unfenced, but ongoing arguments over who should pay for the work meant that the situation had never been resolved. If Mother had been in charge she would have banged their stubborn heads together and had it sorted long ago.

Sighing, I headed back to the stall and took over from Mother so she could look around as well. I felt safe here and the repetitious work prevailed over the darker memories lingering in my mind.

I was sorting out cups during a lull when I became aware that a customer was waiting. I turned to serve him, and immediately forgot what I was doing . . . I forgot everything.

I had never considered that a man could be beautiful, but the one in front of me now couldn't be described as anything else. He was so physically perfect in every way that I was momentarily struck dumb. His long, wavy, golden hair was tied at the back with a bright red ribbon, while his deep blue eyes made me think of a still loch on a hot summer's day. When I eventually regained my wits, it turned out that some had been left behind.

'Ale?'

'I would be pleased to try some, thank you.'

His voice had such a rich quality it was as though each word was not so much spoken as performed. An image of sunlight, sparkling through thick, warm honey poured slowly—

Stupid!

I tore my gaze away to focus on the task, as if pouring ale from a jug into a cup needed concentration, and silently cursed myself for behaving like a foolish young girl with nothing more in her head than air and damn sawdust. I was aware of him staring at my hand. I was used to this and it rarely bothered me unless someone also made a hurtful comment, but having this man watch made me feel ugly, useless and angry. I couldn't understand these unexpected, strong emotions and became so flustered that when I spilt ale on the bench, an almost unheard-of event, my temper erupted without restraint as if it didn't belong to me at all.

'I have another hand to match and two feet that are similarly disfigured if you would like to see them!' I spat out the words while I cleaned up the mess with a cloth and it was only afterwards that I once more looked at his face.

What have I done?

I had never seen such an expression of anguish. The man made no move to hide his tears, which rolled gently down his face where they gathered together on his chin as if reluctant to leave. Father once said that a falling tear is the loneliest thing in the world. My heart melted in shame within my chest.

'I'm sorry,' I said.

'No, it is I who must apologise. I wasn't staring at you ... That's not true. I was, but I was thinking of someone else. She was the closest person to me I've ever known and I lost her in a fire. I'm truly sorry for my rudeness. Your injury brought back a memory that ...' His voice trailed away and I knew what he meant; knew why he couldn't finish what he was saying. 'It's not something I've ever spoken about.'

'I lost my father to a fire.'

Why did I say that? I never speak of this willingly.

'Did you see it happening?'

'I was burned trying to save him.'

He nodded, and I felt that this total stranger instinctively understood an intimate part of me that no one ever saw.

'And the image comes back, often when you don't expect it?' he asked.

'Yes.'

'With me also. I always try to force it out of my mind, but ...'

'Sometimes it's too strong and consumes you, at least for a short while.'

Nobody else had approached the stall and we studied each other for several moments in silence. I've rarely known a man cry and never one who so openly showed it. I felt he had revealed to me a secret part of himself.

'I haven't even given you your ale. There's no charge.'

He reached up and wiped his face then took the cup, but he laid this gently on the bench and held out his hand. He had such sculptured fingers, fingernails that were so clean and well-kept that they would not have been out of place belonging to a wealthy lady.

'Please may we start again? My name's Jack.'

No one had held out a hand to me since the accident. This time it was me who stared, not moving or speaking. That I should place my ruined flesh into his perfect hand was more than I could bear.

'I would be delighted to know your name.'

'Aila.'

'Well then, I'm pleased to meet you, Aila.'

He was still holding out his hand and in the end I could do nothing else but put mine in his. Instead of appearing repulsed he held it firmly for a long time ... and smiled.

* * *

'Who was that?'

Mother had returned to the stall as Jack was walking away and we watched his broad back for a moment in silence. Even when simply moving amongst the stalls this stranger had a grace about him that was rare to see, particularly in a man.

'Just a customer.'

'Mmm,' she said.

Father had often warned me that it was pointless to try to hide anything from Mother because she had the uncanny ability to see things when not appearing to look at them. Sometimes, he said, she even knew when she was not present.

'A handsome-looking man,' she added.

'Do you think so? I hadn't noticed.'

We were teasing each other. She knew fine that I had noticed, that I had Father's habit of constantly studying people.

'What's his name?'

'Jack.'

The word was out of my mouth before I realised my error. Mother smiled. 'Well, you didn't waste any time in finding that out.'

'I didn't ask, he told me.'

'Mmm.'

Mother had this irritating way of saying 'Mmm' which had many different meanings depending upon the conversation and I took this 'Mmm' to mean that she didn't believe me. I let it go.

'He's with a troupe of performers that have just arrived in Dornoch.'

'Travelling folk.'

'They're putting on a play tonight, in the Drovers' Inn.'

'Just a customer then.'

'Mmm,' I said.

* * *

Dornoch was busy. After wandering around for a while Jack found Sim watching their blacksmith friend and the opponent he was about to take on in a tug-of-war.

'Christ, he looks as though he's eaten an entire hog just for breakfast,' said Jack.

'They obviously breed them big up here.'

'He makes even Hector look small. At least there's only one of him.'

'These Highlanders are proud folk. They would never consider pitting more than one man against another.'

The two were silent while they watched Ellen and Bess walking amongst the onlookers, chatting and taking bets. Jack was concerned about the older woman. Once they were certain of being clear of any pursuit, their initial frantic journey from Edinburgh had settled into a more sedate pace. But Bess was still struggling at times, and so he had allowed longer and more frequent rests as they had travelled north. Jack wasn't sure what Dornoch had to offer, but he felt they needed to remain in one place for a while. And, of course, now there was also the extraordinary girl on the ale stall.

'Will Hector win?'

Sim hesitated before replying. He had been studying the local man in some detail as he joked and drank with friends.

'His opponent looks bloody strong and is at least a couple of stones heavier. Sometimes men like that are all strength and little stamina, though I can't judge that from his appearance. In the end it will come down to technique. So, yes, Hector will win, but don't let him take on anyone else today even if he suggests it.'

Jack took the warning seriously. Although he led the group overall, he was wise enough to defer to the experience of the others, which was often much greater than his. Ellen's voice carried clearly to everyone nearby. She had raised a handkerchief in the air.

'Take the strain.'

* * *

After a brief rush of business, the customers to our stall had fallen off sharply and we suspected there might be some event or entertainment that was occupying people elsewhere. Mother suggested I take myself off for a walk and the words had barely left her lips when we heard the noise of shouting on the other side of the square.

'Well, I think that's your first destination.'

I followed the sound and moments later came upon the astonishing sight of two huge men straining against each other in a tug-of-war. They were quite opposite in many ways; one was obviously a Highlander, his plaid worn proudly upon a giant body that spouted a wild black beard and hair. He was the epitome of passion, pride and power, determined to show the superiority of his clan.

The other man was bald, at least ten years older, and he was a mountain of muscle. I wondered if he belonged to the troupe that Jack had told me about. It would make sense as I had never seen a competition like this in Dornoch before. Whereas the Highlander's friends called out encouragement and praise, the newcomer had no one to urge him on and, from the way he held himself, I suspected he didn't need it.

I looked about the crowd and quickly spotted Jack standing next to a small, swarthy man who could hardly have appeared more different. He looked dangerous. Yet for all that, this man stood close to a rotund woman and as I watched he subtly took hold of her hand, as though he didn't think anyone else would notice. It struck me then that they were in love; there was just something about the way they stood and stole glances at each other. I thought how lucky they were. It was unworthy, but I couldn't prevent the envy that tapped at the edges of my consciousness.

'Your hair's lovely.'

I turned then stared in surprise, not just because of the highly unusual comment but because I was facing probably the most beautiful girl I had ever seen. Yet many would likely not consider her so attractive. Her hair was too ginger, and she was small; too small I guessed for her age; like so many children who hadn't grown properly because of hunger and deprivation. Yet she shone with an inner joy that was captivating.

'Thank you, but I like yours more.'

'Hector's my friend,' she said, indicating the huge man struggling with his Highlander opponent. 'What happened to your hand?' She gently took hold of it to inspect and although I was taken aback I didn't feel offended by the gesture or question, nor did I recoil at the touch.

'A fire.'

'Does it hurt?'

'It did at the time.'

The girl placed her other hand on top of mine. They were tiny. She seemed unbothered by the sight or rough texture. This was a new experience for me since the accident and now it had occurred twice within a few hours. The day was becoming unreal.

'My name's Malie.'

'I'm Aila.'

'That's pretty. Look, Hector's won. He always wins.'

I followed her gaze and saw that the two men were speaking. I had been so fascinated by the girl that I hadn't seen the end of the competition. The winner slapped the other on the back and headed towards us as the crowds dispersed to seek other entertainment or collect their winnings if they had bet using their head and not their heart.

'You needn't be afraid of him.'

'I'll try not to be,' I said, just as the huge man reached us. He knelt down on one knee so that he wasn't so far above Malie.

'This is Aila. Isn't she lovely?'

'I'm pleased to meet you, Mistress Aila. I must warn you that my young friend here hasn't yet learned anything of tact or the art of politeness.'

'I would rather have her honesty any day. Oh ... I don't mean that I'm agreeing I'm lovely!'

Hector laughed heartily at my embarrassment and I couldn't help but join in. Malie let go of my hand and went to him. They looked like figures out of a children's story, a giant and a mysterious fairy-like creature.

'Hector doesn't have any hair!'

With this comment Malie rubbed her hands vigorously across the top of his scalp. From a distance I thought that he merely followed the habit some men had of shaving their heads, yet now he was closer I could see that he appeared to have no hair anywhere. There was none on his arms and he didn't even have eyebrows. Father said he once had a sailor like this, but in every other respect the man was the same as anyone else on board the ship.

Hector indulged her, smiling fondly and I instinctively liked him. They were so completely different that I couldn't believe Malie was related to him, yet there was real affection between them.

I miss Father so much.

'Here's Jack. He's got nice hair, hasn't he, Aila?'

I turned and there he was again, just in front of me and without a bench between us.

'It's very long,' I said, making my face appear rather stern. 'It's what I would expect to see on a young woman.'

Jack looked at me, uncertain how to take the comment.

'She's teasing you, Jack,' said Malie, laughing.

She was right. I was.

* * *

'Mother will you stop saying "Mmm" and tell me what you think?'

'I'll speak to Mistress Hamilton. We are guests in her house and I don't want to appear rude.'

I was desperate to attend the drama that the troupe was putting on that evening and had talked about little else since returning to the stall. As it turned out our host was also keen to go and later that evening the three of us found ourselves amongst a boisterous crowd in the large yard at the back of the Drovers' Inn. I had taken the stool from our stall and was fortunately still high enough to see the stage as everyone else was standing.

Afterwards Mistress Hamilton was happy to return home while Mother and I met up with the troupe, and the eight of us were later squashed around a table at the inn.

Mother sat next to the large woman, who had introduced herself as Bess, and the two of them soon looked as deep in conversation as conspirators must have appeared in the infamous gunpowder plot. I had no idea what they were talking about, but I noticed their immediate friendship had caused a few smiles between the others.

'Bess doesn't take to everyone and rarely as readily as she has with your mother,' said Jack, who was next to me.

'Mother's travelled a lot and is good at talking to people.'

'And you, Aila,' said Sim, 'have you travelled much?'

I was wary of the man sitting opposite, although I had no reason to be other than his appearance, which was unworthy for I had complained often enough about being judged solely upon physical characteristics.

'No, although my father was a ship's captain so I grew up hearing stories of his adventures around the world.'

'You must miss him,' said Jack, which might have partly been to warn Sim not to say something that could unintentionally be hurtful.

'Every minute of every day.'

'I never knew my parents in order to miss them,' said Sim. 'I'm not sure if that was a good or a bad thing. I suppose it depends what they might have been like.'

'I'm lucky in having sixteen years with my father and, of course, my mother is very much around.'

Our conversation was briefly halted by the arrival of food. I couldn't help taking this opportunity to study the people around the table. Ellen sat next to me but we had spoken too little to form an opinion. Hector was large in every sense and he had a gentleness about him that reminded me of my father. I had only said hello to Bess, however, the fact that Mother was enjoying her company was proof that she was intelligent and interesting.

My mother's frustration at those she considered foolish tended to reveal itself a little too readily at times, a trait that could prove awkward as she thought most people in authority fell into that category. I wasn't sure about Sim and I didn't understand how Malie fitted into the group. Then, of course, there was Jack.

Everyone was involved in a conversation apart from the two of us and we fell silent, not even touching our food.

'Thank you,' I said, eventually.

'For what?'

'For trusting me enough to reveal your grief.'

Jack bowed his head and I feared I had opened a wound that was too painful. Whatever joy and laughter was going on around us, at that moment we were in a world that was inhabited only by us. He gently placed his hand on mine, as if feeling the same, that what we said and did could not be heard or seen by any other person. Finally, he looked at me.

'I think,' he said, 'that I could trust you with anything.'

9

Kintradwell, 5 April 1727

I RODE ABEL TO LOCH BRORA because he needed exercise and I needed time alone, a chance to reflect and calm myself. For days I had been a jumble of conflicting ideas and feelings, hopes and regrets. In the end Mother had told me quite firmly to get away from the croft for a while. She knew me so well, although I was beginning to wonder if I knew myself anymore.

My meeting with the troupe of performers had felt like a turning point in my life, yet in what new direction could I possibly head? Malie, Hector and the others had accepted me without hesitation or making me feel uncomfortable, as was so often the case.

It was my meeting with Jack that was troubling me, for I had never been attracted to anyone before. I cursed myself a thousand times over for the stupidity of the emotion. Jack was a man who could have the choice of a wife from any level of society and not just because of his beauty. I suspected he had the ability to speak to people regardless of their background; put him in the right clothes and he could walk the corridors of the richest and most powerful houses in the land without tripping up. My feet tripped me up constantly.

I had spoken to him in a way that I had never spoken to anyone, told him of feelings and hopes that I had never told anyone. He had been equally open with me. And when, much later, we emerged together from our secret world to become aware once more of what was happening in the tavern, I realised with shock that everyone else around our table had gone, and not even my mother had interrupted us to say that she was leaving.

Abel picked his own way along the track as the ground was extremely rough and full of dangers, a bit like walking through life . . . Take the wrong step and disaster was waiting its chance to pull you down. What choice of paths did I have? Mother wouldn't be around forever and there had been an increasing number of incidents recently where she seemed to forget what she was about to say or do. For most of the time she was the same strong, dependable, wise woman whom I had always looked to for advice. However, I feared greatly what would happen if the person giving guidance became lost.

'Oh Abel, what am I going to do?'

Abel snorted and threw back his head.

'I know, my darling, there are plenty of people much worse off,' I said, stroking his neck. 'It's just that when you see what could have been, it's difficult to accept at times.'

We stopped at the side of the loch. High in the sky there was a large bird of prey. A golden eagle? I had seen them on several occasions, but it was too far away to tell. I wondered if it could see me more clearly, wondered if this particular bird was one I had spotted before, wondered what on earth I was supposed to do about falling in love with a man who looked like a Greek god, at least how I imagined such a person might look. When we had reached my secret place I dismounted and went to sit on my rock to consider these strange new feelings.

* * *

I returned to the croft a couple of hours later having made no decisions about anything. Not long after I had put Abel in his stall and was sorting out his food I became aware of a minute change in the air, as if another presence had disturbed the balance of my surroundings. Turning around I was confronted with Reverend McNeil standing a few yards away, watching in silence. My immediate unease was made worse when I realised that I couldn't easily get past him.

'Reverend McNeil.' I left the comment hanging, not quite a statement or a question.

'Aila, we meet again.'

'Well, you are in our barn, so perhaps it's not a huge surprise.'

'God guides all our actions. If we meet alone then it was meant to be.'

Somehow I doubted that God had really gone to the bother of arranging for me to be alone in a barn with the temporary minister. I had a sudden suspicion that unsettled me greatly . . . That he had been secretly watching the croft and seeing me return he had followed.

'I've been hearing much about your mother that concerns me.'

Say nothing.

'Several people have expressed their unrest at seeing her muttering when there has been no one close by, and on other occasions she has been heard to speak in a strange tongue.'

'English can seem strange to those who only speak Gaelic, and my mother will occasionally use a phrase in Italian as she loves the language, but in every other way these "mutterings" are no more than any person might say as they go about their daily business. Also, my mother is becoming slightly confused at times because of her age. You will understand this, Reverend, I'm sure.'

'I understand much, Aila. I understand the need to be vigilant, to be ever watchful for the Devil working his evil through others.'

'I suppose you mean women?'

'It is well known that their many weaknesses make women much more susceptible to his will. And, of course, there is the physical side of the demonic pact.'

When he took a step nearer, I instinctively moved backwards into the stall. Abel shifted nervously, sensing this new visitor was unwelcome.

'The idea that the Devil has suddenly taken a carnal interest in my elderly mother is utter nonsense!'

'Perhaps, but what about you, Aila?' he said, taking another step. 'Such a beautiful body would be appealing indeed. Has the Devil promised to make you whole again? Have you already lain naked with him, felt his strong arms around you, his hands upon your thighs? Have you renounced your baptism?'

'No.'

'Did he give you a new name?'

'No.'

'Tell me what the Devil was like! Tell me!'

He was now at the entrance to the stall and I was backed up against Abel with nowhere to go. If that wasn't bad enough his face was contorted into such a twisted, frightening expression that it made me think of a particular gargoyle on a building in Inverness that used to scare me as a child.

'Please move away,' I said, trying to sound firm and calm. 'Your closeness to me is not proper.'

'Proper!' He was in the stall. 'That is not the word for what you are doing! Renounce your pact with the Devil and you might yet be saved!'

What happened next was so confusing that it was difficult to make out his intentions or, indeed, if he actually had any and he was instead completely lost to madness. As the minister lunged, I rushed towards Abel's head, shouting at the horse to save me. Abel swung the back end of his body around, which unfortunately resulted in Reverend McNeil being catapulted into me with such force that I crashed against the side wall, where we immediately became a tangle of arms and legs, both of us fighting to keep our balance.

Eventually, I managed to get my hands on his chest and pushed him with all my strength. He was lightly built and staggered backwards several yards, then he stood, panting and staring at me with an expression of loathing, yet in truth I didn't believe he knew what to do next. Neither did I. My heart pounded and my mind went blank. I couldn't think of anything to say or do that would get me out of this perilous situation. We seemed somehow locked together by our inability to make a decision, and it didn't get better as the seconds ticked past.

Without any warning, the minister was suddenly soaked – his hair, his face, his upper clothing. We were both so surprised that it took a moment for either of us to realise that my mother was standing just the other side of the low wall of the stall. In one hand she held an empty chamber pot.

'I think it's time you left, Reverend McNeil, don't you? I'm sure there are other members of the congregation who need saving more than we do.'

The minister was so astonished that he simply glared at her open-mouthed. I didn't even trust that my own eyes accurately conveyed what had just occurred in front of me.

'You ... stupid ... old ... hag!'

'Call me that if you must, but I'm not the one standing here with warm piss dripping off the end of my nose!'

Reverend McNeil instinctively reached up to his face and I instinctively burst out laughing, which set Mother off as it always did. He was so livid he could barely get his words out.

'I'll—'

Unfortunately for the minister he was by this point standing near the back of Abel and before he could tell us what he meant to do, the horse farted loudly in his direction. Mother shrieked and I had to hold onto Abel's neck to stay upright. Reverend McNeil hesitated for a moment then stormed out of the entrance, his threats drowned by our laughter, plus Abel giving him another fart to send him on his way. It took several minutes before either of us could speak and I was able to ask the question that was puzzling me. We normally relieved ourselves in the gully by the stall and the chamber pot was used only once we had locked up for at night.

'Mother, why did you have the chamber pot?'

'Well, I saw you return earlier and go into the barn, and then sometime later I was aware of the minister's horse being outside, but neither of you were visible. For some reason I decided that a fresh pot of piss might come in handy.'

It was a long, long time before we made it back to the house.

* * *

I didn't really know why I continued to sleep next to my mother after the weather had turned warmer; perhaps it was because I couldn't shake off the feeling of unease that had hung over me for many weeks. Maybe it was because I felt she was slipping away. Mother increasingly did and said things that were perhaps not uncharacteristic, but rather an extension of what might be expected, like throwing the contents of the chamber pot over the minister.

For her to have done such a disrespectful act six months earlier would have been unthinkable. She wouldn't have hesitated to come to my aid and challenge him, but to cover him with piss ... It was as though she was losing some of her understanding of the normal rules that governed our lives. Whatever the reason, neither of us had suggested I should return to my own box-bed. We missed my father and it was a comfort to lie next to each other during the night. So I stayed.

'We've made a dangerous enemy of Reverend McNeil today,' I said. My head rose and fell gently on her chest as she stroked my hair. It was something Mother had recently taken to doing much more often, almost absentmindedly at times.

'Mmm.'

'I wish Reverend MacDonald would return and this strange man could move on to another parish then maybe our lives could be like they used to be.'

'Mmm.'

'What are you thinking?'

109

'That this afternoon was the best laugh I've had in a long while.'

'It was funny once you arrived and saved me. It wasn't so amusing before that.'

'No. You're right, yet we can't stop attending the weekly service or our temporary minister will have a reason to turn suspicion upon us.'

'What can we do?'

'Just carry on as the good Christian people we are, doing exactly what we've done these last few years.'

Mother pulled me tightly into her, but for once her comforting assurance and warm embrace did little to settle my fears.

10

Lothmore kirk, 6 April 1727

AFTER THE UNWELCOME ENCOUNTER WITH Reverend McNeil the previous day, Mother and I were concerned at what he might say that Sunday. Since his arrival in the parish even those few people who dared to miss the occasional service seemed to be attending regularly and, as we made our way inside the kirk, I thought it had never been so full.

Later in the summer a lot of families would travel south to the Lowlands, where they could be assured of paid work helping to gather the harvest, but for the meantime everyone remained in the area. The one person I didn't see was Peggy, but she was so near to giving birth that no one could possibly complain at her absence.

Mother tugged my sleeve and I bent down slightly so that she could more easily whisper into my ear.

'I think if someone died, they would still come along while we have this minister. They're all so terrified of him.'

'Be careful what you say.'

'I wonder if he's dried out yet.'

'Shh.'

'I hope he's not smelling of—'

'Mother!'

We sat down in our normal place, three rows from the front, acknowledging with a comment those we knew fairly well and greeting others with a nod and a smile. As usual, there was a mixture of dress.

Several men wore the *fèileadh-mòr* so there were plenty of bare knees amongst the breeches. Few could afford a set of clothes that were only worn to the kirk and people did what they could to demonstrate respect, with women donning their best hat or shawl and some men attaching two pieces of linen known as 'neck and sleeves' to hide an otherwise rough shirt beneath their jacket. Mother and I wore our woollen arisaids. It depended upon how mischievous we were feeling just how much of our faces we covered.

The one difference was that there were no dogs. During his first service Reverend McNeil had banished them, and although some owners grumbled, nobody was willing to disobey. It was the one thing he had said that Mother and I agreed with, for we had always felt the inclusion of animals was wrong, even though our dear Reverend MacDonald allowed it. The only information that had reached us about him was that his sister remained gravely ill and he wouldn't leave her side until she died or recovered.

This would be Reverend McNeil's fifth Sunday service, and in between these he had been extremely active in visiting properties within the Loth parish. Stories had reached us about how he asked strange questions concerning objects around the house, interrogated families about the behaviour of neighbours and wanted to know whether anyone had unusual marks upon their body. People were becoming wary of friends they had known and worked alongside quite happily for years. As my mother had predicted, mistrust was a dangerous seed to plant.

My mind was brought back to the present by Murdo calling for silence and then starting 'All people that on earth do dwell'. As we repeated the lines I realised that behind us Agnes Munro was singing the correct melody and not the one she usually sang. Even this eccentric old woman had been frightened into trying not to stand out in any way. As with previous occasions, Reverend McNeil walked into the pulpit and studied us as if trying to see the darkness in our souls.

'God guides my hands. He guides my feet upon the path He has revealed that I must tread. The quest He has set me is difficult and perilous yet I have walked this journey for many years and shall never weary. I tell you this . . .' He paused, sniffed loudly then thrust his head forwards as if this would help him see faces more clearly. 'I smell the evil of sulphur! I feel the presence of witches in this parish, sense them corrupting the very air we breathe.'

With great showmanship he clasped a hand over his mouth. A couple of women gave a little cry of alarm and followed his example. I wondered how long they thought they could hold their breath. The minister had a powerful hold over the congregation, more so, I had to admit, than the convivial Reverend MacDonald. Mother tapped my thigh, but there was no humour any more in these secret messages. He slowly removed his hand.

'No, you cannot protect yourself so easily. Do not be fooled. When you search for a cure by visiting a supposedly sacred well at sunrise, it is the Devil who moves your legs. When you call upon fairies or spirits for help with your harvest, it is the Devil who puts the words in your mouth. When you walk three times around a particular tree because you are with child, I tell you the Devil sits in the branches above your head and laughs!'

Almost everyone I could see around me appeared uncomfortable. Rituals and the beliefs of parents and grandparents were as much a part of everyday life in the Highlands as the passing of the seasons. No one considered it a conflict to be a Christian and also to follow the customs of previous generations, particularly when rites were carried out in private.

The minister pointed at the congregation, slowly moving his arm as if he wanted to include every single person. 'The Devil doesn't seek people with badness in their hearts because he already owns them. The Devil seeks good people. He seeks righteous people. He seeks people like you. And I say you must constantly search your hearts for signs of evil temptations. Repent and seek God's forgiveness.'

His finger made its way along our pew, and when it was aimed at me he stopped. It wasn't long before others began to take notice and I assumed this was exactly what he intended.

'Yes, there are those amongst us who are already in league with Satan, if not in actual deed then in thought and wish and desire.' He gave another theatrical sniff. 'And I promise their stench will be burned out of this parish, out of this world, because I shall protect you from the evil that limps along by your side.'

Bastard. Bastard. Bastard.

'Now, let us pray for the good Lord's help in the dangerous task that lies ahead.'

* * *

Peggy gave birth early the next morning, and Reverend McNeil visited several hours later. He had been to many such hovels over the years and had long since become hardened to the horror of the dirt, damp, hunger and misery. Yet there were still occasions, admittedly rare, when he was moved to pity. He felt it now as he looked down at Peggy sitting listlessly by the fire. Tiny, pitiful cries came from the grey bundle in her arms.

'Your husband has asked me to visit urgently because you fear your child will not live?'

'He's ill, Reverend, even though the midwife passed him through the reek of our fire.'

The minister had come across so many superstitious beliefs since arriving in the area, he marvelled that anyone could get their daily work completed because of the things they were meant to avoid or the rituals they had to regularly perform. Passing a newly born baby through the smoke of a peat fire was supposed to avert the 'evil eye'. He sighed. It wasn't this woman's fault she was so ignorant.

'May I see?'

Peggy was too weak and lost in despair to be surprised that the minister should want to actually hold her baby, and he took it tenderly from her then sat on a stool that he had pulled up close.

Reverend McNeil had once had a baby, a beautiful boy called Calum, and an even more beautiful wife. In reality, Peggy was nothing like his Iona, yet there was something about this poor, beaten woman that reminded him of her. He had thought it the morning they met after his first Sunday service in Lothmore. A feature of her face perhaps, or the way she tilted her head when talking.

He had been a young man then, freshly ordained and freshly married to his childhood sweetheart. They had quickly become proud parents, with such plans to make a difference in the world. But within days of the birth the only two people he loved were gone.

The local midwife was known to them and had always appeared to be a good woman. No one had suspected the truth and only the following month she was discovered to be a witch. How could he have been so naïve and ignorant? As a man of God he should have realised, should have seen the signs or at the very least had some suspicion of her evil. But instead he had willingly handed over the care of his wife and son, and the Devil had stood by his shoulder and laughed.

At the execution, Reverend McNeil had studied every detail closely, willing himself to remember each tiny part of the witch's rightful punishment. Once she had been bound securely to the stake, the executioner had approached from behind and slipped a rope around her neck. He tied a knot in this then inserted a piece of wood which he turned so slowly that the stick hardly appeared to be moving.

The minister was pleased that the man was experienced because too much pressure would have snapped the neck, would have made the end too quick. Instead, her eyes had bulged and her tongue turned purple, while there was gurgling and twitching and the foul stench of disgrace. Everything was as it should be.

The flames that later consumed her body had seared into the minister's soul a determination to seek out and destroy these enemies of God. This was his purpose, the reason he had been put on earth. It was during those terrible early weeks that he decided to study law in order to be more effective in his quest, and he wouldn't stop for a single day until God welcomed him to rest in heaven.

The tiny scrap of humanity in his arms took hold of one of his fingers and wouldn't let go. Reverend McNeil felt a tear run down his cheek. It couldn't be seen in the gloom; a secret like that of his earlier life. Suddenly, the dim light that entered via the doorway was reduced even further when Butcher appeared, standing as if uncertain whether to enter his own home.

'I've seen to your horse, Reverend.'

'Sort out this fire and boil some water to make tea for your wife. She needs feeding up. What food is in the house?'

'Well, times have been hard—'

'Don't talk nonsense to me, man! Here.' The minister took out several coins from his pocket. 'Ride to Sinclair's. He's close and has a well-stocked pantry. Tell him I'm paying for food for Peggy and that his wife is to make up a good selection, as she thinks best.' As Butcher took the money, the minster, with surprising speed and strength, grabbed his wrist and held it. 'If one single farthing of this goes towards ale, I promise you will not like what I do.'

Butcher was so taken aback at the unexpected aggression that he stammered in response. 'Yes . . . yes, of course, Reverend. I would never think of such a thing. Let me quickly fix the fire and put the kettle on.'

With the fire properly tended to it was far less smoky, while the departure of Butcher also seemed to make the air easier to breathe. Reverend McNeil didn't need to be able to see what was around him. These properties were all the same, the misery all too familiar. Yet the land was good and the only reason for this wretchedness was because Butcher drank away the money and was too lazy to care properly for his animals or crops beyond ensuring he could pay the rent.

117

'Have you chosen a name?'

Peggy appeared almost hesitant to answer, and he guessed that the fear she had of her husband made her reluctant to make decisions. 'I wanted David, after my father. Mister Butcher didn't like that. He never suggested anything else and now I don't know what to say.'

They sat in silence for a while. The baby seemed content in his arms, although every so often the boy gave a pitiful cry that sounded so weak it was heart-wrenching.

'I agree with you that he should be baptised immediately and we will need a name to do that.'

'Perhaps, if he was named after you, Reverend, then Mister Butcher would have no reason to complain.'

Reverend McNeil's own baby had been called Calum, after him, and he had died within a few days. But he was a man of God, and superstition had no hold over him.

'I would be honoured. My name is Calum.'

'That will be a first in my family, but it's a good, solid name.'

The minister had brought a small pewter flask of water to use as a sign of cleansing. He removed this from his coat and took out the stopper. Outside, the wind was increasing in strength and blew in through the open door, making the air clear further.

'For you, little child, Jesus Christ has come, he has fought, he has suffered. For you he entered the shadow of Gethsemane and the horror of Calvary. For you he uttered the cry, "It is finished!" For you he rose from the dead and ascended into heaven and there he intercedes – for you, little child, even though you do not know it. But in this way the word of the Gospel becomes true. We love him, because he first loved us.'

He took hold of the flask and poured a little water on the baby's head. 'I now baptise you Calum Butcher, in the name of the Father and of the Son and of the Holy Ghost. Amen.'

Reverend McNeil paused for a moment then held out the baby towards Peggy. As she took back her son, a sudden gust made the fire flare and Calum Butcher began to cry.

11

Kintradwell, 8 April 1727

YESTERDAY AFTERNOON MIDWIFE JENKINS HAD called and told us that Peggy's labour had been long and difficult, so that Tuesday Mother and I set out to see what we could do to help. We had only been inside Butcher's dwelling on a few occasions and each time had come away despairing at the conditions. Butcher was a sub-tenant, renting land from the local tacksman who in turn leased a much larger area from the owner. This situation was common in the Highlands and there was generally little incentive for people to carry out any significant improvements to properties.

'Dear God above, it's like facing the entrance to the underworld,' said Mother.

The house was near enough to our home for us both to have walked and now that it was in sight we were filled with a sense of dread, for crossing the threshold was to leave behind all sense of joy and hope. Putting this off for a little longer, we stopped a short distance away. I stroked Abel, who seemed nervous. His pack harness was filled with food and other items we hoped would be useful. There was one jug of ale to keep Butcher occupied.

The building ahead of us was long and low, only the first couple of feet were built of stone as people could rarely afford to do more than use materials that were readily to hand. Above this level the walls were simply sod and mud. There was one small window, the thick glass so blackened that even the strongest sunlight must surely retreat in exhausted defeat.

The hearth was in the centre of the living area and there was no opening in the turf roof, so smoke had to find its own way out. It could be extremely hesitant to do this. As we watched, black clouds drifted reluctantly through the open front door, almost as if they were considering that if the weather was unfavourable they would head back inside until it improved.

'We must be positive for her sake,' I said, though in truth I was also saying this for ours.

'I know, but I already fear for this baby. Her first at thirty-one; Peggy must have thought it would never happen. Well, Aila, we must do what we can.'

Shortly afterwards, carrying the heavy pack harness between us, we stepped into the gloom and in an instant my eyes were watering. It wasn't merely the smoke, for the light in the room was provided by candles made of pig fat, which was the most obnoxious of all the tallows. The rancid stench and taste of pig caught in my throat, so much that I thought I would choke. Peggy sat by the fire in a wooden chair, its short legs designed to keep the user lower to the beaten-earth floor where the air was slightly clearer. A pitiful cry could be heard coming from the dirty bundle in her arms.

'Peggy, it's lovely to see you and we're so excited at meeting this new addition,' said Mother, trying to sound cheerful. 'Aren't we, Aila?'

'It's good of you to come,' said Peggy, her voice sounding unnaturally flat. 'I don't think my boy is well.'

'May I see?'

Mother gently took the baby and went outside into the daylight, while I began unpacking on the nearby table, having first cleared away filthy plates and a hen that protested noisily when I threw it outside. The thickness of the smoke made it difficult to see the dirt as they were both a similar grey and black, but it I knew it was there. It was everywhere.

'We've brought some candles, Peggy, so that you can have better light for the next few days, and my mother has made some baby clothes. I'm sorry I can't do that anymore.' I laid the knitted items on her lap, but she showed little interest. 'I'll lay out the food for you to put away later, when you're ready,' I said, moving back to the table and continuing my task. 'There's also a jug of ale.'

'Thank you,' said Peggy quietly.

I couldn't help feeling that her thanks were more for the ale than anything else, and it was all I could do to keep sounding cheerful. No one had bothered to sort out the smoky fire, so I bent down near Peggy's feet and chatted about anything I could think of while coaxing more flames from the peat.

From this position I could study the surroundings without making it obvious, although I doubted that Peggy would have noticed or cared. Like many similar properties, animals were kept inside during the winter and I knew that beyond the flimsy wicker wall there was an area where Butcher's cow, pig and pony would be kept. The unwholesome smell must have clung to hair and skin as stubbornly as the worst dirt, while there was little to stop the hens from coming into the living area and spreading a mess of droppings and feathers.

Mother had brought the baby back into the gloom. 'Is your baby feeding well?'

'I don't think so.'

'Right, let me see.'

I took away the new clothes then Mother put the bundle into Peggy's arms and made her uncover a breast so that she could watch. She was extremely practical and wise about such matters, despite only ever having had me. My natural curiosity would have had me watching and listening to see what I could learn, but I also felt that two of us standing over such a vulnerable woman was unfair.

'I'll make some tea,' I said. I filled the kettle and hung it from the *slabhraidh*, the metal chain hanging from the ceiling directly above the fire, then I lit a couple of the candles we had brought and snuffed out the ones in use. They gave extra light, although they did little to immediately improve the air.

'Apart from anything else you need feeding up,' said Mother. 'You've hardly got enough fat on you to keep yourself going, so it's no wonder that this wee mite is struggling to obtain any milk.'

We had brought cloths and soap with us and it wasn't long before Mother set about cleaning while I sat on a stool beside Peggy and fed her the pease broth we had made earlier and since reheated. It was a strange scene, me trying to feed Peggy while she tried to feed her baby. I think I was having more success. After a couple of hours Peggy looked and sounded better and the baby, having been washed and changed, was asleep nearby.

'Will you have the baptism on Sunday?' asked Mother. It was the custom for a baby to be baptised in the kirk on the first Sunday following its birth.

'It's been done. I feared for him so much that I begged my husband to fetch the minister. Reverend McNeil came yesterday. He was very kind.'

Mother and I expressed our surprise with a glance towards each other, which we hoped would go unnoticed.

'Well, that's good then,' said Mother, 'and what name did you choose?'

'I wanted David but in the end I asked Reverend McNeil to tell me his first name.'

'You named your baby after the minister?' Mother's tone gave away how taken aback she was at this. I doubted that Peggy noticed. 'What is it?'

'Calum,' she said. 'Isn't it lovely?'

* * *

Once we were outside we fitted the empty pack harness to Abel then looked back at the house. Our mood was as gloomy as the inside we had just left.

'Is it bad, Mother?'

'I'm afraid so. I fear Peggy's too undernourished to provide milk and I don't see that changing, not in time anyway.'

'We could bring over more food.'

'Yes, but unless we're going to feed her every meal, I don't think she'll eat it. I've known women in these situations appear to lose all hope and interest in anything around them, including their own baby. However, Peggy's problems go back long before this birth.'

'Is there nothing we can do?'

'Well, unless we were to have Peggy and Calum in our home so that we could care for them day and night over the coming weeks.'

'Butcher would never agree to that.'

'No.'

'Are there no other recent mothers in the area?'

'I've been thinking about that but no one comes to mind. I would have been happy to pay someone to be a wet-nurse, but the last new mother is over at Lothbeg and she must be long past that stage.'

'What about Brora? There's surely someone suitable amongst the population there.'

'Yes, that's worth trying. It's too late to leave today. Ride over first thing in the morning. You'll probably have to negotiate with a husband as he'll likely consider his wife's breast milk as his property to sell. Take some money and see if you can agree to bring back the mother and her baby to live with us for the next few weeks.'

We fell silent. I couldn't bear watching the smoke hanging around the front door as though it was a ghost from some Shakespearean drama about to foretell a terrible tragedy. When I moved to stroke Abel's neck, I was confronted by Butcher standing only yards away.

'That baby won't live beyond the next few days.'

'Mother!'

She turned quickly and we all stared at each other without speaking for several moments.

'You've brought things?' he said, giving no hint as to how much of our conversation he had been listening to.

126

'Food, clothing and other items that may help,' replied Mother. 'There's also a jug for you to help celebrate your son's arrival. He's a bonny wee boy.'

'Aye, I suppose he takes after me in that.'

'Well then, you'll be keen to see them both, so we'll be on our way.'

With that we walked away and didn't look back, yet I felt the hostility in his eyes boring into me with every single step until we had gone around a corner and were finally out of sight.

12

Kintradwell, 10 April 1727

MY TRIP TO BRORA THE day before had been
successful up to a point. Having asked around in
the town, I had soon found myself outside the
house of a new mother. I consider myself a good judge of
character and I liked this woman, who was quite willing to live
with us and feed both babies.

However, her husband wouldn't return from work until that
evening and she couldn't leave without discussing it with him.
She didn't expect there to be any objection and was so certain
he would bring her to us today that I left money as a sign of
trust and to make up for the lost pay he would have. Then I had
ridden Abel home, fretting all the while over whether I had
made the right decision and if I should perhaps have tried harder
to find someone who could have returned with me.

Mother and I had been busy that morning making butter,
but upon hearing a sound outside we went to investigate.
Butcher was sitting on his pony. It was difficult to tell which
one looked the most unfriendly or the least intelligent. Peggy's
husband obviously wasn't intending to get down and had been
waiting for us to come out.

'You need to go to my wife.'

'Why?' asked Mother. 'Is she ill?'

'No.'

'Is the baby ill?'

'No.'

'Thank the Lord. It's good that you're here because yesterday we managed to arrange for a new mother to live with us. She'll feed both her baby and your Calum until Peggy is feeling better and able to do this herself. It won't cost you anything and her husband should bring her here soon.'

'There's no need to be bothering with all that.'

'Why? What's wrong with the idea?'

'He's dead, that's what's wrong.'

'What! Calum's dead?'

'Yes, and it's women's work to sort out bodies so you need to be there. She just sits. It's not right. My son was never cared for properly. Now he's dead you two must do what has to be done.'

'We'll leave straight away and see you back at your house.'

'Me? It's not my place to be involved in such matters. A man needs to be able to grieve in private.'

'And where will you be?' asked Mother, anger nudging aside her initial shock.

'That's my business and nothing to do with anyone else. The least you can do is let me have a jug of ale to help me with my sorrow.'

Mother looked as if she was about to drag Butcher off his pony and lay about him with her fists. I wouldn't have bet money on him winning such a fight. She stared for several moments without replying until even he became uncomfortable at the silence.

'Well, woman, am I to be expected to bear this day as dry as chaff in the field!'

Slowly, Mother turned her head to me, fury and sadness fighting for control of her expression. 'Prepare our horse, Aila. Fit his pack harness. I'll fetch a jug.'

By the time I led Abel out of the barn, our obnoxious neighbour had gone. We were silent as we loaded food and other items into the large carrying bags. When we had finished I took hold of my mother and held her tightly. The death of babies was a common occurrence, yet I knew that this one would affect her deeply. Eventually, she patted my back and pulled away, regaining some of her usual composure.

'We must control our emotions so that we can best help Peggy, and we must keep our thoughts to ourselves, at least for now. But I'll tell you this, daughter: if I were your father, Butcher would currently be hanging by his heels in the barn.'

* * *

Peggy was sitting by the smoky fire, holding Calum almost exactly as she had been when we last saw her with the baby. Mother bent down and took one of her hands. Even in the gloom it looked dirty.

'Peggy, my love, Calum is with the Lord now and He will see to all of his spiritual needs. We must see to the needs of his body, for that is our task on earth. May I take him to wash and change into clean clothes?'

Peggy let Mother take the bundle from her arms and we both walked outside. She tenderly pulled away the shawl from the tiny face and I couldn't prevent the tears that flowed down

131

my cheeks. Calum was so beautiful, so perfect, it was difficult to believe he wasn't just sleeping.

'Oh, dear Lord.' Mother sighed. 'Leave me here. I'll see to Calum and Peggy.'

'She doesn't seem to know us.'

'No. We'll have to take charge and it's probably best that Butcher isn't here. Ride to the carpenter and tell him to make a coffin and bring it to us, then carry on to Murdo and explain what's happened. Tell him you want to buy a plot in the cemetery and also pay for his services to dig the grave. Here, you'll need this.' Mother was still holding the dead baby, but she pulled out a small bag of coin from a hip pocket and handed it over. 'The next few days will be terribly difficult. We must remember that they're much worse for Peggy.'

* * *

Although Calum and the coffin he rested in were barely any weight at all, I felt crushed by them. This was a sorrow that could not be measured on any weighing scales.

After we had completed our tasks and returned home the day of Calum's death, Mother and I had debated long into the evening about how to get to the Lothmore kirk. In the end the only sensible option was for me to ride Abel and have the tiny coffin balanced in front of me on the horse's back. And so, two days later I rode, while my mother and Peggy walked. Butcher had taken himself off somewhere and we suspected it was to the tavern at Brora, where he would hope to get free drinks throughout the day from sympathetic customers.

As well as paying Murdo for his services, I had hired the kirk's mortcloth. This one was for children, yet still too large for the tiny coffin. I was certain that Reverend MacDonald would not have charged a fee in these circumstances, but only the minister could make this decision and in his absence I decided to pay rather than make a request to Reverend McNeil, despite his surprising recent display of kindness.

Abel seemed to sense the importance of the burden he carried, and he plodded along without showing any of his usual frustration as such a slow pace. We passed few people, but those that we did meet respectfully stepped to one side or stopped work, men removing their bonnets. Most of the local population would have already heard of the tragedy and, even if they hadn't, everyone recognised the kirk's black mortcloth.

The cemetery was empty apart from Murdo. The small pile of soil near where he stood seemed only to emphasise the desperate sadness of the situation. He came over and took the bundle down from Abel, then helped my mother unwrap the mortcloth, which she folded carefully and gave to me. I went into the kirk and put it on the table just inside the door, the one that normally held the collection plate.

Murdo was a kind man, and although he remained silent there was a gentle courtesy about his manner and movements. Once he had laid the coffin in the freshly dug hole, he stepped away to give us some privacy.

The fierce reaction against Roman Catholicism following the Reformation meant that Church of Scotland ministers did not conduct funeral services; the idea of saying prayers for the dead went totally against reformed tradition. Indeed, many families didn't attend burials, even of loved ones, and would sometimes leave it to the carpenter to bring the body in the coffin he had made and bear the responsibility of seeing both put into the earth.

Our presence exposed us to dangerous criticism from the community and kirk elders because the generally accepted practice in the Highlands was that women didn't attend funerals, regardless of their relationship to the deceased. But Mother was completely against this line of thinking and would not leave Calum in the keeping of strangers.

I did have some doubts about what we were doing. Mother and I were strong enough to endure any potential conflict but I worried about Peggy, who simply went along with what was suggested. I guess we make our decisions in life and have to face the consequences, so the three of us stood, holding hands, near the edge of the grave.

'Dear Lord,' said Mother, 'we ask you to accept into your keeping baby Calum, whose body we now lay to rest in your sacred soil. We don't understand why he was taken from us so young. He can be guilty of no crime against God or man. His innocence cannot be disputed. And we ask, Lord, that you look over his poor mother, Peggy, who now grieves with such despair that her spirit is in a dark place. Please help her to find the light.'

We remained in silence for many minutes, each lost in their own thoughts, in their own prayers. I had been too ill to attend my father's funeral and at the time was only vaguely aware of it happening. It was one of the few occasions when Mother got a trusted neighbour to sit with me while she travelled to the Inverness cemetery. It must have been the loneliest journey she had ever made. I realised, looking down upon the coffin, that we had never spoken of that day.

Why did I never visit Father's grave?

'Peggy, we have done what we can for Calum and must leave the remaining tasks to Murdo,' said Mother.

He may not have been able to hear what was said, but Murdo had been involved in enough funerals to know what point we had reached. He walked slowly towards us.

'I will see to wee Calum's last needs with respect, Mistress Butcher.'

I liked him for that, for the way he addressed Peggy and for mentioning the baby by name, not merely considering it as another paid job. She nodded to him and Mother shook his hand.

'Thank you, Murdo. Your help and kindness are much appreciated.'

With that the three of us left; the part-time gravedigger, precentor, schoolmaster and session clerk waiting patiently until we were out of sight before he put his shovel into the small mound by his feet.

13

Dornoch, 30 April 1727

ONCE WE BEGAN ATTENDING THE Dornoch market again our fortnightly trips seemed to come around more quickly on each occasion. As usual, we travelled from home the day before, Abel pulling our sledge loaded with barrels of ale. If the track was particularly good, Mother would join me on the horse's back.

The market square early that morning was a place of frantic activity. Stallholders moved stock and animals in a seemingly endless procession of confusion, adding to the mayhem by pushing through the crowds with baskets, hand barrows and sledges pulled by ponies and sometimes simply manhandled.

Birds, legs tied together and carried upside down, spread fear and feathers as they flapped in panic, while pigs rooted around unchecked, upsetting everything and everyone around them. Items got dropped and knocked over. People got angry with their animals and each other. They hurried to pay fees and rushed to lay out stalls to show off products to their best advantage before competitors could beat them to it.

Excitement, irritation, good-humoured blether and shouts of warning fought with each other constantly. I loved every second, yet throughout it my mind felt detached, in its own state of conflicting thoughts and emotions; worrying about poor Peggy who we hadn't been allowed to see since Calum's funeral, remembering how I had carried his tiny body in front of me as I rode Abel and, I could not deny it, thinking about Jack.

Mother and I had seen the troupe again two weeks earlier. Amidst the sorrow of baby Calum's death, I was drawn towards their world of make-believe and performance like a moth to a candle. But this attraction was much more than a single flame, it was a beacon of light that had unsettled the rhythm of my life as surely as if night no longer existed and there was only continuous sunshine. I knew Mother sensed it, these new feelings within me that tinged our lovely croft with an aura of unrest that it never had before.

Lately I went to the beach or took myself away on Abel much more often than normal. Mother let me go without comment, without reminding me that my help was actually required with some particular task. She knew that I was aware of it and if I felt the need to be alone that strongly then she was willing to let me go.

'Aila, are you going to stand there daydreaming for the whole of the morning!'

Of course, her patience wasn't endless.

'Sorry, Mother.'

There was no sign of Duncan or any of the officers, so I took Abel back to Mistress Hamilton's property. On my return I met Jack. Instantly, the noise and bustle around us melted away into silent mist, and only his beautiful face remained.

'Aila.'

'Hello.' I was struck dumb for a moment until I remembered that Bess had not been well the previous fortnight. 'How's

Bess?' His smile disappeared and I was almost sorry for asking.

'Not good. She's as stubborn and tough as an old mule and won't slow down. At the end of the play the other night we almost had to carry her off the stage. We've rented a room for her in Dornoch. Of course, Ellen had to stay with her and that meant Malie as well. The rest of us are still at our camp outside town. It's odd not being with the women. It's the first time since the troupe was formed that we haven't spent every night together.'

'You're here early.'

'I wondered if you might like some help setting up.'

His smile had returned. And so had mine. We weaved our way through the crowds to our stall, where Mother was waiting.

'Good morning Jack. Are you here to put those impressive muscles to use?'

'I am indeed, Mistress Horne. Just tell me what to do.'

'It's always a pleasure to instruct a lovely young man what to do.'

Mother had a strange expression of amusement, and for an instant I thought that she was being terribly rude. I was already dismissing the uncharitable thought when Jack laughed as if it had indeed been a ribald joke of a very base nature. I knew I wasn't worldly about private matters between a man and a woman, but I could feel my face flushing with shame at the very idea that Mother should imply, even in jest, that ...

'We need these barrels on the bench,' I said, perhaps a little too loudly.

With Jack's help the stall was set up quickly. Duncan walked by as we were working and, seeing we didn't need his help, he nodded and carried on. Jack updated Mother about Bess and she offered to remain on the stall while we went to see how our friend was doing.

The women were staying in a room at the Drovers' Inn. When we got there, I suggested that it was more appropriate for me to go up to the bedroom so Jack went to find a table. Ellen answered my knock and I could tell immediately that she was worried. She stepped into the corridor and quietly closed the door.

'None of us have had much sleep. We're all in one bed and Bess has been coughing and restless throughout the night, sweating one minute and shivering uncontrollably the next. Now she's exhausted and finally asleep along with Malie.'

'How is she?'

'Oh, young and used to a lot worse than a night of unrest. Malie will be fine.'

The two of us went downstairs and Ellen relayed her news to Jack.

'We'll have a terrible time trying to get her not to do any performances today,' he said, a frown deepening on his face. 'Once she's set her mind to doing something I doubt that even Hector could prevent her.'

Bess proved her hardiness and determination, getting out of bed regardless of how she felt and sitting with the troupe that noon when I joined them at the Wolf's Head.

'I'm telling you it's true!' For the last twenty minutes I had become increasingly irritated at their complete refusal to accept a word I was saying. The problem was that they were such good actors I couldn't decide if anyone was merely pretending or indeed if they all were, which made me even more insistent. I suspected that this is what they intended. 'Jack?'

'Aila, I believe there are sea monsters that can swallow a ship and its crew whole, and men who can turn base metal into gold. I could almost be persuaded to believe that Sim once bought a round of drinks, although he would have had to be very drunk at the time, but this story of yours . . .?' He spread his hands and shrugged.

'My father told me!'

'Ah, and haven't you already explained to us what a good storyteller he was,' said Sim. 'And I wasn't *very* drunk.'

'He wasn't making this up. And I can prove it!'

This was why, soon afterwards, I led four of them a short distance from Dornoch, Sim and Bess remaining at the tavern so that they could talk privately and Bess didn't exert herself. Within a few minutes of arriving at the place I had been describing, we saw two figures that I was sure would confirm everything I had been saying.

'Look! Look! Those two men there.'

'Oh, they're fine gentlemen and no mistake,' said Ellen.

'I can't see what they're doing,' said Malie.

'Get up on my shoulders,' said Hector, bending down.

Malie shrieked when he stood up. 'Don't drop me! I'm so high I can almost touch the sky. What are they doing?'

'Well,' said Hector, 'that man there has just put a small leather ball on the ground.'

'Why?'

'According to Aila, he'll beat it with a wooden stick.'

'It's a club, and he's not going to beat it, but hit it,' I said, and even to my ears I sounded like a frustrated schoolmaster.

141

'Why's he going to hit the ball?'

'Because Malie,' I continued, 'he's going to try and put it in a hole.'

'A hole in the ground. Like a rabbit hole?'

'No! Not a rabbit hole. Weren't any of you even listening to me! It's one that's been made specially.'

'Did those men make the hole?'

'I don't expect so ... More likely some other men.'

'Why does he want to put his ball in another man's hole?'

I couldn't answer straight away. Next to me, Jack was standing with his hands on his hips, laughing loudly, while Ellen had almost collapsed against Hector. The blacksmith himself was rocking with mirth so much that Malie shrieked again in fear.

'Hector!'

'Just ... Watch.'

I was desperately trying to retain some shred of dignity. The man, who had been practising his swing, took his shot, sending the ball disappearing into the distance. His companion laid down his ball. Hector's laugh was so loud that the man looked over and shook his fist. Ellen waved back as if they were old friends. Moments later he took his shot, the club swishing through the air and not making contact with anything.

'Was he just trying to frighten the ball this time?' asked Malie.

For the first time I began to suspect her innocence about this subject. I was losing control, while the man lost his temper and shouted something at us that we couldn't hear above our own noise.

'You're ... all ... putting ... him ... off.'

142

'Heaven save us,' said Ellen. 'They appear to be intelligent, at least for men, yet they're doing this of their own free will?'

'They are! It's a game of skill.'

'What I don't understand,' this was Jack, 'is what they do once the ball has disappeared down a hole?'

'Maybe he produces another one?' suggested Hector.

'Christ, how many balls do they have?' asked Ellen.

The desire to laugh was washing over me so fiercely I could hardly take a breath to speak. 'He removes the ball and he ... he ...'

'Hee, hee!' said Jack.

'Stop it! He ... puts it back on the ground ... and ...' I couldn't get the last few words out of my mouth. I had completely lost the fight to retain any self-control and tears were streaming down my face. Malie, now a crumpled heap, had wrapped her arms around Hector's head in order to keep balanced, while Ellen had sunk to her knees and seemed to be crying into her hands. Next to me Jack was bent over, speechless.

'And hits it again!'

* * *

'I wonder how Aila is getting on trying to prove her story?' said Sim, still sitting next to Bess in the Wolf's Head.

'Poor Aila. You were all awful to her.'

'Not entirely. I don't think everyone knew about the game. More ale?'

'Not for me.'

'You don't look well. Do you want to go back to the Drovers' Inn to rest?'

'With my theatre already set up for the children! I can't let them down.'

'You try so hard not to let anyone down.'

They fell silent, listening to the murmur of voices and the sounds of people eating and drinking flowing throughout the tavern. There was a part of Sim that was so ingrained he couldn't prevent himself subconsciously checking out other customers for potential danger. He decided that the only unpleasant sight was the head hanging above the bar, said to have belonged to the last wolf in Sutherland.

'I think,' said Bess eventually, 'I've let you down.'

'Why do you say that?'

'Because, you foolish man, I've loved you all these years and never spoken of my feelings. Now, my days are numbered.'

'You've a long while yet.'

'No, Sim, I haven't. There's no time left for anything but complete honesty between us.'

'Sorry. I'm a coward.'

'You're no coward.'

'I was too afraid to tell you how I felt.'

'In that, we were both at fault. Yet I've embraced every minute . . . Acting on stage, working, eating and laughing side by side. Our love might not have been openly acknowledged, but we've lived more closely than many married couples.'

'Aye, that's the truth. It's been fun, just as you promised it would be that night we met.'

'Ah, Stirling, the start of our new life. I remember when you walked into that room with Ellen as if it was yesterday, and feeling immediately jealous that she was with you.'

'Jealous? Of Ellen with me!'

144

'Don't put yourself down, Sim. I saw beyond what others see on the surface. While you were so engrossed with Hector and Jack, I asked Ellen if you were a couple.'

'I never knew that!'

'It was women's talk, not meant for the ears of men.'

'I would be speechless at that revelation ... if it wasn't for one thing.'

'What?'

Sim grinned, taking his time finishing off the tankard of ale.

'Sim! You tell me this instant what you're talking about!'

'Later that night, Hector and I were out at the ... Well, we were standing next to each other. There was no one else around ... and I asked him.'

'You asked him what?

'If you were attached to anyone.'

* * *

I felt terribly guilty as I approached our stall, particularly when I saw how busy it was. Mother had generously offered to let me join the troupe for a noonday meal and the subsequent trip to watch the men play golf meant that I had been away for a great deal longer than should have been expected. She was, as ever, not only kind and loving but wise.

'I'm sorry not to have returned sooner,' I said, feeling and sounding almost like a small girl again, expecting to get into trouble for misbehaving.

'I've been selling ale since before you were born and I'm not past it yet. And for you, sir?'

It was a fact that since the accident Mother could run the stall more efficiently than I could on my own. She made no more of my absence and I quickly settled back into our routine. During the occasional quiet moments I told her about our adventure and she laughed for a very long time, echoing my own suspicions that some of them, if not all, had been teasing me.

* * *

It was later that afternoon when I bumped into Jack again. Perhaps it wasn't such a surprise as I had gone looking for him when Mother had told me to take myself off for a walk. She knew that at times I got frustrated on the stall and, having seen markets in some of the most beautiful cities in Europe, she wasn't too bothered about looking yet again around the one in Dornoch. I think it almost made her sad, what she had seen in her life and what she was now able to experience.

'Hello.'

Jack was standing a short distance from Bess's tiny theatre, positioned so that he could see her setting up behind the stage as well as the large group of children gathering in front of it.

'Hello, Aila.'

'Have you stopped laughing at me yet?'

'If I don't think about it, otherwise I'm likely to start again.'

It was fascinating to watch Bess setting out various hand puppets on the ground nearby and I assumed they were laid out in the order that she wanted to put them on. Jack and I talked for a little while longer as we waited, but our conversation stopped mid-sentence when we saw Bess slowly slump backwards. We were with her in seconds.

'What's happened?' asked Jack, concern etched into his face.

'It's just a touch of the ague,' she gasped. You could see sweat coming through her clothes. I was kneeling on the other side of her and she grabbed my arm with surprising strength. 'Aila, promise me you'll entertain the children.'

'Me!'

'Yes, you can do it.'

'I don't know how, I'm sorry.'

'You do. They mustn't be left disappointed. Promise!'

Bess became agitated at my refusal and then started coughing. I had no choice but to agree, although what I was supposed to do with a bunch of children was beyond me. Hector and Sim arrived almost together as if the troupe was connected by invisible threads that alerted them all when one was in trouble.

'Let's get you somewhere more comfortable,' said Hector.

Bess was helped away and I was suddenly left alone at the back of the little theatre wondering what on earth I was meant to do now. From this side there was an obvious peep hole that allowed the audience to be viewed without them realising. I looked through this and saw children staring at the stage, waiting for something magical to happen. There seemed to be even more of them than only a few minutes earlier.

I felt helpless. Since the accident children normally ran away from me and these days I felt awkward in their presence, as if I was always waiting for something bad to happen. There was nothing I could do to help. They would just have to come back another day, when Bess had recovered.

Honour can only be achieved by the way we live.

I heard my own voice when I was seven years old, telling Mother how Father had explained the concept of honour.

You have given your word, Aila.

I was beset by guilt and panic. Frantically, I examined the puppets scattered about my feet, almost hoping that one of them would suddenly jump up and explain what to do. I had no conscious thought, certainly no actual plan, as I pulled off my leather glove and forced my hand into a figure representing a young girl. There was just enough movement in my fingers for it to work.

Then I found a puppet of a man, which I had to pull onto my right hand using my teeth. I still had no idea what I was doing and glanced once more through the peep hole. A couple of children were crying and one had stood up. Anxious parents had moved closer. My heart was pounding. This was madness! I raised my arm a fraction, hesitated, then committed myself to a journey that had no visible path, lifting my hand higher so that the puppet popped up on to the stage. There was a gasp from those in the real world.

Now what do I do?

My body, my entire being, felt as though it no longer belonged to me. Before I was even aware of it, the second puppet was on the stage. It was as though they both had a life of their own and I had become merely the prop, as unimportant as the wood holding up the tiny curtains. My mind was as blank as newly fallen snow. The figures looked at the audience, each other, and spoke.

'Father?'

'Mmm.'

'How do we become the people we are?'

'Now that's a very good question. You see, we should all examine who we are, because then we can discover how to become a better person.'

'But what about me, Father? How did I become me?'

'Well, let me think ... Imagine you're an apple.'

148

14

Kintradwell, 1 May 1727

WHEN MOTHER HEARD THAT BESS had collapsed, she insisted that her new friend should be brought to our croft where it would be much easier to care for her. This was my mother as she used to be, and I was pleased to see her keen to take on a role that had played such an important part of her earlier life. Neither Sim nor Ellen would be separated from Bess, and without them there was no troupe, so in the end it was decided that they should all come and stay for whatever length of time was required.

The day after my performance with the puppets, Jack and the others travelled with us north along the ancient drovers' trail. We stopped a couple of times for rest and refreshments and once to gaze upon the impressive Dunrobin Castle, seat of the powerful Earl of Sutherland.

As soon as we reached Kintradwell, our home was transformed with noise, chatter and excitement in a way I hadn't thought possible. Although Bess had ridden all the way, the journey had exhausted her so she was tucked up with blankets in an armchair while Sim relit the fire using our tinderbox and pieces of charred linen that we kept handy for the task. Mother and Ellen sorted out my box-bed, which still hadn't been used since the previous autumn.

I was helping to unload one of the sledges with Jack and Malie when we overheard Hector talking to the three ponies. We stopped to listen. With great politeness and formality he explained to each animal that this was Abel's home and while they were guests, they had to be respectful. Malie was immediately helpless with laughter and had to lean against Jack to stay upright. He put his arm around her and smiled fondly, then he looked at me above her head and my world felt complete. We were still being entertained by the animal conversations when Sim came outside.

'Hector's been speaking to the ponies as though they were gentlemen at a ball,' said Malie.

'Ah, the big man is always a stickler for correctness. He's probably got them bowing to each other.'

'How's Bess?' I asked.

'Arguing with Ellen and your mother about being put to bed in the middle of the day. As the fire's going well I thought I would make a tactful retreat. I see that your stack of peat is low.'

'Yes, we have to rely on our neighbour for supplies.'

'Well you won't be doing that this summer,' said Sim. 'We men are going to need work to do while we're here or we'll be going soft above the neck and below it.'

'I suppose ...' I hesitated, thinking about Butcher's likely violent reaction at losing the profit he made each year.

'That's settled then,' said Jack. 'In the morning we'll make a proper list of all the jobs that need doing. We have to earn our keep. Back to work, young ginger top.'

'Yes sir!'

Malie stood to attention and saluted like a miniature soldier, then the four of us set about finishing the task of moving all of the items indoors that weren't going to remain on the sledges, like the parts of the stage and props. Hector joined us, and as we worked, talked and laughed everything felt so perfect that somehow it didn't seem real.

*　*　*

By mid-afternoon animals, people, items and food were settled and stored away. Once Bess had felt the comfort of the heather-filled mattress with a clean sheet and fresh-smelling blankets, she announced that while they remained at the croft, my box-bed would do quite nicely. It was decided that Ellen and Malie would sleep near the fire each night and the men would be in the barn. Mother and I would continue where we had been, and this suited everyone fine.

Two of our hens had all but stopped laying and so Sim wrung their necks and proceeded to demonstrate to Malie how to pluck them. She sat by his feet, enthralled by his explanation. The day was warm and apart from Bess we were all outside enjoying a rest and ale while watching the two figures increasingly surrounded by feathers.

Every so often Malie would lay her head on Sim's thigh so that her face was only inches from the bird. In these rare moments, I could study her surreptitiously, and I began to understand something that I hadn't fully appreciated before.

Malie didn't just crave affection, she was desperate for human contact at every possible opportunity. In fact, I hardly ever saw Malie physically unattached to one of the group; she usually had her arms around someone or they had their arms around her. I remembered how she took my hand that first day we met and didn't let go until she went to hug Hector and make fun of his baldness.

I instinctively understood her need following my own experiences after the accident. But I had Mother and we were extremely close. Until recently Malie had no one. I tried to imagine what it must be like to go through life without anyone to hold you, never to feel the warmth of another person's body. It was a terrifying image and I had a glimpse of my life once Mother died.

Unnoticed by anyone, Sim had gathered feathers in his hand and he suddenly pretended to pluck Malie, releasing feathers every few seconds as if they were being pulled out of her hair. It was cleverly done and we all laughed.

'Now it's your turn,' he said when his performance was over.

The two swapped places and much to everyone's delight she began plucking the second hen, her nimble fingers quick and efficient. I found this task a huge challenge and I couldn't prevent a moment of envy, although it was quickly gone.

* * *

Later on, Hector set up a fire and the troupe's cooking pot outside, which meant that we could all sit around and enjoy the unusual warmth of that May evening. Mother remained inside. She had made a barley broth and was patiently feeding this to Bess, who sat propped up in bed. Our meal was still bubbling away, but the jugs of ale were already going around and so were questions about the croft. I was equally fascinated by their lives and we were deep in conversation when Mother joined us.

'Bess says to tell you goodnight.'

There was a shouted chorus of 'goodnight Bess' and a few moments later a voice could be heard through the open doorway.

'For goodness' sake stop making so much bloody noise!'

Jack had mentioned that he played the harp, but I had no idea he was so incredibly gifted until after our meal when we sat around to listen. I was filled with awe. The music seemed magical, as if it transported us to another place. Ellen sang and afterwards she suggested that I should sing. To do this while accompanied by Jack was a thrill I couldn't believe. However, the best singing had been saved until last. Mother and I looked at each other in astonishment when Malie began.

I had never so wanted an evening to last. If I could have stopped time by halting the pendulum on Father's clock I would have done it, and perhaps never have started it again.

* * *

When we had eventually come inside Bess had been restless and Ellen had spent quite some time soothing her. Now we were all trying to settle down. It was strange to lie next to Mother with other people in the room. We often prayed together before undressing and I normally left this decision to her, but she didn't suggest it.

She had been fussing around Bess since we had arrived at the croft and had looked very tired a little earlier. I supposed it was another sign of ageing. She stroked my hair. There had been no chance to speak together, which was highly unusual, and now we couldn't easily talk without disturbing the others. However, she whispered in my ear.

'Happy birthday.'

'Thank you.'

I was born on 1 May 1707, the date generally being remembered as the day the Acts of Union between England and Scotland came into force, rather than for the arrival of a small, red and rather noisy baby. Father always said that the tiny scrap in his hands was far more important than any agreement between countries.

'Jack's pleasant.'

'They all are,' I whispered back.

'Mmm.'

I poked her gently in the ribs and she chuckled quietly.

'Go to sleep, Mother.'

* * *

I slept soundly, although I was once aware of movement during the night, and when I got up in the morning I saw that Malie was next to Bess. Ellen was already dressed and had the fire burning brightly. I was surprised at how silently she had moved around. My mother was still asleep, so I dressed and went over to the other end of the room where Ellen was making tea.

'Bess became restless, so I got Malie to lie beside her. It seems to have calmed her down.'

'You're very close.'

'Yes.'

'How did you get together with the troupe?'

Ellen poured tea into cups and it felt odd that she had so naturally taken on this role, almost as though I was the guest. I sensed that she was considering what to say. The blankets had already been neatly tidied away, but we unfolded one and laid it on the floor in front of the fire so that it was easier to sit together and speak. Even then Ellen remained silent for quite a while.

'I was a limmer.'

I convinced myself I had misheard. I couldn't equate the thoughtful person in front of me with the commonly held beliefs about such women.

'You heard right,' she continued. 'I sold my body. When my father died my mother took up with a man. Let's just say that he wasn't a good man. I ran away with nothing more than the clothes on my back. I was young, yet well aware of being attractive and ended up working in a Glasgow brothel. It was very upmarket. I did have my standards.'

My jaw was hanging open. I had never been so lost for words. When Mother used to go on about standards, she had something completely different in mind. What would she say about this? Could I even tell her? Ellen was amused at my reaction. She reached over, placed her fingertips under my chin and gently closed my mouth, which made me feel foolish.

'It's not something that's talked about. Malie doesn't know and I would like to keep it from her.'

'I won't tell anyone. Do the others realise?'

'Of course. It's how I met Sim. He was ... Well, that's his story for him to tell. There was some bother ... There was always *some* bother locally, but there were killings among a few of the more violent city gangs that got out of control. Sim had to leave in a hurry and he asked me to go with him.

'Despite his fierce appearance and reputation, he had always been kind. Being alone with me was the only time he allowed himself to show a side of his character that he couldn't risk

155

revealing to anyone else. Anyway, we left the very day he suggested it and never went back.'

'But, don't you mind?'

'Mind?'

'About Sim and Bess?'

'Lord above, Aila, Sim and I were never in love. There had been an intimacy and there was a trust between us. I wouldn't have gone with him without that. We made good travelling companions, but it was never anything more.'

'Oh.'

'A couple of months later we arrived in Stirling and one evening in a tavern we came across Jack, Hector and Bess. They had recently met each other and were trying to put together a travelling troupe of performers, who could also put on plays. The idea seemed like it might be fun.'

'And has it been?'

'My God, it's certainly been that . . . Fun, tough, dangerous. There've been plenty of tears and arguments. I've known us have lots of money and no money at all, on occasions the five of us existing only on what one of us could earn. Yet we've always been there for each other, looking out and protecting as fiercely as if we were all close blood relatives.'

'Your experiences have been so different to mine,' I said. The observation sounded weak. By most standards I had led a privileged life.

'We all do what we have to in order to survive. That period of my life in Glasgow is not one I would have chosen, no woman would, but it's behind me now and whatever the future holds I'll never go back to it. Besides, I no longer have the figure.'

'You're still attractive, Ellen.' I meant it. I had seen the way men watched her with desire in their eyes.

'That's kind of you, but I'm not what I was to look at.'

'Well, I can understand that.'

'You are far lovelier than you realise.'

With that she took hold of my hands and kissed them. I was so taken aback at the contact that I flinched. Our conversation was brought to an abrupt halt by my mother waking up.

'Have I slept in? That's not like me.'

'Good morning, Janet. I think you spent so long yesterday taking care of everyone that you're worn out. I'll bring some tea over.'

'Oh, I rather like this service,' said Mother, sitting up. 'I could get used to it. Are you taking note, Aila?'

15

Kintradwell, 3 May 1727

UNLESS THE WEATHER WAS UNNATURALLY wet, local people made their way every May to a large open hillside about a mile from where we lived. This was the month to start cutting peat. Each man normally worked the same patch that the generations before him living at that particular dwelling had used, a matter of tradition rather than ownership. Over time the land had been turned into a mosaic of oblong troughs of varying lengths, widths and depths.

It was common for entire families to be involved in the hugely important event of *buain na mònadh*, and I had often ridden out to watch the activities. The old men were always keen to explain what was happening. People worked in groups, particularly when they had to dig deeper into the earth. When the area around a hole was being extended, the first task was to remove the turf at the edge, which was then put to one side. The material underneath could range in colour from light brown to black, and everyone wanted the latter because it dried more quickly and burned hotter.

'You cut it to the size of the good Lord's Bible,' an ancient Highlander had once told me before demonstrating how to use the *tairsgear*, which made the task of cutting the layers easier. Once cut, each block was laid on the ground to dry. At this stage the peat was too wet to be moved or handled, and it was normally left for a couple of weeks before people returned to take it home. The work was gruelling and time consuming, with cutting, travelling and stacking continuing over several months.

Butcher always seemed to work alone, and I was never certain if this was his choice or because the other men refused to be involved with him. When we had first arrived in the area, Mother wanted to agree a daily rate, to pay him for the time he spent obtaining our peat. Butcher had demanded to charge us as if it was his product to sell. Of course, this made it much more expensive. She had lost the argument, much to our irritation.

Sometimes poor people paid the most for their peat because they were forced to purchase it from someone with a means to transport it off the hillside. On many occasions I had seen women bent almost double under the weight of the creel on their back as they struggled to walk home with as much of the free fuel as possible.

Yet even these folk were better off than those who were forced to burn dried cow dung, along with whatever suitable material they could find locally such as brushwood, gorse or broom. Coal was generally too expensive for the majority of people, despite there being a mine near Brora, and cutting trees wasn't permitted on land owned by a laird even when there were substantial woods.

A few days after their arrival I rode out with Jack, Hector and Sim, the latter's pony pulling a sledge loaded with tools, plus food and water for the day. The frantic activity going on meant that it was easier to leave the animals and sledge, and carry the tools for the last hundred yards.

'I swear the three of you look like small boys about to be given a great feast,' I said, as we stood around the edge of the hole that Butcher had worked the previous year. His own patch was a short distance away, and although I hadn't spotted him, he could easily have been hidden from sight. 'If you grin any wider your smile will meet around the back of your heads!'

'That's a great line,' said Jack. 'Can I use it in a play?'

'Only after you've dug this peat.'

'You're a hard woman, Aila,' said Sim.

'You have no idea how hard I can be,' I said. However, my attempt at sternness was soon destroyed by Hector, who moved to stand behind me then gently laid his chin on my shoulder so that our faces were side by side. It felt so utterly ridiculous that I couldn't prevent myself from laughing.

'Come on, boys,' he said, removing his jacket and waistcoat. 'There'll be no food until we've got this task well under way.'

I watched for a while then walked around, speaking to a few of the other men before returning to Abel. I hadn't been with the horse for very long when Sim joined me.

'I need some water,' he said, picking up and drinking from a stoneware jug that we had filled from the Kintradwell burn on our way over. 'I can't tell you how good it feels to be doing simple outdoor work with those two, away from the stench of cities and towns. We can become so caught up in performances and our desire to entertain that we sometimes lose ourselves. Maybe that's a good thing, maybe not. I don't know if that makes sense?'

'Yes, it does. You have a huge, sensitive heart, Sim, and you care deeply about others.'

'Don't tell anyone. I have my reputation to consider.'

I laughed, but the sound died in my throat because I saw Butcher approaching us and even from a distance I could see the anger in his face. Moments later he stood in front of me, having given the slightly built figure nearby a dismissive glance. Sim appeared strangely detached as if he didn't want to be involved.

'What are you doing? You buy your peat from me!'

'We have no contract with you and we're free to do as we wish.'

'Don't try using your clever words! I'm not having it. And who do you think you're looking at?' he added, glaring at Sim.

Sim shrugged his shoulders in what was, I suspected, an uncharacteristic show of subservience. I could guess why, because what we could see, and Butcher could not, was that Hector was striding towards us. He tapped Peggy's husband lightly on the shoulder, and when he turned around his face was only at chest height to the huge man. Hector grabbed Butcher's jacket and lifted him so high he was forced to stand on his toes. People nearby had stopped work in order to watch, and more than one man was smiling.

'Aila's my friend, and if you threaten her in any way I will pluck out your eyeballs and boil them in my broth! I will slice your liver and eat it on my bannock! I will tear out your filthy heart and pound it with a rock until it is pulp, then I will stuff it down your ugly gullet! And my vengeance will fill me with joy such as has never been seen before!'

I couldn't believe the transformation in Hector. He was terrifying. There was nothing of the gentle giant that I knew him to be. Butcher appeared to be almost fainting in fright and could hardly speak coherently.

'I ... I ... You've ... no right.'

'Right!'

Hector suddenly let him go, but Sim had stuck out a leg and moments later Butcher was flat on his back looking up at the three of us in horror.

'Maybe you should pluck out one eyeball now?' suggested Sim helpfully. 'The left looks the tastiest.'

Butcher whimpered, and if he had been anyone else I would have felt sorry for him.

'No, I ate a couple of babies for breakfast and I'm still feeling quite full. Now crawl away and never threaten my friends again.'

My violent, bullying neighbour turned himself over and crawled away in the dirt on his hands and knees. When he was several yards from us he stood up and ran off. Hector was grinning from ear to ear.

'I've always loved that scene,' he said, 'particularly the bit about boiling eyeballs in the broth.'

'Act three, scene two,' said Sim, 'just before the villain rides off on his horse. The big man's normally saying it to me, Aila. Nice to see it done to someone else.'

It was only then that I understood, for the threat had appeared so real I had almost been holding my breath in shock.

'It's from a play!'

Sim shook his head. 'I can't understand why I'm always the villain in these dramas. It doesn't seem right to me.'

'But, my small friend, you act the part so well,' said Hector, putting a consoling arm around his shoulder. 'It's almost as if you were made for the role.'

'I'm going to speak to the playwright.'

'Ah, the golden boy's quill is a thing of great power.'

'Well if I don't get any satisfaction I shall hide his bloody quill, and where I put it will make his eyes water!'

'What do you say, Aila?' said Hector, who was now laughing loudly.

'I say that you've both had your fun and we should be helping Jack.'

In response, they put an arm through each of mine and we walked back, blethering as though we had known each other all our lives.

I was so happy.

* * *

The following morning it seemed that every inch of indoor and outdoor space at our croft was filled with activity, noise and laughter. Sim had decided to make a couple of new besoms and sat amongst piles of hazel twigs plus two ash handles, which he had made longer than our existing ones so they were more suited to my height. Jack was making trips to the beach, leading two ponies fitted with pack harnesses to bring back seaweed, while Hector was cleaning out the barn, having repaired a hinge on one of the large doors.

Bess's health had improved enough for her to leave my bed for short periods, sitting outside when the sun was shining or near the fire when it wasn't. Sim was often by her side and they could be seen deep in conversation on many occasions; their obvious affection for each other was lovely to observe. That morning she was near the front door, appearing quite content to sit quietly and watch Sim work.

Malie was like a small child, wanting to explore everything, and I decided this might be a good opportunity to get an idea of what she knew about the countryside. I began by taking her to the farthest part of our croft.

'Last month we planted this with pease,' I said, pointing to an area in front of us, 'and that over there with oats.'

'It's just soil.'

'The seeds need time to grow into plants ... Time, warmth, water and seaweed.'

'Seaweed?'

'For a plant it's like food, just as you would eat porridge.'

'I don't think, when I was younger, that I had enough porridge,' she said, in a rare moment of being openly sad.

'I think you didn't get enough of many things, Malie, including hugs.' I took her in my arms, and when we eventually pulled apart she kept hold of my hand. 'We'll harvest the pease in August and the oats in September. Come on, there's much more to learn.'

We found Jack digging, the ponies grazing nearby on rough ground. 'You've come to watch a man hard at work,' he said, smiling.

'You're putting seaweed into the soil because the plants need their porridge.'

'Well, that's certainly one way of describing it.'

'When this is ready we're going to grow bere,' I said, adding, 'A type of barley,' in response to Malie's puzzled expression. 'It's good for making all sorts of foods. However, now it's our turn. A lot of the vegetables such as carrots, onions and beans have already been put in but you and I, Malie, are about to start planting kail.'

'Are we?'

'We are.'

'And I,' said Jack, 'am off to the beach for more porridge.'

* * *

After the noonday meal Sim presented a new besom each to Mother and me as though they were great gifts. Everyone applauded and it was good to see that Bess still felt able to be outside.

'Sim, that is the best besom I have ever held,' said my mother, demonstrating its effectiveness by giving the floor in the doorway a quick sweep. 'I can see Aila and me fighting over who will be the one to clean!'

Later that afternoon I found Malie at our table carefully turning the pages of my father's large family Bible. We owned a huge number of books, more than a dozen, kept safely on a high, sturdy shelf, with titles covering subjects ranging from medicine and travel to astronomy and the law. There was some poetry plus one work of fiction, *Robinson Crusoe*, which Father had given me for my sixteenth birthday. There was no one else in the house, so I sat opposite Malie, silently watching as she continued, so lost in concentration that I initially misunderstood what I was seeing.

'Is this yours?' she said eventually, without looking up.

'It was my father's.'

'Do you mind me looking?'

'It would be wrong to forbid someone to look at a Bible. He would be pleased. Do you know your scriptures?'

'I've never held a Bible.'

It was only then that I realised, and I couldn't believe how slow I had been. 'Malie, can you read?'

'No. But the pages are beautiful and they're so thin. I never knew there were so many words.'

'Some of them are the same, but repeated, to make sentences.'

'What does ... that say?' she said, pointing at a line from Exodus. I knew it well enough to be able to read the text upside down.

'And if thou refuse to let them go, behold, I will smite all thy borders with frogs.'

'Frogs! What does that mean?'

'Oh Malie, how do I even begin?'

I did begin, in teaching Malie how to read and write while Mother, thankfully, took on the much more difficult task of explaining the Bible.

* * *

The most exciting event on the croft was the impending birth of our cow's calf, and as Hector accurately predicted this happened within the first week of their arrival. Highland calves were normally born during April or May in order to benefit from the growth of fresh pasture. As Mother and I had never kept a cow before this one, we were happy to leave the black-smith to provide any assistance that might be needed.

Although everyone wanted to be present at the birth, he would only allow Malie and me to attend as he didn't want the animal to be upset by a large group of people. Sim had shaken his head and Jack had laughed, but no one disagreed, and so I found myself that afternoon standing with Malie outside the stall.

'Malie, do you know how babies are made?' I had been surprised at how highly intelligent she was. She grasped new ideas quickly and absorbed information like a sponge with water, yet I was often speechless at her ignorance.

'Aila, I'm not that stupid.'

'Sorry,' I said, smiling and feeling a little foolish.

She took my hand and we watched in fascination at the cow lying on its side. It wasn't long before two small white hoofs appeared, followed by thin legs, and then suddenly there was a wet, slimy body on the floor in front of us. It hadn't taken long at all. Hector gently wiped the animal with some of the clean straw that had been laid, while the cow busied itself eating the birth sac. The sight made Malie squeal in disgust, but her expression didn't change from one of utter wonder.

A short while later, while the trembling calf was being licked clean by his mother's rough tongue, Hector began to gently milk the cow, which seemed quite unconcerned by his touch. The scene reminded me of my father, watching such a big man being so tender. When he had finished with the teat he emptied the jug into a nearby pail and repeated the process with the other three, then he turned to us.

'Now, you two, take notice. We need to get the calf used to drinking from the pail rather than the mother's teats.'

'Why?' asked Malie.

'Because otherwise it's much more difficult to get milk for our own use, and without that what do we not have?'

'Butter or cheese.'

'That's right, but the first milk and the next is only for the calf. It's nature's way. See how it's different to what we're used to?' He tipped the pail slightly so that we could see the frothy liquid, which looked a bit lighter in colour than beaten eggs. 'Watch carefully, Sim is not the only one who can perform magic.'

Hector opened a jar of honey that he had requested from me earlier, although he wouldn't reveal why it was needed. He coated three fingers. The calf wobbled on its spindly legs as the cow continued to clean it. Hector moved the pail nearer and very carefully put his fingers into the mouth of the calf, which immediately started to suck. Then he slowly moved his arm and the newly born animal followed until its nose was almost in the milk.

'This is the most difficult part because its instinct is to suckle direct.' Hector submerged his hand so that the calf's mouth was drawn down into the liquid. When it began to drink, he lent back against the wall with a satisfied sigh. 'This will have to be done several times over the next few days until it becomes natural for the calf to drink from the pail and then even in the field he won't suckle from the mother. As long as I'm here or Aila is present then you can do it, Malie.'

'I can!'

Malie danced around the barn then ran out of the door, and for the next hour all anyone heard from the girl was about the magic that Hector had performed and how next time she was going to put her fingers in the calf's mouth.

*   *   *

Jack was on the bay, the pony following Abel as the horse picked its way carefully along the rough ground towards Loch Brora. This was our first day out together away from the croft and although I had suggested that we all came, everyone else immediately announced that they were busy with jobs that had to be done that morning. Even Malie said she couldn't leave the calf as she was still training it to sook from the pail and without her guidance Hector might not do things correctly.

And so there we were, just the two of us, with food and ale to see us over the next few hours. I knew the land well and the weather was fine, yet I had never felt so nervous. Why? What was there to be nervous about? We were only going for a short ride to exercise the animals.

During the journey I had been unable to think of a single subject that we could discuss, something my father would have found difficult to believe. However, Jack had also been quiet and I wondered if he had only come along because no one else would, and now he was resentful at leaving behind the lively entertainment that would inevitably be occurring back at the croft.

Well, he didn't have to accompany me.

We followed the path between Socach Hill and Killin Rock, but then went up to the top of the latter to admire the view across Brora and out to sea.

'It's stunning,' said Jack, after many minutes of silence. 'We're so busy living our lives, often just trying to survive, that there's little time to notice the beauty surrounding us.'

He looked at me and smiled. I thought that the surrounding beauty was nothing compared to the sight upon that pony.

'What are you thinking?' he asked.

'Oh, how lovely it is. I ride here sometimes when I want to be alone. There's a spot farther along where we can tie up the animals by the side of the water.'

About half an hour later we were sitting on a rock in a sheltered area, Abel and the pony happily foraging amongst the vegetation behind us. Nearby, a robin was singing, although I couldn't see it. I had never brought anyone here before, not even my mother.

'You like to be by yourself at times, Aila?'

'Yes, when I can be spared from the croft, which isn't that often.'

'And what do you do?'

'Do?'

'When you're alone.'

'Enjoy the views, sounds and smells. I love it all . . . The lochs hiding between the hills and mountains waiting to be discovered, the heather, the ancient trees, the birds. Over there! It's an otter with a trout. The loch's full of them.'

We watched it eat, which made the following silence less awkward.

'You know a lot about animals and birds,' said Jack.

'Most of what I know has come from my mother. My father's passion was the sea. You've never married?'

Aila Horne, you idiot! Asking such an intimate question!

'No. I won't lie and say that there haven't been women, but no one I wanted to spend the rest of my life with. And you?'

I assumed he was merely being polite. 'There haven't been any men knocking at the door.'

'The parish of Loth must be stocked with fools.'

'Just men who see.'

'I think they might look, but they don't see.'

We fell silent again. I didn't trust myself to speak. My heart was pounding at my foolishness and I hoped Jack didn't notice. Eventually, he spoke.

'I want to ask you something.'

'Ask me then.'

'I've been thinking about it for a while, but I don't want to offend or upset you in any way.'

'I haven't a clue as to what you're talking about.'

'I know you haven't, which is actually pleasant, but once I've asked . . . Well, then it can't be unsaid, can't be taken back and I couldn't bear to lose your trust and friendship.'

What on earth is he on about?

'Jack, I can't imagine that you're going to say something that's offensive and, believe me, my mother wouldn't have allowed me to ride up here with you alone if she thought for one second that you weren't a man of honour. And she is an extraordinary judge of character.'

'Your mother's a wise woman, that's for certain. Christ, I've never hesitated at such a thing before. I feel like an awkward boy.'

'For goodness' sake, what is it?'

'I would like to kiss you.'

'What!'

'I'm sorry, please don't be alarmed. I can see I've been too forward. You're not a woman to be kissed lightly . . . No, that's not quite what I mean either. I can't believe how much of a mess I'm making of this.'

'Why do you want to kiss me?'

I simply couldn't accept he had said what he had. The truth was, I had never been kissed by a man, only Father, and that was obviously in a different way altogether to what I guessed Jack meant.

'How can you even ask? I've wanted to ever since we met at the market.'

For a long while I simply stared at him in shock and confusion. 'You cried that day,' I said. 'I've never forgotten our conversation and how I felt that you instinctively understood a part of me that no one ever sees.'

'It was the same with me, and I hadn't experienced that before.'

'I've never kissed a man.'

'Really?'

I shook my head. 'I wouldn't even know what to do.'

'I've never kissed a man either, but—'

'Kiss me then.'

The reality was that I had wanted him to kiss me so much it had been like a physical ache. We moved around on the rock so that we were face-to-face. I didn't put my hands anywhere as I didn't want to spoil the moment. My heart felt as though it would burst.

'So, what do we do?'

'I move my head closer to yours.'

'Yes.'

'And I brush these strands of hair from your face.'

'That's sensible, otherwise they might get in the way.'

'Then I bring my lips towards your lips.'

'I see.'

'And ... they come together ... like this.'

Oh, dear God.

* * *

While Jack and Aila were away from the croft, Sim took Malie for a walk around the local land.

'Are we going somewhere in particular?' she said, after they had been wandering for about fifteen minutes.

'We are.'

'Where?'

'I don't know.'

'Then how will you know we've reached it?'

'Because I'll smell it.'

'Sim, you're really strange at times.'

'That is likely quite true, but on this occasion I don't believe so. Ahh, there you go.'

Malie looked about her and sniffed. 'What is it?'

'Fox. See there, in that open vegetation. That's where he crosses the track, and he goes out the other side just here.'

'So what are we doing?'

'We're going to set traps because the fox has eaten too many of Aila's hens. It's time he paid the price for his thefts. In the end, we all have to pay for our actions in life.'

Malie was suddenly unnaturally quiet, and he could tell by her changed expression and posture that there was something on her mind. He waited patiently.

'Sim.'

'What is it?'

'Thank you for saving me that night.'

She gazed at the ground as if feeling guilty or ashamed, and although he remained silent in order to allow her to continue, Malie didn't look up.

'Come on, let's go and sit over there.' He indicated a large flat stone on the top of a slight rise in the land. The position gave them an excellent view, so they sat side by side and stared at the horizon.

'Isn't the sea big?' she said. 'There's no end.'

'I've never been on it.'

'I thought you had done everything.'

Sim laughed. 'No. I grew up in Glasgow with no desire to have just a few pieces of wood between me and the ocean. I was never that brave.'

'Were you a bad man in Glasgow?'

'Aye, I was, lass. I did many terrible things. There are few choices I've made in my life that I'm proud of. Do you know the one that fills me with the greatest joy?'

'No.'

'It was being able to save you, not just from those men but giving you a home and a new chance amongst us. I hope it helps to balance the scales of justice when I finally meet my maker.'

Malie leaned against him, resting her head on his shoulder. 'I'm sorry I was frightened of you at the beginning.'

'Hah, don't go worrying about that.' He put his arm around her, feeling more protective of this girl than any person he had ever met. 'I've known hardened men, four times your size, who were frightened of me. And they had good reason to be. The troupe ... Ellen and Bess, Hector and Jack ... They allowed me to be a different person. They're good people.'

'You're a good person.'

'Well, I'm not sure about that, perhaps better than I used to be.'

'Will we eat the fox?'

'No. But we'll eat the rabbits that we're going to catch. Let's start setting those traps, then you need to get back to your calf.'

'The calf! Come on, there's no time for just sitting about.' With that she ran back down towards the fox's trail. Sim watched for a moment. Before standing up to follow her, he quickly wiped the tears from his eyes.

16

Kintradwell, 13 May 1727

BESS HAD ASKED TO SPEAK to me privately, without making it obvious to anyone else, and that afternoon presented the first opportunity. She was in Mother's chair by the fire and I sat in my own opposite, although these days it often felt that we didn't have 'our own' of anything.

'The others are all busy outside and I doubt that we'll be disturbed for a while,' I said.

Bess didn't speak for several minutes, so we sat looking at each other. I was wondering what was on her mind, but really had no idea.

'Thank you for entertaining the children on the day that I collapsed. I heard afterwards that you're a natural performer, as good as anyone who has been using puppets for years.' I made to brush off her compliment but she put up a hand to stop me. 'I can't speak for long, so let me talk while I'm able. This isn't why I asked to see you. You're a very intelligent and practical woman and will understand that what I say is out of necessity.

'I'm dying, Aila. Shh ... I am, even if no one else realises it yet. These old legs won't be taking me on any more journeys. There will be a terrible sadness amongst the troupe when I'm gone, but Sim is the only person I'm worried about. His grief, and his personality, might make him a danger to himself. Watch out for him if you can.'

Bess paused for a moment before continuing, as if gathering her thoughts and her strength. 'Your mother is a most inspiring woman, but you know as well as I do that she is losing her grasp on reality. I've lived long enough to see this in elderly folk. And your mother knows it herself, although she hides her ailment well. I think Janet will not be able to manage with my death as well as she might once have done. When my time comes, you will need to take charge of much and take care of many. If you are willing, I would like to be buried on your land, perhaps somewhere with a nice view. I'm not a religious person, although I was brought up as one, so do as you think best.

'I know you love Jack.'

'No, I—'

'Aila, I've never seen anyone's face light up so much in another person's presence. Don't let your injuries blind you to your feelings ... or his.'

Bess began coughing and had to stop. I handed her a cup of ale and waited for her to recover. This was one of the strangest conversations I had ever known and my eyes were rapidly being opened to Bess's huge wisdom and insight. Mother had been drawn instinctively towards these characteristics. I had made the mistake of seeing only a large, funny person and not considering what depths lay beneath the surface. My father would not have been pleased at such an unforgiveable error. Eventually, she settled enough to continue.

'In the six years we've all been together I've seen Jack grow from not much more than a boy into a man and I can think of no finer one. Yet, behind his beauty he is haunted. None of us have ever been able to understand the reason, for he has always been reserved about that part of his life. One day he will need your help, but you must wait for that moment. Don't be tempted to press him before he is ready to talk of it.'

The effort of speaking so much had exhausted Bess: she looked horribly pale and her chest was heaving with the need for air.

'You need to rest. Shall I help you to bed?'

'Yes and no. I've almost said what I wanted to. I would like you to have some of my puppets.'

'Why?'

'Because it's what I wish. You can say they're in memory of me, if that helps give you an acceptable reason. There . . . Quite a speech! Worthy of one of Jack's plays. I'll rest now, though some more ale would be quite acceptable.'

I refilled her cup, adding some nutmeg before warming the liquid with a flip-iron from the fire. 'I'm sorry we've not spoken more,' I said, and I meant it. 'It's my fault and my deep regret that I haven't got to know you better.'

'Child, your attention was fixed on someone with a more appealing countenance.' She managed a weak smile. 'Now, let me be. Go and find the man who is the man you must find.'

*　*　*

The next day I rode Abel out to the moss bank. Jack, Hector and Sim followed on ponies and all four of the animals were pulling sledges. We were going to start bringing back the peat, a task that had taken several months for Butcher to do during the previous two summers. Upon arrival we paused to study the scene before us, which was dominated by the numerous piles waiting to be removed. The place was deserted.

'I thought there would be lots of others here,' said Jack.

'Today is the fourteenth of May,' I said, although that didn't appear to mean anything to him. 'It's considered an unlucky day to begin a task or job of importance.'

'Now you tell us,' said Sim. 'If I had known I would have stayed wrapped up in my blanket.'

'Not for long, you wouldn't,' said Hector.

'Well, it's a good thing that none of us is superstitious,' I said, getting down off Abel. 'Isn't it.'

Although the animals were well cared for and strong, we could only put a limited amount onto each sledge as they couldn't be used to transport heavy weights over such rough ground, so we didn't even retrieve half of the peat that had been cut from our patch. There would be several more trips. Back at the croft the men stacked the turfs into the traditional curved shape which let air circulate throughout to aid drying while ensuring only the outer edges would get wet when it rained. As was the custom, the best peats were laid in the centre.

I had gone inside to make some refreshments, and when I came back out Mother was talking to a stranger who was standing next to a pony he had obviously just dismounted. A dog sat obediently nearby. I put down the tray I was carrying and headed over as Hector was making his way there, no doubt checking that everything was alright.

'Aila, this gentleman is a drover.'

Of course, everyone had heard of these men who, every summer, gathered Highland cattle, often many hundreds, and

180

drove them south to the huge markets in Falkirk and Crieff. I had never met one and assumed that last year and the one before, our neighbours had made clear that we had nothing to sell. In stature the man was like Sim, and I suspected his size was misleading as their reputation for toughness was legendary.

'You're seeking potential cattle?' asked Hector, who I could see was immediately interested in speaking to the man.

'Agreeing on animals, timing and prices, then I'll be back in a couple of months to round them up.'

'We have one cow and a calf,' I said, 'but that's only a few weeks old.'

'Too young for this year's journey,' said the drover. 'Perhaps next summer?'

'Yes,' said Mother, 'but you're welcome to see it and take some refreshment while you're here.'

'That's kind of you, Mistress . . .?'

'Horne. Janet Horne.'

The man retrieved a small book from his pocket and wrote down some details. I was impressed at his precision and he noticed my curiosity. 'I write everything or I would have no chance of remembering what was said where.'

We all stopped work and enjoyed taking our refreshments with the drover. Mother and I helped as best we could in advising him on who might have livestock for sale. Almost everyone sold spare cattle to the drovers as it was difficult to sell them otherwise, simply because most people already had what they wanted. As well as their hardiness the drovers were renowned for their integrity. They would be responsible for people's livestock on the outward journey and would be carrying considerable sums of money on their return. Before leaving, the man had one piece of information to give to us.

'I've heard rumours about a particularly violent gang of reivers working an area south of here. Hopefully, they won't reach this far north.'

'We've never had any trouble and I doubt we'll have any now,' I said, patting one of Hector's enormous arms.

'Well, best to be watchful.'

'Thank you.'

I was being overconfident; my belief that no one would bother us making me boastful and rudely dismissive of the drover's warning. But I should have heeded his advice. We all should have.

17

Kintradwell, 20 May 1727

JACK'S EYES SNAPPED OPEN WHEN he felt the hand over his mouth and he was on the verge of jumping up from where he had been sleeping when Sim's voice whispered so closely and quietly that it seemed as though there was almost no sound, just a gentle tickle of air across his ear.

'Reivers ... At least six of them. Hector goes first, then me. You go right.'

Jack nodded to show he understood. The darkness inside the barn was broken only by the few stray beams of light that crept in from the outside, where there was a full moon. It was enough to move around quietly when the three of them knew the layout so intimately.

Jack could make out the bare-chested figure of Hector standing near the large doors. He felt something touch his hand and realised that Sim was holding out a stout piece of timber nearly three foot long. He took it, checking the feel and weight of the makeshift weapon, then the two of them joined the blacksmith in his vigil.

Someone on the outside had slipped a thin piece of metal between the doors and was lifting the wooden locking bar. A second tool had been pushed through higher up and between them the wood was being moved smoothly out of the bracket on one side. Jack had to admit it was skilfully done. He thought the pounding of his heart was probably making more noise. The horse and ponies certainly were, but the reivers would expect their presence to make the animals nervous and start moving in their stalls.

The three stood, watching and waiting as the intruders worked stealthily at their evil task. In his mind, Jack prayed that his friends would not be harmed, that death would not be brought that night to Janet and Aila's home, that he would not have to kill.

Then the bar was free. There was a slight pause before one door was pulled cautiously outwards about an inch. The recently greased hinges gave nothing away. It moved a little more. Jack sensed Hector's body stiffen next to him, and seconds later the huge man charged. Violence shattered the stillness inside the barn. Like an unstoppable boulder, Hector smashed against the door then continued into the main body of men, his huge fists flying this way and that amongst the startled reivers. Sim flew outside and Jack followed, turning right and immediately coming upon a man momentarily stunned in surprise.

Jack thrust the timber hard so that the end smashed into the stranger's face then he pushed him over before spinning around. A man who had been knocked to the ground by the door had just got to his feet. He wasn't big but looked tough and dangerous.

'You bastards will pay for that,' he snarled, holding out the metal tool that had been pushed between the doors. It looked a very effective weapon and he came forward without hesitation. Jack stepped back so that he had more space to swing the timber and felt a hand grab his angle. He couldn't risk looking down so kicked out blindly with his other foot. There was a grunt and the hand released him.

Jack instinctively knew his opponent would be fast, and so he weaved the timber back and forward in front of him, which prevented the reiver getting close enough to use his much shorter weapon.

'You should go before anyone else gets hurt,' said Jack, though with little hope of his comment having any effect.

'Scared, boy? You should be!'

They circled each other, trying to find a chance to make the first strike. Then a voice shouted out.

'Stop! Stop!'

Jack's opponent backed away and looked towards the source of the command. Around them, the fight was already over. Two figures lay motionless on the ground near Hector while a third, cursing wildly but completely helpless, was pinned under his foot. Close to Sim, a man was bent over moaning and another, standing a few yards away, was clutching his shoulder. The one who had called out the order was on his knees. Sim was holding a handful of his hair to force back his head while the other hand held a knife to the leader's throat.

There was a moment that seemed unreal as enemies and friends stood around, chests heaving, no one speaking and nobody appearing quite sure what to do next. Sim spoke and Jack was chilled to his core by what he heard.

'Listen carefully, because I've always killed when I said I would ... Always. None of you will die from your injuries tonight, but if I hear that you're still in the area tomorrow, I will come hunting and I promise you will not know I'm by your side until you're already dying. I will soak the earth with your blood until not one of you is left alive.'

Some men make idle threats and others make boasts that they cannot achieve, but everyone outside that barn knew in their hearts that the words they had just heard were true. There were utterly, terrifyingly true.

Jack felt shocked, sickened ... saddened. He loved his companions; loved, trusted, admired, respected them. In all the years they had lived together he had never seen this side of Sim, had never realised such a large part of his friend's soul was owned by the Devil.

*　*　*

We were all shaken after the incident with the reivers, and for the next couple of days the women stayed close to the house, despite Sim's insistence that we were safe. At first, I thought the men were understandably subdued because of the violence that had been thrust upon them in the dead of night, but I began to realise this wasn't quite accurate. They weren't subdued, they were ... sad, particularly Jack.

I tried to get him to tell me what happened, but all he would say, all I heard any of them say, was that no one had been seriously hurt and the reivers had been so scared by the unexpected attack that they agreed to leave the area immediately. From what I had heard of reivers over the years, this seemed unlikely. There was a part of this story that was not being told, but I couldn't find out what it was. I doubted I ever would.

*　*　*

Since arriving at the croft, Bess had lost so much weight that she looked like a different person, and now she only managed to get out of the box-bed with help. Mother and Ellen had taken on most of the role of caring, as Malie wasn't strong enough to do much and I was too clumsy to do more than a few basic tasks. The mood was sombre. People tried to occupy their minds by keeping busy, taking care of the animals and of each other.

That Friday morning was sunny and Bess had wanted to sit outside, so with help from Hector she was bundled up in a chair near the front door. Sim brought out a stool and sat close to her, while everyone else found things to do elsewhere to allow them some privacy.

We had come to accept that the reivers wouldn't return, so I took Malie to the beach to collect cockles. There had been a glut of them recently and we each carried a pail. The best place was farther along the shore. I wished so much that I could walk barefoot in the sand, but my one experience of trying this since the accident had been extremely unpleasant. In truth, the cockles were partly a pretext, for I wanted some time alone with Malie in a situation where she could talk freely about any subjects she wanted. We had almost reached our destination before she broke the silence.

'What do you think happens to people when they die?'

I decided against trying to explain the concept of predestination. She had asked for my beliefs and so that's what I gave her. 'Well, I think that those who've lived a good life and have followed the teachings of Christ will go to heaven.'

'Who decides if they've been good?'

'God, I suppose, perhaps St Peter at the gates.'

187

'Not ministers?'

'I don't think so. They're really only people like the rest of us.'

'I've never been in a kirk.'

Mother and I had continued to attend the Sunday service in Lothmore, and although none of the troupe came with us it hadn't entered my head that anyone could reach Malie's age and actually never have entered a kirk. 'Did your parents not take you?'

'I don't remember them.'

'Who brought you up?'

'An aunt and uncle, but they never wanted me and were so horrible that I ran away when I was quite young. I got together with other children living on the streets of Edinburgh. I was constantly hungry, but I was lucky and always managed to avoid any real trouble. Sometimes friends disappeared and were never seen again. There are some bad people about, Aila.'

I didn't know quite what sort of conversation I had expected but it wasn't this. In so many ways Malie had a greater under-standing of life than I had and she knew things that I would never know, that I would never want to know.

'The night that Sim saved me, some men came to where we children used to hide out at night. I was asleep when there was suddenly a lot of screaming and scuffling. There seemed to be figures everywhere. Those of us who could just scattered into the darkness. That was how I ended up alone in an alley and those men got hold of me. If it wasn't for Sim I would never have been the same person again after what would have happened . . . Assuming I even lived.' She paused before adding, 'I was frightened of him for a while and that makes me sad.'

'It's difficult not to judge people by their appearance.' I thought of my own recent discovery about Bess. 'We can all be guilty of it, even me, and I should be the last person to make that mistake.'

Malie took hold of my hand and we walked a little farther without speaking. A cool breeze blew gently inland from the sea yet the weather continued to be surprisingly warm.

'Look,' I said, pointing. 'It's a seal.'

'What's a seal?'

'A creature that lives partly in the water and partly on the land. He's watching.'

'Why? Would he eat us?'

'No. He's curious, that's all. My father used to tell me stories, myths really, about seals.'

'What's a myth?'

'Oh, where do I start? Let's sit down on this rock so that I can rest my feet and I'll tell you about the selkies.'

18

Kintradwell, 27 May 1727

BESS'S CONDITION HAD BEEN STEADILY getting worse, and the mood around the croft that day was one of such despair and sorrow I think we all felt that a dark presence had settled upon the house. Ellen and Mother did what was needed to keep Bess clean and dry. She was largely unconscious and didn't respond as they tried to make conversation; instead they simply made comments about everyday events so that their friend might take comfort from the sound of their voices.

None of us wanted to be far away, but actually being in the room for any length of time was almost unbearable. People would sit by the bed for short periods. I watched them as they stepped outside afterwards and immediately took a huge breath of fresh air as if it had been difficult to breathe inside. Only Sim remained constantly beside her; hour after hour he sat there.

Mother and Malie cooked the noon meal on an open fire outside and we sat around in silence trying to eat. The food stuck in my throat and I'm sure it was the same for everyone else. However, we attempted to keep a sense of normality. Afterwards, Hector put Malie on a pony and gave her a lesson in riding. I think people were trying to make sure the girl was occupied and doing this also helped them. I went into the barn to see Abel and moments later Jack followed me in.

'I feel like a coward hiding in the barn,' I said.

'I know what you mean, but listening to her laboured breathing is ...'

'Yes. Sim looks awful.'

'He'll stay with her until the end.'

'We must all watch out for him.'

'You know, afterwards the troupe will move on.'

I could feel panic rising in my chest, so I turned towards Abel and began brushing his coat in an attempt to calm myself.

'Of course, I expected nothing else. You only came here for Bess to recover and now that isn't going to happen you obviously won't want to stay.'

'It's not that we don't want to. Despite the reason for coming, I've never seen the troupe so happy.'

'I'm pleased.'

'Don't be angry.'

'Why should I be? It's nothing to do with me, Jack.'

'We need to make most of our money during the summer so that we can survive the winter months. To start with we'll go back to Dornoch. The annual fair in June sounds promising.'

'Well then, there's nothing to debate is there. I might even see you at the market!' I was angry because I was weak, and I was crying because the man I loved was about to leave, and the magic that had entered my life would be gone. The thought filled my soul with dread, for I knew that our home would never again be the place it used to be, no matter how tightly Mother hugged me at night.

'Please don't cry.'

'I'm not crying!'

Tenderly, he put his hands on my shoulders and turned me around to face him. I dropped the brush and threw my arms around his waist, wailing like a child as he held me.

'What will I do when you've gone?' I sobbed. 'I will be so much less than the person I was before.'

'You won't.'

'I will.' I pulled back to look at his face and he gently wiped the tears from my cheeks. 'I've seen what might have been and that will be a torment I will have to endure for the rest of my life.'

'I wish I had an answer. I have a responsibility to the troupe and now we also have Malie to think of.'

'I can't leave my mother and I would be no use to your troupe anyway, only an extra mouth to feed. I wouldn't even be able to travel on foot as you do.'

'Oh Aila, I'm so sorry.'

Jack held me again and we said no more, for, in truth, there was nothing more to say.

* * *

It was evening. Sim sat on the stool that he had been on for almost the entire day and held one of Bess's hands, while Ellen sat on the edge of the mattress. The entrance into a box-bed was relatively small, so it was impossible for more than two people to be physically near the person inside. The rest of us stood. Mother had an arm protectively around Malie, who was clinging to her in fear. I assumed she had seen death and bodies before, but perhaps not of anyone she had been close to.

Jack had lit some candles and stoked up the fire. We left the front door open as the weather was calm, and with so many of us close together it felt better to have a slight breeze blowing in. I had never known minutes drag by so slowly. Every agonising breath taken by Bess was so unnaturally loud, so horribly painful, it seemed to me that I could feel the movement of air on my skin. I closed my eyes, but this made the sensation worse.

Jack brought over two chairs from the table. He set one by my mother and she sat down gratefully, pulling Malie onto her lap so that she could cuddle her. Jack set the other chair by me, and when I sat down he stood behind so that he could place a hand on my shoulder. I was glad of the reassuring touch of those sculptured fingers. Ellen glanced towards us. When she turned her head again she reached over and took hold of Sim's other hand.

Only Hector stood alone, like a statue of some ancient Greek mythological giant . . . One with tears running down his cheeks. I was trying to work out how he could be included in some form of physical contact with someone when Malie reached out to him. He smiled, then took a step towards Mother so that he could stand close enough to take hold of Malie's hand. I blessed the child for her thoughtfulness.

Despite the despair that overwhelmed our small group, I suddenly realised in that moment that I loved them, every one. They had become a family and I simply didn't know how I would cope once they were gone from my life. As if reading my thoughts, Jack stroked my hair and the side of my face. I nestled my cheek into his hand and he left it there. Of course, I loved Jack in a different way altogether.

And so those agonising minutes passed one by one by one; each an hour, a day, an eternity. It turned cold outside; Jack quietly closed the door then fetched a spare blanket to put around my mother and Malie, who had fallen asleep in her arms. We spoke in whispers, thought in whispers, breathed and moved in whispers. I suggested putting Malie in our bed but Mother wouldn't let go of her. It was only then that I saw the slightly puzzled expression on her face, and although this worried me there was little I could do.

Ellen got up and started to make tea for everyone. Hector sat on the floor, still holding Malie's tiny hand. Jack knelt down near me and rested his head on my lap. For a moment I was shocked at the intimacy, and it was in full view of the others. No one had ever done such thing before. Yet at the same time it felt completely natural, and nobody appeared to take any notice. Beautiful, strong, reliable Jack had a need to be held and reassured, something that I suspected was normally hidden.

What haunts you my love? I wondered, putting one hand on his back and stroking his hair with the other. My heart was a battleground between love and grief, and I thought it would burst as they competed with each other for dominance.

During the previous few hours our emotions had been bound together in that room as if forged in a great fire, then they had been beaten and stretched as though hammered on an anvil. Now they were thin and fragile, ready to snap apart at the slightest touch and perhaps each of us secretly feared that we would be cast adrift, alone. Heavens knows, we were all in need of comfort.

Bess's breathing became even more laboured; the increasingly long pauses in between were heart-stopping for the rest of us.

More than once I thought she had died, only for her to take another slow, deep intake of air. It was awful.

Throughout it all Sim held on to Bess's hand, speaking quietly to her and occasionally kissing her face. Then the pause didn't stop. It simply went on and on. I saw more heads look up, including Jack's.

'Bess? Bess?' Sim's words were spoken softly at first, but they quickly became more urgent until he was screaming her name and crying uncontrollably by the side of the bed.

Ellen threw herself on top of Sim and held him tightly. Malie woke and immediately began to cry. Through my tears I saw Mother gently pull Hector's head towards her chest and the huge man sobbed as she tried to console him and Malie together. Jack and I fell into each other's arms.

The sound of crying echoed throughout our home, beyond the barn and across our croft and, I imagined, out to sea where the selkies stopped to listen.

* * *

Our outpouring of grief left us exhausted yet strangely also more at peace. Each of us in turn leaned into the box-bed and quietly said our own farewell to Bess. Sim was the last, and when he had finished he slowly closed the heavy curtain across the opening; the final curtain of the final performance.

No one was likely to sleep that night apart from Malie, who was almost dropping with fatigue. Mother insisted she went into her bed, and despite Malie's protests she was asleep within minutes of being tucked up. While I replaced a couple of the candles, Jack got the fire blazing once more. Ellen made more tea and Hector poured ale for those who wanted it. Mother sat in her armchair and I made Sim sit in mine. We shared out blankets. I sat on the floor by Mother and Ellen did the same with Sim, which allowed her to hold his hand at times or simply rub his leg, little gestures of kindness.

Several days earlier Mother and I had agreed on a suitable place for the grave, however, we hadn't spoken about this to anyone as neither of us wanted to talk about Bess dying. Once we had sat in respectful silence for a while, I decided to broach the subject.

'Bess spoke to me about being buried on the croft, and my mother and I have since selected a secluded spot that we feel would be suitable.'

Everyone was quiet for a while until Hector spoke, his voice hoarse with emotion. 'I had wondered. It's good that you had this conversation with her, Aila. Deep down, we all knew there could only be one outcome.'

'I loved her,' said Sim quietly.

'I know, sweetheart,' said Ellen, taking hold of his hand. 'We all did, but your love was special. It meant so much to her.'

We spoke then of Bess and there were stories of past events, plays and performances that had gone well and some that had been a disaster. There were moments of humour amongst the sorrow and tears. After an hour or so Jack caught my eye and indicated that I should check on my mother. She was almost asleep, her head nodding as she fought to stay awake. I knew that simply suggesting she went to bed wouldn't work. I stood up and gently shook her shoulder.

'Mother, Malie needs you to comfort her. Do you think you could help?'

She looked up at me, her eyes unfocused. 'Malie?'

'She needs your help, Mother.'

'Oh, yes, of course.'

Over by the bed I helped her to undress down to her shift. No one bothered about such a break with respectability. As she climbed in, Malie stirred and whimpered, which had my mother instinctively wrapping her arms about the girl and whispering soothing words. As I tucked them in, it struck me just how odd the sight was. I wondered if part of my mother thought that she was holding me, perhaps as the young girl I had once been. I leaned over and kissed them both before returning to the others to sit out the remainder of the night by the fire.

* * *

When it was light Mother and Ellen washed Bess while I took the men out to the area we had chosen. They began digging immediately, as if there was a terrible urgency to the task. Malie had gone into the barn where I suspected she felt safe being with the cow and its calf. I found her sitting in the corner of the stall, crying, so I sat down and pulled her into my arms.

'It's alright to cry. We'll all be crying over the coming days.'

'I didn't want to see Bess being washed.'

'Everyone will understand. But we shouldn't be too sad, for she lived the life that she wanted and not many people get to do that.'

'Can we all stay here?'

'It's a lovely idea but the croft isn't big enough to support the troupe. You could remain if that's what you want. My mother and I have already discussed this idea and we would willingly give you a home.'

'It's what I used to wish for all the time when I was sleeping on the streets of Edinburgh, but the others need me. I couldn't let them down after everything they've done.'

'You're a wise wee thing.' I stroked her beautiful hair, realising how difficult it was to imagine the filthy, terrified girl Sim had rescued.

We sat there until the men returned, and when I judged that they had had sufficient time to wash and tidy themselves we went into the house. Mother and Ellen had wrapped Bess tightly in a clean sheet and she had been laid on the floor on top of a thick, dark blue material that I recognised as one of the rolls of cloth purchased on the day my father died. Mother caught my eye and I nodded my approval at its use. We both understood. It would never have been made into a winter coat.

Everyone looked grim but no one was crying. I think we were all determined to do this task with as much dignity as possible. Each of us took hold of part of the material. Sim was at the front of our procession, holding the head of the woman he loved. I was near her feet with Malie and the other four took the main weight of the body. And that's how we carried our friend to her final resting place, a little way beyond our cultivated land to a raised area that provided a good view out to sea. I hoped that Bess would approve.

Once we had lowered her body into the hole we stood around without speaking. A few cried quietly. Eventually, Sim reached up and wiped his face of tears then nodded to the other men. The rest of us moved a short distance away as they put back the earth. We remained. This was a journey we would make together. The final act was for Sim to place the small wooden cross he had made into the ground.

Hector and Ellen reached the house first and they waited until we had caught up. People appeared hesitant to go inside. I didn't know where the strength came from. Perhaps it was because Bess gave me permission and told me I would have to take charge, but I began speaking with such authority that nobody seemed inclined to disagree.

'Right, we hardly ate yesterday and the first thing we're going to do once we've washed and sorted out a few things is sit around the table and have a proper breakfast. Bess said to me that we were to make sure we took care of ourselves during these difficult days and I'm not about to disobey her wishes. Sim and Jack, we need some more water from the burn please. Mother, I can hear the cow mooing.'

'I'll milk it now,' she said, setting off immediately.

'Ellen, can you collect eggs. Hector, can you bring more peat and sort out the fire, then I'm sure you'll want to check on the animals. Malie, you and I are on cooking duty.'

I made sure everyone ate well and, indeed, no one was in a hurry to leave the table, so our breakfast was an unusually long affair. I wondered about setting people specific work, but then decided that they would all make themselves useful around the croft and so kept quiet on this point. It was the right thing to do. Sim took Malie with him to set traps and I was glad that he wasn't going to be by himself.

While Hector and Jack cleaned out the barn, I helped Ellen and Mother bring out all of the bedding from my box-bed. This included the mattress: Mother unpicked the stitching at one end so that we could remove the heather and wash the cover, along with all of the blankets and the sheet. When the cover was dry it would be refilled with heather from the barn, where we kept a supply on an area high off the floor.

We kept ourselves busy that day, but the next morning I was aware of the men checking the sledges and having discussions that I guessed were about leaving. When Jack suggested we go for a walk on the beach, I knew what he wanted to talk about.

'You're preparing to go, aren't you?'

'Yes. It's time for the troupe to move on, although in reality I'm not sure if we are a troupe anymore.'

'What do you mean?'

'We can't perform any of our usual plays with just four of us. There's no way Malie could replace Bess. We'll have to work out what we can still do, and what new material I may have to write. Of course, everyone then has to learn their parts. So, Hector can earn money beating men at trials of strength, Sim can dazzle people with his juggling and I can play the harp, but we're not the group we were.'

'Will no one work the tiny theatre?'

'No. Ellen isn't Bess and performing with puppets is a talent you either have or haven't got. And to be honest it never brought in much money.'

We walked in silence for a while. I felt that both of us were avoiding the real discussion. Then again, perhaps this was the real discussion because there was no 'us', there was no 'Jack and Aila' as if we were a couple. So, what was there to talk about except the practicalities of their departure.

'Well, thank you for all the work you've done around the croft. Mother and I have never been so set up with peat and jobs completed.' I sounded formal, as if merely speaking to someone at the market.

'The care you and your mother gave to Bess will never been forgotten.'

'We were only sorry we couldn't do more.' *Aila, stop sounding so cold and distant. Say that you love him. SAY IT!* 'Well, when you've gone, my mother and I will need to get back to brewing so that we can start selling again at the Dornoch market.'

'Aila . . .'

'Yes?'

The pain on his face was clear. The grief in his voice made it sound unnatural. Inside, I was a wailing mess of misery, but on the surface I must have appeared as hard and unforgiving as granite.

'I'm sorry.'

'There's nothing to be sorry about, Jack. You have your life to live and I have mine. We should turn back now. There's a lot that needs to be organised.'

19

Kintradwell, 31 May 1727

THE FEELING OF SADNESS AS the troupe prepared to leave that Saturday morning was more than I thought I could bear. It seemed as if the heart of our home was being ripped out and all we would be left with was a shell, just walls and windows and an empty silence. Everything would be filled with that empty silence; the house, the land, the sea . . . me.

Most of the troupe's possessions had been securely tied down on the sledges the day before, so the main tasks left were sorting out food and the ponies. It was done too quickly and the animals were soon in their harnesses. Malie had said goodbye to the calf. I think Hector had as well, though he made less fuss about it.

I had never experienced anything like this, saying farewell to those I had grown to love. We stood around talking of nothing important, nothing of our real feelings. Hector, Ellen and I hugged and said our goodbyes then we hugged again. We were waiting for Sim. During the previous afternoon people had made their way to Bess's grave and said whatever words they needed to speak – all except Sim, who was there now, and so Hector and Jack pretended to find odd jobs to do, tightening ropes that didn't need tightening, checking harnesses that didn't need checking. Ellen talked quietly with my mother. I stood a short distance away with Malie, who had wrapped her arms around me and was crying softly.

'The others will look after you,' I said. 'You're only going as far as Dornoch and we'll be there in a couple of weeks for the annual fair, so we'll meet up again then. The fair will be really exciting.'

'But what will happen after that?'

Yes, what after that? The troupe would move on, I would stay behind and never again meet a man such as Jack. I didn't want another man. I wanted him. I knew in my soul that for the rest of my life there would only ever be him. Then Jack came over and Malie went to my mother.

'Well, almost ready to go,' he said.

'Yes.'

'I'll never forget my time here.'

'No.'

'I'll never forget you, Aila.'

'I don't expect I'll forget you either.' *Too late now to talk of love.* 'I hope the fair is successful.'

'Aila—'

'Look, there's Sim.'

When Sim came over to me, Jack moved hesitantly away. I could tell Sim had been crying. He didn't say anything, just hugged me. And I held him. Of everyone in the troupe, the person I least thought I would hold on to the longest was Sim, yet there we were, neither of us wanting or willing to let go. Around us people were saying another round of goodbyes to Mother, but we were only delaying what had to be faced. Eventually, he pulled back.

'Thank you for what you did for Bess.'

I couldn't speak. I had heard and guessed enough to know that the man facing me had lived a life so alien to my own that it seemed impossible we should feel any sort of connection. I leaned forward and tenderly kissed his forehead. A single tear ran down his cheek. He managed to smile, then turned and walked briskly away towards the leading pony. Sim took hold of the rope around the grey's neck and led it forward without looking back. The others followed. There were a few waves, a couple of last comments of thanks and farewell.

Or course, we would see them again quite soon, but the magic in our lives would never be recaptured while speaking amongst busy stalls at the market or sitting around a noisy table in a Dornoch tavern.

It was gone.

* * *

'I have a bad feeling about this.'

Jack and Hector were sitting in the Wolf's Head. Sim had gone outside to the privy and the two men were taking the brief opportunity of his absence to discuss their concerns.

'He's going to get even more drunk and then look for a fight,' said Hector.

'That's what I'm worried about.'

'Sim's seeking a relief from his grief and anger.'

The two men had remained sober, each drinking only a cup of ale while Sim had been downing whisky and ale as if trying to put out a fire.

'Well it's likely to land him in the tolbooth, and we might not be far behind if things get out of control. Hector, if he pulls a knife—'

His sentence was interrupted by the return of their friend, who appeared to deliberately knock into a man at the next table as he came to his seat. The man looked up. He was with four others and Jack thought they were just ordinary workers having a quiet drink after a long day of labour, but he knew how quickly violence could erupt in these situations. Sim called loudly to one of the serving women.

'Christ woman, am I in a tavern or a desert! Whisky and ale for the three of us.'

'Not for me,' said Jack.

'The three of us,' repeated Sim, 'and I'll have theirs if they don't want it.'

The woman went off to the bar and Jack saw the large barman, who no doubt had a large cudgel under the counter, watching them closely. Sim had been getting increasingly noisy all evening and attracting the attention of several customers.

The troupe had arrived from Kintradwell that afternoon and set up camp about a mile out of Dornoch. Ellen and Malie had remained there when the three men had left for the town. Sim was not going to be denied alcohol and Ellen had told Hector and Jack to go with him. She would watch out for Malie and the ponies.

'What are you looking at!'

The man Sim had knocked into had make the mistake of glancing in their direction. He shrugged and turned away.

'Don't you turn your back on me when I'm speaking!'

Sim stood, immediately followed by Jack and Hector, the latter grabbing Sim's arm.

'Leave them alone,' said the blacksmith. 'They're not looking for trouble.'

'Someone is always looking for trouble.'

Sim yanked his arm free and took a step forward. The five men at the table jumped up, sending chairs crashing to the floor and overturning a couple of tankards. Jack could see others nearby stand up, getting ready to defend themselves if the fight came their way, while the barman was striding towards them with a weapon that was about half the size of a small tree.

When Sim's hand moved towards his belt, Jack knew that they were only seconds away from potential disaster. The punch Hector threw was so unexpected that even Sim had no chance to react, and as he fell Hector caught him, slinging the unconscious body over his shoulder in one fluid movement.

'Our apologies, gentlemen,' said Jack in a loud voice. 'We're sorry for the unfortunate disturbance. We mean no disrespect and we'll see our friend is taken safely away without any further bother.' He pulled out a small bag of coins and made a big show of emptying some of them on the table. Jack was performing, capturing everyone's attention while Hector walked casually towards the door before anyone could think of trying to stop him. 'Drinks here please, barman, and for anyone else we have unintentionally caused upset to this evening.'

The barman looked around. People were already sitting back down at their tables and he could see that the threat of a possible fight was over. He decided it was much easier to let the three strangers leave and make sure that some of the money went secretly into his own pocket.

'And one for yourself, of course,' said Jack, as if reading the man's mind.

'Don't come back,' he said, slapping the wooden cudgel he held into the palm of his hand for effect.

207

Hector was already outside. Jack spoke while walking to the door as if exiting the stage at the end of a scene.

'Indeed, we will ensure that such an incident is not repeated. Goodnight to you all. I wish you a pleasant evening in this fine establishment.' Hector was waiting several yards away. 'How is he?'

'He'll be alright. He'll have a sore jaw, a bad head and a grumbling stomach, but in the morning he'll say sorry. However, for now I'd prefer to head back to camp. I hope we can get there before he wakes up. I don't fancy my chances of knocking him out a second time.'

* * *

The first day of June was a Sunday and that morning Mother and I travelled to the service as we had done throughout the weeks that Jack and the others had stayed on our croft. We had never commented on the fact that none of them ever joined us. I assumed that by constantly moving around, the troupe managed to avoid the wrath of the kirk, which otherwise had such a firm hold over every aspect of people's lives.

Although Reverend McNeil had referred to witches during the previous month, his sermons had become much more 'ordinary' and these references were brief, as though merely a reminder to the congregation to be generally wary. He also ignored me, but, despite my relief at this sudden and unexpected lack of attention, for some reason I couldn't explain, this made me nervous. I expressed my concerns to Mother as she walked alongside Abel. The conversation was partly because I couldn't bear the silence.

'Just be glad that the minister seems to have moved on, Aila. He's no doubt discovered that we've nothing to do with witchcraft and is searching elsewhere for a victim.'

'And don't you think it's odd that he's never once mentioned anything about the troupe? News must have reached him quickly that they were staying with us and he was well aware that they didn't attend any Sunday services. I would have thought they provided him with an ideal target, such strange, evil people living in the parish.'

'When you put it like that, it is a bit surprising. But as they've moved on it would surely be difficult for him to start complaining now.'

We were both puzzled. It made no sense, unless Reverend MacDonald was about to return and the temporary minister had decided he simply didn't have time to follow through with any accusations. I made this point.

'I suppose that could be the reason. Let's see if he sheds any light as to what he's thinking at this morning's service.'

The surrounding hills were bright with the yellow blossom of broom and whin, interspersed with heather that was yet to reveal its glory. The track passed close to a small loch and we stopped to watch a roe deer drinking at the water's edge. The animal didn't appear concerned by our presence.

There were a large number of birds nearby, and in years gone by Mother and I would have challenged each other to identify as many different kinds as possible. She always won, which used to make me so mad and determined to win the next time. I never did. Those innocent times of my youth, with Father laughing by our side, seemed no more than a distant memory.

I couldn't prevent my mind going back over the previous day's events. After Jack and the others had gone I went for a walk on the beach, yet somehow it felt as though this other sanctuary of mine had become a sad place, the large expanse of empty sand merely emphasising the fact that I was so small and insignificant, so by myself.

Had all of the places I used to love visiting become sad? Was my secret rock by Loch Brora now just a lump of cold stone that offered no comfort? Would birds still sing in my presence? If they did, would I hear them? It had been a desolate day, with Mother and me going around the croft and finding little jobs to do following the troupe's departure. Unable to find any peace of mind, I had suggested visiting Bess's grave, but while we were there Mother had seemed distracted and distant, which left me more unsettled than ever.

* * *

As we made our way towards the front of the kirk I couldn't help feeling that something had changed, that some people reacted differently to us than they normally would. I couldn't say what it was exactly ... Replies that were perhaps less friendly than we could have expected, people appearing to avoid us that would usually have been pleased to talk. It may simply have been my own state of mind. When there was no sign of Agnes Munro in her usual seat, I merely thought she had been delayed or maybe taken ill, so when I looked around before the service I was astonished to see her in another seat.

'Agnes is sitting near the back!'

'What?' Mother found this so difficult to believe that she glanced over her shoulder to check. 'Well, I can hardly trust my own eyes. What goes on there, Aila?'

'I don't understand it. I've never known someone move like that, unless Agnes has fallen on hard times and can no longer afford to pledge a subscription.'

'That could explain why she's had to move. It's also odd that the MacGregors haven't yet appeared.' The pew immediately next to Mother was still unoccupied. Otherwise the kirk was full and the service about to start. 'Let's try and find Peggy afterwards and see if she's heard something that we should know about.'

The Sunday service was similar to those we had experienced during the whole of May, yet through it all I felt increasingly that something was wrong, something was *false*. Yes, that was the word that came to me. What we were seeing and hearing was not the true Reverend McNeil. The zeal and passion that he presented to us during those early weeks, that was the real man. I was sure of it. This was not him, yet for the life of me I couldn't make sense of this different version.

Afterwards, outside, we managed to find Peggy by herself, although I felt that even she was trying to avoid us.

'Peggy, how are you?' said Mother, hugging Peggy, who flinched so much that I held back from doing the same.

'Janet, Aila. I'm fine, just fine. I don't need any help, thank you.'

She looked ill. I let Mother take the lead on the conversation.

'It's been too long since we've seen you. Perhaps we'll come over during the next few days, in between brewing.'

'No, please don't. Mister Butcher, he's very unhappy about the peat and being threatened. He's told me not to see you anymore and I think that's for the best.' Peggy kept glancing around the crowd. She seemed terrified. 'Things are difficult.'

'I'm sorry to hear it. You know that if you ever need our aid, we will be there to give it. Aila and I will respect your wishes. Your husband can be reassured that we will not visit.'

Mother sounded hurt and I wanted to hug her, but this was not the time or place for open demonstrations of affection. That Butcher should give up his access to free ale showed just how serious he was about this break in our relationship. It worried me, although I couldn't see any way forward for the moment.

The three of us fell silent and as I looked around it struck me that there was an unnatural amount of space between us and the nearest groups. Also, people turned away quickly if they saw that I had noticed their attention. I thought Peggy was too frightened to reveal anything she might have heard about us and Mother obviously felt the same, for only a few moments later she suggested we make our way home, even though we hadn't spoken to anyone else in the congregation.

20

Lothmore kirk, 6 June 1727

MURDO TOLD US. WE HAD been summoned to Lothmore to attend a kirk session in order to be questioned about ... Well, that part was still to be revealed. So, Mother and I stood in the kirk, facing men we had exchanged pleasant words with most Sundays for the last two years, yet now they appeared to regard us as strangers. The men were seated; Reverend McNeil next to a man I recognised as the Dornoch minister, along with Murdo, who was obviously prepared to take notes, and six elders. For several minutes no one had spoken and I wondered if this was intended to intimidate us in some way.

'I am the Reverend Fraser, minister of Dornoch, and the parish of Loth falls within my presbytery. Concerns have been brought to my attention about your strange behaviour and the fears within the local community that you are involved in witchcraft.'

I sensed Mother stiffen next to me. Before arriving we had agreed that I should try to speak on behalf of both of us. We had discussed the possibility of such an accusation, but it had seemed so ludicrous that we couldn't bring ourselves to consider it further. I began to wonder if Reverend McNeil's recent lack of references to witchcraft during his services and his apparent loss of interest in me had been a deliberate ploy to put us off our guard.

Being ordered to attend a kirk session was a serious matter for the person involved. Offences generally concerned someone having missed Sunday services without a valid reason, an accusation of working on the Sabbath, drunkenness or, much worse, fornication, even adultery on occasions. Hearing the word 'witchcraft' was terrifying. Those found guilty of not adhering to the strict moral standards demanded by the kirk could be fined or given a punishment that was humiliating, like being dressed in sackcloth and made to sit on the 'stool of repentance' in front of the congregation over several Sundays.

People suspected of witchcraft could face a court trial and possible execution.

'Before we continue, is there anything you would like to confess?'

'I swear before God and before you, Reverend Fraser, that my mother and I have not been involved in any form of witchcraft at any point in our lives. Nor do we know anyone who is a witch or is associated with one.'

We weren't sure what lies Reverend McNeil had told the Dornoch minister, so I knew it was important to try and counteract any damaging mistruths right from the outset. I spoke clearly and with conviction, trying not to think of the meeting as an interrogation, although it certainly felt like one.

'I had heard that you were unnaturally confident in your speech and manner. I see that this information is correct.' The Dornoch minister paused as if considering the next point. 'It's known that you are disrespectful to ministers of the kirk.'

This was a dangerous comment because it was difficult to argue against, or to explain the sort of man Reverend McNeil really was, without appearing to be disrespectful and thereby confirming the accusation, at least in the minds of the men opposite.

'If we have ever appeared to be disrespectful to any good minister of the kirk then we are truly sorry, and I'm sure that if you were to speak to our own minister, Reverend MacDonald, who has known us since we arrived in the area, you would learn we are God-fearing, regular members of his congregation who have never given any reason to have complaint laid at our door.'

'I had been told that you were tall for a woman.'

'My father was a tall man and I take after him. Surely there is nothing unusual in that.'

'You hold strong opinions, Aila Horne.'

It was clear that Reverend McNeil had provided a list of our 'faults' and that he was going to leave the questioning to the more powerful Dornoch minister. I was still trying to work out a suitable reply when he continued.

'You both recently attended the graveside at the funeral of your neighbour's baby.' He turned to Murdo, who looked extremely uncomfortable but nodded in confirmation. 'You know well that this goes totally against accepted local practice. And I believe you feel you are equal to men.'

What has any of this to do with witchcraft?

'I admire and respect all men as they each of them rightly deserve to be admired and respected.'

The minister scrutinised me with intelligent eyes, though I thought they weren't unkind, not black and heartless like those belonging to the man next to him. 'You're clever with your words. Is that why your mother remains silent?'

I didn't answer and Mother immediately picked up the clue that she should speak. 'I mean no disrespect by my silence, Reverend Fraser, but my mind is not as agile as it was when I was younger. I hope you will forgive an elderly woman in letting my daughter speak on my behalf.'

Well done, Mother.

'Several people have expressed their concern at seeing you talking when there is no one nearby to listen, Mistress Horne. People fear you are conversing with the Devil.'

'No, Reverend. Elderly people tend to mutter when they are trying to remember what they are meant to be doing. Old age brings with it a poor memory, I'm afraid. And sometimes I revert to English without thinking, because that is a language I used for many years after I had left the Highlands. Of course, I am very pleased to have returned to the land of my birth.'

My mother was playing her cards well, for she was far from being a frail old woman and in reality could probably have knocked half of the dithering kirk elders opposite to the ground, if she had to.

'Your husband died in a fire?'

'He did.'

'And your daughter was burned in that fire.'

'She was.'

'Accidents and misfortune seem to follow you around.'

'I think . . .'

Mother's reply trailed away. After a few moments of silence I turned towards her and saw her expression of confusion. This loss of concentration in the middle of a sentence was happening more regularly and I knew her puzzlement could last for seconds or minutes. I had to take over.

'It's obvious that you are a man of mercy and compassion, Reverend Fraser. I know you will understand when I explain that my mother can sometimes become confused quite suddenly, particularly when faced with lots of questions. I beg that I may answer for us both.'

There was some debate between the ministers and the elders before the man from Dornoch continued. 'You have also been noticed to behave strangely. More than one person has reported seeing you talking to your horse. In addition, you have been known to stand completely still, staring at another person and even closing your eyes as if perhaps recanting a silent curse.'

I assumed Reverend McNeil had spoken to someone I had been with when overwhelmed by the terrible images of my father burning. I hadn't realised someone might consider my behaviour in such a dangerous light. Yet how could I explain my reasons? I felt unable to think logically. Then I recalled how often Mother used to talk about honesty and realised that the only explanation these men might believe was the truth, regardless of how painful this would be.

'When my father was trapped in the burning building in Inverness, I tried to save him. It was extremely foolish, a young girl's love and loyalty overcoming common sense. That was how I burned my hands and feet. The image of him, Reverend Fraser, lying under a huge beam, his body surrounded by flames, his utter despair at knowing he was about to die horribly ... That image haunts me, sir. It can take over my mind, even during the middle of a conversation with a friend or neighbour, and I have to force it out of my head. If on these occasions I have appeared odd then I swear that is why and there is no evil or malice involved.'

I wiped the tears from my cheeks with a corner of my sleeve. I had never spoken about this to anyone other than my mother, and even then never in such detail. To be forced to explain my secret torment felt like an intrusion into the most private areas of my soul. However, they couldn't doubt my sincerity, and a couple of the elders nodded in apparent sympathy. The minister was silent for so long that I began to wonder if he had understood what I had said.

'Over the years I have counselled members of my congregation, often soldiers, who have seen or done barbarous acts which haunt them in the manner that you describe, even hardened men used to their trade of war. I am not surprised that such a terrifying sight would so affect the mind of a young woman. There is no shame in it, Aila.

'For today, I am satisfied that we have heard enough.' He held up his hand when Reverend McNeil tried to speak. 'I must warn you that I intend to investigate these allegations and rumours further. Do not leave the area or this will be taken as a sure sign of your guilt.'

*   *   *

Mother was back to her normal self as we made our way home. I walked part of the way leading Abel by his reins as I wanted to be beside her while we discussed our experience at the kirk session.

'What do you think, Mother?'

'I think that if Reverend Fraser had been our temporary replacement we wouldn't have been forced to be involved in this nonsense.'

'I can't recall ever hearing of a witchcraft trial.'

'I remember your father once coming home from Inverness angrier than I had ever seen him. He had been at the coffee house and the story of this poor woman's execution for witchcraft was in the newspaper. Some of the men he often met there were in favour of it and this had led to such a huge argument that William was never again friendly with a few of them.'

'Father would always hold true to what he believed.'

'Yes, but you would have been a child at that time and I've not heard of a case since, although I suppose there may have been.'

We carried on walking for about ten minutes in silence, acknowledging occasionally a shouted greeting from someone working in a nearby field who either hadn't heard the rumours or didn't realise who we were.

'I lost my concentration part way through ... didn't I?'

'Only for a short while.'

'A short while too long. You need to start telling me when I lapse like this or I may not realise.'

I didn't answer or at least not quickly enough for my mother. In truth, I was becoming frightened of these 'lost' moments.

'Aila?'

'Yes, I'll tell you.'

'I know you're scared. So am I. But I'll increasingly need your help and support. You must become the strong one.' She took my hand. 'You miss Jack.' It wasn't really a question, so I didn't reply. 'Fate has been extremely kind to you, Aila, and extremely hard too. I don't know what to say other than follow your heart.'

'That's what I did when I ran into that burning building, and look at the outcome.'

'Would you do the same again?'

I considered this, as the point deserved proper thought.

'Yes, just as Father would have gone into that building to try and save me, or you would have done in order to reach either of us if we were trapped. Love binds us as much as it can blind us. Thank God it does, for without it what are we left with?'

21

Dornoch, 12 June 1727

WE HAD HEARD NOTHING FURTHER after our appearance at the kirk session and the following Sunday service was similar to the previous ones, although this time people didn't hide the fact that they were avoiding us; there was almost an empty sea of wood around Mother and me as we sat in our pew. News about our summons would have spread throughout the area, and the story had no doubt been expanded with each retelling.

Fortunately, Mistress Hamilton stood by our friendship, Dornoch being far enough away for her to feel safe, at least for the present. As a widow, even a wealthy one, she was highly vulnerable to persecution if associated with someone accused of witchcraft.

The annual fair had brought in large numbers of visitors as well as merchants from far away. Over the coming days there would be sales not just of unusual items like quality linens and rare spices but also large numbers of animals, in particular horses. The event had gained a reputation as being an important place for horse trading. We were lucky in being able to set up our stall in the usual place, particularly as we hadn't attended the regular market since April, and the familiar stallholders greeted us while we all went about laying out our produce.

'May I help?' a familiar voice said.

'Jack!' Beaming, Mother embraced him. 'How lovely to see you.'

He turned to me. 'Hello, Aila. How have you been?'

How could I even begin to explain the turmoil and conflict within my heart, standing here in the noisy market with people around us?

'Everywhere feels lonely. How's Sim?'

'There was almost some bother the first night we came back. He's settled since then, but he's not the same.'

'It's too early for his grief to have left him, or for any of us.'

'No. The troupe isn't what it was. Malie's the one who keeps us more cheerful and provides a distraction.'

Mother gave a rather theatrical cough to attract our attention. Left by herself, she was unable to move the barrels easily.

'Sorry, Mistress Horne.'

With Jack's help our stall was soon set out. I had already taken Abel back to the Hamilton property, so we stood around for a moment, not sure what to say or do.

'Oh, take yourselves off, the pair of you. Here.' Mother handed me a small purse of coin. 'You know what we want, Aila. See what you can buy.'

I was about to ask if she could manage alone but stopped myself just in time as she would have pointed out, yet again, that she had been brewing and selling ale since before I was born. Jack and I walked away. Even this early in the morning Dornoch was bustling. There were stalls everywhere, merchants and vendors trying to outdo each other as they shouted to early visitors. The noise and smell from the large numbers of livestock added to the confusion.

'How are the others?' I asked. We had walked in silence for several minutes, pretending to be interested in whatever happened to be near.

'Looking forward to seeing you and your mother. We'll meet them as we walk around, although they might not easily be able to speak. I've missed you.'

'Really?'

'You know I have.'

'If you say so.'

'You're angry.'

Recently it had felt that I had a mountain of anger weighing upon me. I sighed loudly, releasing some of the tension in my body, which was so stiff that my gait was more uneven than usual.

'Not with you, Jack ... With life.'

'You're too hard on yourself, Aila. Bess was right when she said so to me.'

'Did she?'

'You weren't the only one to be summoned to a private conversation during those last few weeks. I think she actually spoke to everyone, including Malie and your mother.'

'Mother didn't say.'

'And did you tell anyone you'd spoken to Bess?'

'Well ... no.'

'There you are then. Why should other people have told you?'

'I wish I had known her better.'

'There were deep and mysterious waters running through Bess's life. Even after all those years together, I never really

223

knew the background of her early years. Sim probably knows more, but he's never said.'

'What else did she say about me?'

'I can't tell you, otherwise it won't have been a private conversation.'

I remembered how Bess had told me about Jack being haunted by something from his past and that I shouldn't try to force him to reveal what it was. He was right. We all had our secrets and it would be unfair to push him further about what had been spoken.

'Look, there's Sim,' I said.

We had been wandering with no particular aims, despite the list of items I knew we needed at home. There would be time later to purchase those. Sim had a large crowd around him and it was immediately obvious why. With astonishing dexterity, he was juggling four flaming touches. I watched with a mixture of horror and awe as the torches moved faster and higher in the air. The crowd were mesmerised. Then one torch fell to the ground.

'Damn!' Jack cursed under his breath. 'He's never done that before.'

Sim caught the other three and extinguished them in the tub nearby. He bowed. Some people clapped. Some jeered. He bowed again, and I could see him trying to make light of the mistake but, to those who looked, the pain was clearly visible in his eyes.

Nearby, Ellen and Malie were going around with buckets to collect coins, but the crowd was already dispersing to find new entertainment and avoid paying for the flawed performance. Jack and I went over as Sim douched the last torch in the water.

'Aila!'

We hugged each other for a long while, which only emphasised the fact that Jack and I hadn't embraced at all.

'Sorry, Jack,' he said, eventually pulling away from me. 'I lost my concentration for a second.' He sounded embarrassed and I guessed that was an unfamiliar experience for him.

'Don't worry, there'll be plenty more opportunities to dazzle audiences with your display of dancing fire.'

Any potential for further awkwardness was avoided when a small figure hurled itself into my body with such force that Jack had to put a restraining hand against my back before I lost my balance.

'Malie!'

'Aila! How's my calf?'

'Growing bigger by the day, a bit like you. I'm sure you've grown taller even since leaving the croft.'

'I miss my calf, and you and your mother. Is she on the stall?'

'Yes, you can see her whenever you want.'

'We could go now.'

I looked at Jack. He shrugged. Our brief time alone was already over.

*　*　*

Soon afterwards I was busy selling and serving ale while Mother smothered Malie in hugs and kisses and found out every detail of what the girl had been up to since she left us.

'Well I don't see any purchases, Aila,' said Mother eventually. She had immediately spotted that I had returned empty handed. 'Why don't you and Malie go around the fair and perhaps this time you might be able to buy the items we need.'

'Yes, Mother.' I knew well when I was being chastised. She was quite right. I had been given a job to do and so far hadn't achieved any of it.

'Where's Hector?' I asked Malie, when we had left the stall.

'He's working at the local forge. The Dornoch blacksmith has hurt his hand and Hector came to an agreement with him to do the work. There's a lot, with so many people and horses. Jack said I should stay away, but that's where Ellen went after Sim's performance.'

'How are you, Malie?'

'Oh, I'm alright. I miss Bess. What shall we buy?'

Malie and I went around the fair. First we visited the basket weaver, who had a huge array of products, from something delicate that would hold a few freshly made bannocks to a sturdy pack harness for a pony. I bought a basket that was comfortable when carried with my arm under the handle and used this for our subsequent purchases: tea, spices, candles, a new bridle for Abel, a couple of wooden bowls; the list was long and varied.

This annual event was much more open to outsiders than the tightly regulated weekly market in Dornoch, and we stopped to examine the display of one of the many chapmen present. These were men who travelled the country throughout the year, buying products to resell at the large fairs. This man sold linen, most of which he would likely have purchased from individual weavers, providing them with ready coin to help pay their rent while obtaining high-quality materials that could subsequently fetch a much higher price. Some of it was beautiful, yet we soon moved on as Mother always enjoyed purchasing linen, so I left this task to her.

Curiosity drew us towards a large crowd and a wave of anger washed over me when I saw the lines of neat bottles on the table. We caught the end of a very different type of list.

'... king's evil, scurvy, sibbens and all types of ague.'

Everyone lived side by side with disease and illness, and these travelling 'practitioners' usually claimed to be able to cure almost every ailment known, often by using the same remedy. They preyed on fear. Only earlier that morning Mother had been hearing how the outbreak of chincough in Tain showed no signs of dying out. Although Dornoch now had a doctor, the nearest apothecary was in Inverness and people desperate enough would grab any potion that offered to alleviate their suffering.

'Can we go?' I hadn't appreciated Malie was frightened, so we walked away as those nearby jostled with each other to make their purchases. 'I once watched a man filling bottles from a river and the next day I saw him selling them in the street as cures.'

'One time my father became so angry at a man in Inverness who was little more than a showman that he tipped the table over, breaking most of the bottles on it. Father was later fined in court, but he said it was better that poor folk had kept their money and not been given false hope. Come on,' I said, trying to lighten our mood, 'I've saved the best for last.'

'What is it?'

'You'll have to wait until we find him.'

The annual fair was attended by one of the main booksellers from Edinburgh and I enjoyed a long discussion with the man about the numerous titles on display. I was particularly interested in a beautifully bound copy of Allan Ramsay's *The Gentle Shepherd*; although any purchases would have to wait until

Mother had also visited as we always decided together what to buy.

Malie had stood in mute awe, staring at the rows of books as if they were something magical. She was childlike in so many ways, yet I hadn't been exaggerating when I said she had grown. In fact, since first meeting the troupe she had changed quite a lot physically, as if the growth of her spirit had enabled the growth of her body. I waited until we were alone again to ask a question that had been on my mind for a while.

'Malie, how old are you?'

'Fifteen.'

'Are you?'

'I know how old I am, Aila. I just don't look it.'

'You're starting to make up for lost time. Maybe we need to do something about it.'

'What?'

'Patience is a virtue, Malie.'

'Is it?'

'My mother's always saying so, although I suspect it's because she thinks I've never mastered it!'

Markets normally included at least one stall selling new and second-hand clothes; the latter were nearly always being reused, shortened, lengthened, unpicked and restitched again and again, until finally they could be of no more use than rags. It was an activity that took place in the meanest dwelling and the wealthiest estate. Some people purchased old items to resell, either as they were or with alterations. These stalls usually sold a variety of threads for mending and wools for knitting. I found enormous pleasure in buying for Malie and she was beside herself with excitement.

'I've never worn something that has only ever been mine,' she said.

'You'll be grown up.'

Her demeanour changed instantly. 'Will anyone still want to look after me?'

The seriousness of the question and her level of anxiety took my breath away, and I think that she would have hurriedly returned every single item if there was even the remotest chance of her fear coming true.

'Of course they will, Malie. People don't love you because of what you're wearing but because of who you are, and that doesn't alter by changing a petticoat.'

'If you're sure.'

I was about to answer when the expression on Malie's face changed so dramatically that the words never left my mouth, yet even before I asked her what was wrong I felt a presence behind me that made my skin crawl. Slowly, I turned around, reluctant to face whatever or whoever was standing so close, then my ability to speak seemed to desert me entirely.

'Aila.'

The reptile!

'God has brought us together again.' He stared at me for a long while in silence, then his gaze fell upon Malie as if suddenly spotting a likely prey. 'And is this one of the ... travelling folk?'

Malie appeared as unable to reply as me.

'I haven't seen you in the kirk. Perhaps that's not so surprising ... with such striking ginger hair.'

'My hair?' said Malie. She sounded terrified.

'If you had ever attended the kirk, then you would know!'

I knew. I knew exactly what he meant and I thought my heart would burst with the fear of it.

'Such a colour of hair ... It's the sign of a witch.'

22

Kintradwell, 18 June 1727

DESPITE THE ENORMOUS AMOUNT OF work that had been carried out around the croft by the troupe, it hadn't taken long after their departure for our land to demand attention. That Wednesday morning, after an early breakfast, our task was to plant a leek bed.

'Do you think the new king will make any difference?' I asked, pulling up a stubborn weed from the vegetable plot.

'Not to these weeds he won't.'

'I doubt that he'll speak Gaelic.'

'I don't think the previous one even spoke much English,' said Mother, echoing a common complaint about the old Hanoverian king. 'I shouldn't imagine, Aila, that the new King of Great Britain will make much difference to the lives of folk like us and these leeks here won't care if he has two heads yet doesn't speak at all.'

When Mother suggested we take a break around mid-morning, I wasn't about to say no. My hands were sore. Once we were sitting by the fire and had been refreshed with tea, bannocks and blackberry preserve, Mother fetched a salve from the pantry. She was skilled at making remedies and with her many contacts amongst merchants was sometimes able to obtain herbs, seeds and plants that were not always available locally. I had only managed to learn a small fraction of this part of her knowledge, but I knew that this particular lotion contained St John's wort and aspen.

'Here, give me that hand.'

She pulled up a stool next to my chair and began to gently rub my fingers. I closed my eyes. I always felt so much better after these moments and never knew if it was because of the ingredients, having my hands rubbed or because I was being taken care of so tenderly. Perhaps it was a combination of all these things.

'Your poor hands. I fear this work isn't good for them.'

'We have no option.'

'More often these days I wonder if we were right to come here.'

I opened my eyes. This was a concern I had never heard before. I was still considering how to reply when the door was flung open and three men burst in. One of them was Duncan, who had helped to set up our ale stall on many occasions.

'What is the meaning of this?' cried Mother, standing up to confront them.

Duncan replied, speaking to us as if we were strangers. 'We're officers, here with orders from the sheriff depute to arrest you on the charge of witchcraft.'

'That's nonsense,' replied my mother. 'You know well who we are, Duncan.'

'Don't speak my name. I'll not be cursed by a witch.'

'I'm not a witch.'

'What's that there?' he asked, pointing.

'A simple salve for my daughter's hands.'

'Hah! We catch them using their magic potions and spells and they still deny it. Tie her up.'

One of the men quickly stepped forward. I was immediately on my feet but he thrust me easily back down into the chair, before forcing my mother's hands behind her back and tying them with rope he had ready for the task.

'Let her go!' I screamed, unable to take in the violence that had so unbelievably forced its way into our home. 'You've no right to take my mother. We've done nothing wrong.'

'That's for your betters to decide,' replied Duncan. 'Get her.'

Despite his bulk the third man was fast, and before I could even think of resisting I was being tied up as well.

'What are you doing? Let me go!'

'Release my daughter at once. You've got me.'

'Take me for a fool,' shouted Duncan. 'She's not escaping justice that easily. You're both being arrested for witchcraft.'

'Both of us?' cried my mother in disbelief.

'Yes, and I'll not risk being cursed. Make sure their gags are secure.'

My attacker, for I could think of him in no other way, pulled a filthy rag out of his pocket. It looked so disgusting that I instinctively clamped my teeth together and started frantically twisting and turning my body. However, with my hands tied it was only a matter of time before he managed to force open my jaw. I think I bit his fingers at one point, and in his revenge he pushed the cloth so far inside my mouth that some of it was at the back of my throat. I was left kneeling on the floor, desperately trying to breathe and not to cough or vomit.

Years of shifting barrels meant that my mother was a strong woman, and through my tears I could see her resisting furiously despite being tied. Then the officer punched her in the stomach and she couldn't fight back anymore. We were dragged outside and each thrown over the back of a spare pony like recently killed deer about to be brought down from the hills.

The journey was a nightmare of pain and fear; more than once I almost fainted from the discomfort and lack of air. The taste and smell of the rag made me want to retch. For every single plod of that pony's hooves I had to focus my entire being on simply breathing and trying to keep calm.

The men stopped once to take refreshments and they simply pulled us off. I landed heavily on my shoulder and my mother grunted in pain as she hit the ground. We were left where we lay while the men ate, drank and chatted almost as if we weren't present. They took much better care of the animals than us, which made me feel even worse. When they had finished, they threw us back on and continued.

Eventually, when it seemed as if my body could endure no more, we reached Dornoch. From my position I could see little beyond the animal's legs, but as we walked slowly through the streets our shame was increased tenfold because it was a market day and we were led past the stalls of merchants who knew us well. Conversations stopped mid-sentence to be replaced by gasps of surprise; a drunken voice called out that we should be 'punished properly' even though no one had any idea why Mother and I had been arrested. When the ponies stopped outside the tolbooth we were hauled into the building. A brutish-looking man had his feet up by a fire, drinking.

'Ah, you've brought the witches,' he said, standing. 'I hope they've not caused any trouble?'

'We made sure they didn't,' said Duncan.

Mother and I had collapsed to the floor in exhaustion. There must have been some signal behind our backs because we were both untied. As soon as our hands were free we pulled out the rags. I was helpless, gasping for air as I lay on the floor, but my poor mother was in a worse state and immediately started vomiting.

'Disgusting, dirty witches!'

This was the jailer. The town didn't employ someone permanently in this position and I assumed the man was being paid by the authorities to do this job for the duration of our imprisonment. Everyone had heard stories of people being held for months in appalling conditions as they waited for their trial. Would this be our fate?

'You'll have to watch that you don't get cursed,' said the man who had tied me up.

'They'll get a fist if they even look in my direction!' said the jailer. 'I'll not have anyone putting the evil eye on me.'

This exchange went on above our heads and another silent signal must have occurred because together Mother and I were lifted off the floor, half carried along the corridor and thrown onto the filthy floor of a large cell. The door was locked behind us and we were left alone, as wretched, shocked and despairing as it was possible to be.

* * *

The tolbooth used to be the chapterhouse for the cathedral and I think that the crumbling building only remained standing because of the layer of dirt that covered it. One entire side of our cell had been fitted with bars; some light came in from the corridor and there were two grubby windows high up on the opposite wall. The floor was laid with large, black Caithness slabs, so cold and hard that even though I had kicked the filthy straw away from one area we had so far resisted lying down.

The air felt damp and even the exceptional heat of that June didn't reach Mother and me as we sat on two wooden stools, which we had put together so that we could hold hands. They were the only items of furniture apart from a bucket in one corner for bodily waste. There was no bedding or blankets and we were only wearing what we had been arrested in. It was the first time I had been away from the croft without the leather glove covering my left hand.

'Why have they done this to us?'

'Oh Mother, I don't know . . . Because we sound different . . . Because I look different . . . Because people are desperate to find someone to blame for their various misfortunes, someone who could easily be taken away.'

'Executed?'

'It may not come to that.'

'None of this would have happened if your father had been alive.'

Once we had recovered from our initial shock I had called to the jailer to bring water, but he had merely shouted from the comfort of his fire to be quiet. The journey had affected us greatly: every inch of my body seemed to hurt and I knew it was the same for my mother, in addition to how we felt emotionally. The taste of the cloth still made me want to retch and it was difficult to speak, so we had been sitting in silence for a while when there was the sound of someone entering the building. A few moments later a figure appeared at the bars of the cell. I rushed over.

'Jack!'

'How are you both?' He looked and sounded desperate.

'Frightened ... Thirsty.'

'I'll bring food and water to you.' Jack lowered his voice. 'I had to bribe the jailer but he won't give me long. When I heard what had happened, I made some enquiries. Your trial is set for tomorrow morning.'

'So soon?'

'Aila, listen, years ago I did some copying work for a law firm in Edinburgh. Despite my lowly position I became friendly with one of the partners and I saw him again recently. Now, this is important, Scottish men of influence and culture are increasingly looking to science and there's been a significant shift throughout the legal profession against holding witchcraft trials.'

'Because they no longer believe in witches?'

'It's more because they no longer believe it's possible to reasonably prove guilt in any legal sense. You should attack them on this at the very start of the trial. They won't expect it so you must use that moment of surprise to make your point before they try to silence you. Challenge them with confidence, as if you know the law. Create enough doubt to make them consider delaying the case.'

Jack's comments were so unexpected that I simply didn't know what to say. When he continued his voice was just a whisper. 'You cannot rely on your mother tomorrow. This is all down to you.'

'Yes,' I replied, equally quietly. 'When she's put under pressure, her confusion becomes much worse. At other times she's better. But in court ...'

'I'll be there, near the front, so that you can see me.'

'Don't do anything foolish.'

The jailer shouted from the office at the front of the building that Jack had to leave.

'Don't lose hope,' he said, taking hold of my hand through the bars and squeezing it gently. 'Concentrate on tomorrow.'

Then he left and I felt that there was no hope, not within me, not within that cell, not within the whole world.

* * *

When I turned fifteen Father took me to the courthouse in Inverness on several occasions as he wanted me to have an understanding of how our legal system operated. It seemed that much of it had little to do with justice and I suspected that was partly what he wished me to see. Only wealthy people could afford to have someone represent them, while females accused of a crime were often not permitted to speak in court. This meant that unless she had a significant amount of money or an influential male willing to speak on their behalf, a woman could face a huge challenge in proving her innocence.

I once saw Father defend a neighbour accused of theft when the evidence was so clearly invented by a local man with a grudge against her. He made the man appear such an utter fool that the sheriff later asked if my father had studied law. 'No sir,' he had replied, 'I study people.'

As Mother and I sat next to each other on our stools, I wondered about the people who would be in court the next day. An accusation of witchcraft spread fear in the community faster than an outbreak of smallpox. No one would want to

238

appear to be our friend, to have been associated with us or even to have carried out work for us in the past.

Anyone and everyone connected to a witch could be suspected of witchcraft themselves. The common belief was that if they were suspected then surely their family and friends had to be investigated. And so it went on until it wasn't unheard of for someone to find that they were suddenly accused when they had no connection whatsoever with the original person. Witchcraft was the most contagious disease known, for you could be affected even if you were miles away from the outbreak.

* * *

It was difficult to keep track of time, but it must have been about half an hour after Jack's visit that I heard someone enter the building and a few moments later the jailer appeared at the cell. There was a short gap in some of the bars near the floor so that items could be passed without unlocking the door, and he pushed through a small jug of water and a couple of pieces of stale bread, which became covered in dirt as he slid them along.

'This is not enough.'

'Witches should be grateful to get anything, so shut up and let me rest!'

He was an ugly brute, who so obviously enjoyed inflicting distress that it would be useless to argue. I picked up the bread and jug, and sat next to Mother. As he walked away we could hear him laughing.

'I can't eat anything,' said Mother.

'No, nor can I, and we must conserve some of this water.' I handed over the jug. 'Take a drink for now.'

We each took a little then sat holding hands, trying to give and receive comfort, though God knows there was none to be found in that cell. The sound of people outside talking, calling out greetings and enjoying the sunshine made our predicament even harder. It felt as though we had endured a huge sea crossing and stepped off the ship onto a strange, hostile island that bore no resemblance to the lives we knew. It seemed impossible to believe that it was only that morning when Mother and I had been planting a leek bed and discussing the new king.

Neither of us could sit for too long and we walked about as an alternative to leaning against a wall or getting down on the floor. We gave each other hugs and kisses, rubbed the other's back and shoulders, wept, took tiny sips of water, walked again. Mother became more distressed and her confusion worsened.

Stories about how prisoners were persuaded to confess to witchcraft were legendary, and although I had heard that torture was no longer allowed in Scottish jails, I couldn't prevent tormenting myself with the idea that I was wrong or that the law might not be rigidly adhered to. Mother would have known these tales of horror as well as I did, although neither of us mentioned them.

Terrible images consumed my thoughts. There was apparently a device called 'the boot', which crushed the victim's foot and leg, and 'pilliewinkes' that crushed the hand. If anyone came near me with such evil contraptions I would simply confess to whatever they wanted to hear even before they were fitted. I was weak and couldn't endure pain to those parts of my body, not again.

I tried to calm my fears with the fact that if the court case took place in the morning there could hardly be time to extract a confession using torture or the practice of 'watching', where relays of people kept someone continually awake. Also, a confession was normally used to obtain permission to hold a trial and this was obviously not required, which meant that the authorities must have some other form of evidence. Yet what? Accusations? McNeil by himself surely wasn't enough. There had to be others, but who?

My mind was brought back to the present by the noise of the main door opening and closing, which was followed by the jailer speaking. The office seemed to be quiet for a while then a huge shadow blocked out what little light filtered through the bars.

'Hector!' I croaked. 'Am I glad to see you.'

He smiled, but it faded when he noticed the grim conditions. 'Jack wasn't sure he would be allowed in again and didn't believe that the food would reach you if he simply left it, so he asked me to visit. I explained to the jailer that you are my friends and I don't like seeing friends going hungry. He wasn't keen to let me enter, but once I'd lifted him off the floor to make sure he had heard me properly, he allowed me in without even suggesting a bribe. Here, Ellen's put food together and some extra clothing, and I've brought blankets as well.'

Hector handed us the items through the bars, keeping only the basket. Mother came over and seemed to improve just by seeing the friendly giant.

'Hello, Mistress Horne. How are you bearing up?'

'I've known better accommodation, but your gifts are very gratefully received.'

'I wish I could do more.' He lowered his voice. 'We've broken camp and we'll find somewhere farther away from Dornoch that's well hidden from the track. Ellen and Malie will stay there tomorrow but Jack and I will be in court.'

Hector remained for a short while until even he thought he shouldn't push his luck. It was only after he had gone that it struck me he had made no mention of Sim, but I dismissed this as being unimportant. Hector had brought several jugs of water and one of ale. We used the latter to finally get rid of the revolting taste in our mouths before putting one of the precious blankets on the floor then we laid out the cooked chicken, cheese and bread so fresh it was still warm. It looked like a feast, though we had little appetite and had to force ourselves to eat something.

The smell of the peat fire in the office drifted along the corridor and we occasionally heard the jailer moving about, but he left us alone until much later when he walked along and pushed a lantern through the gap in the bars. He then lit the candle fitted into a niche in the wall opposite the cell door and went back to his fire without acknowledging us in any way. I wondered if, on his way out, Hector had threatened to pluck out his eyeballs and boil them in his broth.

* * *

By evening Mother and I were exhausted, so we decided to settle ourselves for the night. We left the blanket to provide some protection from the flagstones and wrapped the others around us, keeping on our clothes plus some of those that Ellen had packed. I didn't remove my boots because I was worried about the filth, although my feet suffered if left inside them for too long. It was a case of choosing the lesser of two evils.

I laid my head on Mother's chest and she held me tightly.

Even when she became confused her instincts remained strong. Since Jack had left I had been thinking almost non-stop about the following morning and felt that I needed to bring this up before we went to sleep.

'Mother, tomorrow in court I think it's best if I speak on our behalf.'

'You fear that I will say the wrong things?'

'I fear that whatever we say will be twisted and that every sentence will have to be carefully constructed.'

'Well, you are your father's daughter and if anyone can argue our way out of this it's you. I will remain quiet unless I'm forced to speak.'

Like some herald of doom, at that very moment the bell in the cathedral began to ring. It was rung only twice a day, at five in the morning to announce the start of work for some, and eight in the evening to mark the end of work for others.

'The good people of Dornoch will be sitting down in front of their fires,' said Mother.

I thought about those 'good people', many of whom had complimented our ale or had sold produce from a stall near to ours, and considered whether any of them would speak up for us during the ordeal that lay ahead. Somehow, I doubted it very much.

23

Dornoch, 19 June 1727

ROUND THE MIDDLE OF THE morning Duncan and another officer arrived at the tolbooth, and although they didn't tie our hands or stuff our mouths, they were unnecessarily rough as they marched us to the nearby Town House. We entered through a side door and were pushed up three steps until we stood side by side on a small wooden platform, encased by railings. The second officer – I heard him being called Campbell – remained behind us. We hadn't been in the building before but I was far more interested in the people who were present than the impressive architecture.

Captain David Ross, the sheriff depute, sat behind a long bench on a raised area that took up almost one entire end of the room. I glanced at the men either side of him; seven on one and eight on the other. This was the assize who would judge our fate. I recognised a few of the more successful local merchants, plus dignitaries who had been to our ale stall at various times, all landowners and men of wealth and significant standing in the community.

Below the sheriff, the clerk of the court, who would have knowledge of the law, sat at a table upon which were laid several papers plus a ledger of some sort, along with writing quills and ink. There was also a black book, which I took to be a Bible.

The roped-off area for those who wanted to watch was packed, with easily more than a hundred people pressed tightly together. I assumed there were witnesses amongst them, although who they could be, I had no idea. Jack had managed to get a place at the front and we looked at each other for a long time. His grim expression no doubt reflected my own. I returned his nod and carried on with my study. Hector was standing near the main entrance and I knew that Ellen and Malie would be safely at the hiding place. There was no sign of Sim.

My attention was drawn to the centre of the room, where the floor was kept clear for witnesses to give evidence and be questioned. A figure dressed in black had walked into the middle; McNeil must have been hidden by someone as I hadn't spotted him until that moment. He stared at me and I wondered if he was going to act as some form of prosecutor. There was no one acting in our defence.

I don't know what drew my eyes back towards Jack at that moment, perhaps some invisible connection between us, but I was shocked at the change in his expression. It wasn't grim anymore, it was murderous, and I watched in horror as his hand moved slowly towards the hilt of his knife. He stepped forward until being stopped by the rope pulling tightly across his waist. No one else appeared to have noticed and certainly McNeil seemed unaware despite being only several yards away.

'Jack, don't.'

I spoke in a whisper that not even my mother could hear, yet it was as if those words had reached across the room and

246

suddenly made Jack aware of his surroundings and what he was doing. He visibly relaxed, stepping back and lowering his arm. He looked at me, and although our eyes locked, I didn't understand what had just taken place.

'A lot of people,' said Mother.

'Yes,' I replied, forced to give her my attention.

'They don't look friendly.'

'No.'

'Aila, be the person that your father brought you up to be.'

I tried to return the reassuring smile she gave me but the muscles in my cheeks refused to obey.

The constant murmur of the crowd had risen slightly upon our arrival before returning to its original level as those present spoke quietly to their friends and neighbours. Then the clerk stood and everyone was immediately silent.

'The court of the sheriffdom of Sutherland, held in the Town House of Dornoch by Captain David Ross, sheriff depute of the said sheriffdom, on this day the nineteenth of June, seventeen twenty-seven. No person shall enter or leave or speak to another without permission. This assize has gathered to decide upon the innocence or guilt of Janet Horne and her daughter Aila Horne of Kintradwell in the parish of Loth, who are charged with the abominable crime against God and man of witchcraft.'

The clerk now turned to face us. 'Janet Horne, how do you plead to this charge?'

'Not guilty.'

'Aila Horne, how do you plead to this charge?'

'Not guilty.'

For all the good it will do us.

The clerk looked behind him and when Sheriff Ross nodded, he sat down. This was the moment I had been thinking about constantly since Jack last spoke to me, the moment that I had analysed and worried about, dissected into a thousand parts and put back together throughout the entire night.

'By what authority do you try this case?'

I spoke clearly and loudly as if equal in status to anyone in that room. No one expected me to speak, never mind to raise such a point, and the response was a stunned silence. Even my mother looked on with surprise.

'The witches should remain silent!' cried McNeil once he had regained his wits.

'We are not witches, nor have we been convicted of being witches. You have no right to refer to us in that manner.'

'How dare you speak to a minister of God in this way!'

'What I say is true. You of all people should be willing to hear the truth. And this is a court of law, not an ecclesiastical court, so Sheriff Ross I ask my question again. By what authority do you try this case?'

'By the authority invested in me as sheriff depute of Sutherland, and you will be silent.'

'I will not. If you intend to kill us then I can hardly make our sentence worse by speaking. That is not the point here. Trying a person on a charge of witchcraft goes completely against the prevailing advice of legal experts throughout the whole of Scotland, who no longer believe it is possible, in law, to realistically prove someone is guilty of such a crime. This provincial court does not have the legal or moral authority to try a case of witchcraft and certainly not to pronounce a verdict.'

The members of the assize looked at each other in aston-ishment and no one ventured to speak until McNeil found his voice. It was always McNeil.

'See! The witch condemns herself out of her own mouth!'

'How is this?' asked the sheriff.

I was wondering the same thing.

'No mere woman could possibly know of such matters, or speak in the way this witch does. I tell you now that the words we have just heard in this court have come direct from Satan himself!' This caused a stir of unrest, with people glancing nervously about as if expecting to see a horned man with cloven feet and a tail, or whatever image they believed repres-ented the Devil. 'Perhaps, Sheriff Ross, the application of a scold's bridle would make everyone safer?'

I couldn't prevent the fear that flashed across my face, for the suggestion filled me with terror. McNeil saw his attack had struck home and gave me the same little smile he had that day I found him in Mother's armchair. The scold's bridle was a small metal cage that was strapped firmly over the victim's head, its vile, protruding tongue being forced into the woman's mouth so that she could not speak, eat or drink.

When I was a young girl I once saw a woman in Inverness who had been fitted with this hideous contraption because her husband had complained to the authorities that his wife was quarrelsome. She was being paraded through the streets as a warning to others of what could happen to them. I've never forgotten the terrible despair on her face.

I had no idea if the use of a device like this would be allowed, but if McNeil persuaded the sheriff to follow his advice then Mother and I had no chance of escaping execution. I walked a dangerous path. I needed to make McNeil appear foolish yet I couldn't do this with the sheriff or the others. Instead, I had to appeal to their sense of right and wrong ... Appeal to their male pride.

'Sheriff Ross, surely the educated men of honour who sit by your side are not so afraid of being bested by the arguments put forward by a "mere woman" that you would prevent me from speaking at all? I cannot believe that men who guide and uphold our community so wisely would be so easily frightened into taking such an action.'

I spoke respectfully, regardless of what I felt inside, and I addressed each man in turn, a few of them turning away their heads either in shame or because they were afraid to meet my eye. The sheriff conferred with a couple of those nearest to him before announcing his decision.

'Reverend McNeil, may I remind you that this is a court of law and I am in charge.'

The minister's face underwent several changes of expression as he fought to control his temper.

The sheriff then turned to me. 'And the accused will not speak without my permission. This trial will continue without further interruption.'

*   *   *

'I call the first witness,' said the clerk, looking down at a paper to remind himself who it was. 'Peggy Butcher.'

Mother and I looked at each other in surprise. For several moments no one moved.

'Peggy Butcher! Come into the centre of the courtroom.' The diminutive figure of Peggy emerged from the crowd, which

250

parted to let her through as though she was a leper who had forgotten her bell. 'Don't waste our time. Come forward.'

Our poor beaten neighbour appeared terrified and I could only assume that she was even more afraid of her violent husband than she was of lying in court, for I could see no other way that Peggy could be used against us.

'You are Peggy Butcher and you live on the adjoining land to the accused?'

'Yes, sir.'

'Speak up so that all might hear.'

'Yes, sir.'

The clerk picked up the Bible on his desk and walked over to stand in front of her. 'Are you willing to make faith?'

Peggy looked confused, and he gave a sigh of frustration before continuing. 'Place your hand upon the Bible. Are you willing to swear that what you are about to say is true and without malice or prejudice against the accused?' When she didn't reply he continued. 'Say the words "I swear it" if what you are about to tell this court is true.'

'I swear it, sir.'

As the clerk returned to his desk he stopped beside it and announced, 'The first witness, Sheriff Ross,' before sitting down.

'Thank you,' replied the sheriff, studying the trembling figure for several moments before continuing. 'You have recently lost a baby?'

'Yes, sir.'

'You must reply clearly. If you are honest then you have nothing to fear. Shortly before your baby died, you were visited by these two women.' He pointed at us, as if there was any doubt who 'these two women' were.

'They've been very kind to me, sir.'

'You are to answer my questions and nothing else. Do you understand?'

Peggy nodded. So far, she hadn't looked in our direction. I felt only sorrow for her, although I was puzzled as to what she might say.

'As they were leaving, the older of the two women said something . . . What was it?'

Peggy stared at the floor, appearing as if she might actually collapse upon it. In complete contrast, McNeil looked happy watching in silence from the side, for now leaving the questioning to the sheriff.

'Answer truthfully and you will not be in trouble.'

'Janet . . . the mother . . . she said that the baby would not live.'

Butcher!

'She cursed your baby?'

'She said it would not live more than a couple of days.'

'Witch!' shouted McNeil, stepping forward so that he could once more be the centre of everyone's attention. His comment was accompanied by cries of shock from the crowd. 'Sheriff Ross, even if this was not considered a curse, divination is a recognised sign of witchcraft.'

'Anyone with eyes in their head could see that the baby was too ill to survive,' I shouted back across the courtroom. 'Isn't that why you were called to baptise the child the very morning it was born?'

'Foretelling the future is the right of God alone and anyone else who believes they have such a power has entered into a covenant with Satan!'

'So, if I foretell that today will be followed by tonight and it will be dark and that this will be followed by tomorrow and it will be light again, is that divination or purely common sense that any person in this room could predict!'

'Silence,' called Sheriff Ross. He waited for order before continuing. 'And when did your baby die?'

'Two days later, sir.'

The sheriff spoke quietly to the nearest members of the assize and then to the clerk, who dismissed Peggy curtly.

'You will remain in the courtroom until told to do otherwise. Return to your place.'

Peggy turned around and for the first time she looked at us. Her face was so full of anguish that I nodded and hoped that she knew I had no ill will towards her.

'Step forward, John Butcher.'

Butcher stepped out of the crowd, ignored his passing wife, and walked into the centre of the court. He removed his hat and held it to his chest as if trying to look pious, while his attempt at an expression of open innocence made him appear more stupid than ever.

'I am here, sir.'

Once he was sworn in, Sheriff Ross took over. 'I want you to explain to the court what you have already told to myself and the Reverend McNeil, concerning what you saw of the two women who stand accused of witchcraft.'

'I was out one night in March, checking that all was well before going to my bed, and I saw Janet Horne walking up a hill that borders our land.'

'How could you see her if it was night?'

'There was a full moon, sir, and light enough to know that she wore nothing more than a shift. I was shivering even with my full clothing on, but she appeared unconcerned by the intense cold.'

'You suspected some unnatural power at work?'

'I did, sir.'

'Carry on.'

'I don't mind admitting I was fearful, but I followed, making sure I remained hidden. When she stopped at the top I moved nearer, and although not close enough to hear I could see that she was uttering spells.'

'How could you tell they were spells?'

'She was holding both arms up to the sky, as if beseeching spirits, and I suddenly felt a terrible, evil presence. I'm a God-fearing man, sir, but I thought the Devil himself was about to appear before my eyes.'

Butcher glanced up at Mother and me as if afraid. Much as I hated the man, his ignorance and his violence, I believed a part of him genuinely did fear us and that made his evidence much more dangerous because everyone else could also see that he was scared.

'Then the other one appeared.'

'The daughter?'

'Yes, sir.'

'Did she join in this activity?'

'Sir, I was filled with such dread that I closed my eyes and prayed for the good Lord's protection.'

'No one could blame you for that.'

'Thank you, sir. When I opened them, the pair had vanished and I returned as quickly as possible to the safety of my home and my dear wife.'

'Did you see other examples of this Devil worship?'

'I did, sir. I felt it was my Christian duty to keep a watch on them and I saw similar events on other occasions.'

Mother groaned quietly, so I stepped nearer and took hold of her hand. I didn't know how much of the proceedings she was following, but she obviously understood something of how badly things were going. Behind us Campbell muttered a comment I didn't catch, but in the absence of any instructions he made no move to separate us. Sheriff Ross continued.

'And during the time that these women have been your neighbours, have you seen other examples of witchcraft?'

'I have, sir. Apart from our beautiful baby dying, God bless his innocent soul, our previously healthy cow began to give hardly any milk at all while our pig and some of our poultry have also taken ill.'

'These are clear and common signs of the involvement of witchcraft,' said McNeil.

This is too much.

'Your cow stopped giving milk because the poor beast is half starved and I suspect that's what's wrong with your other animals!' I shouted.

'The witch must be silent!'

It was obvious that McNeil was going to use every opportunity he had to refer to us as witches, and on each occasion this idea was going to be further engrained into the minds of the assizers and the crowd as fact. I could only challenge him so many times before the sheriff would silence me, and that might make it more difficult to object to other, more damaging lies. McNeil knew this as well as I did.

I was already surprised at the degree of freedom I had been given to speak. Initially, I had thought that my outbursts had been so unexpected that the sheriff almost hadn't known how to react, but now I began to wonder whether he had been pushed into conducting this trial. Maybe, in his heart, he didn't want to be the person to condemn women to be executed. Whatever the reality, I couldn't stand there in silence.

'Sheriff Ross, are we to be blamed for every beast that is ill, every harvest that fails and every accident that occurs?'

'Such things do not happen without a reason.'

'Perhaps, but was there never an animal or person ill before my mother and I arrived? Did accidents never occur? Are we to believe that people in the parish of Loth were so content and in such continuous, robust health that life was perfect in every way?'

My comment was followed by silence as no one could think of a suitable retort that bore the faintest resemblance to a logical answer. As ever, the way forward was provided by a man who displayed less honour, compassion and kindness than the lowliest of creatures.

'Sheriff Ross, there is other evidence that proves beyond doubt the guilt of the two witches.'

'Butcher, you may return to your wife. Carry on, Reverend McNeil.'

'During my extensive investigations amongst the local population I learned that Janet Horne had turned her daughter into a pony in order to more easily ride around and do evil. The Devil himself shod her feet and the results of that vile deed can be seen clearly by every decent man in this courtroom today.'

Damn him. I knew that he would try to use my injuries against us, but this was madness.

'Reverend McNeil, if I look like a pony to you then you've either known some very strange ponies or some very strange women.'

There was a collective intake of breath before some of the bolder men in the crowd laughed. McNeil was furious.

'This disrespect towards a minister of the kirk is an outrage!'

'And was it not an outrage when you arrived uninvited in our barn and, finding me alone, you threw yourself upon me and were only prevented from going further by the arrival of my mother, who emptied a piss pot on your head!'

This time the laughter was loud and long, and I saw that even a couple of members at the bench were smiling. The blood seemed to drain out of McNeil's face. He was white with rage. We glared at each other with such hatred that it seemed to fill the space between us with a physical connection. It was in that moment I truly understood how everything that was about to happen in the courtroom would be decided between McNeil and me. Everyone else was a spectator; the sheriff and assize, the witnesses and officers, the boisterous crowd, even Jack and Mother. They were merely bystanders.

McNeil and I were each terrified of the other, yet we were drawn together like two ships set upon a course that could end only in collision and disaster. But which one of us would sink? He clung to the power and beliefs of an age that was disappearing and it filled him with dread. And I was a symbol of a threat to all that he relied on to give purpose to his life.

I was a threat not because I was a witch, although he probably did believe that, but because I represented an idea ... That a woman could be intelligent and educated, could hold opinions and challenge the injustices around her. That she did not have to be subservient to the kirk or to men. Yes, we haunted each other's nightmares, but I had pushed him as if I had used a besom to sweep a wildcat into the corner of the house, and now he was more dangerous than ever.

'Enough of this witch's lies! Sheriff Ross, let her show her hands and feet to the court. Let people see with their own eyes the Devil's work upon her body.'

The sheriff surveyed the scene before him. 'Bring her into the centre of the court.'

I was grabbed roughly from behind and dragged down the stairs to stand in the open area, where all could see me clearly. Campbell loved to show off his control and held my arms in such a tight grip that I was grimacing in pain. The officer was playing his part in a game where the rules had been written by powerful men. We all had our parts to play.

'Remove her boots,' instructed the sheriff.

As soon as the officer let go I slapped away his hands as hard as I could.

'I will do it! I will do it!'

He raised his fist to strike me. Fortunately, the sheriff intervened in time.

'Let her do it. Step back so that everyone may see.'

Campbell reluctantly moved away. My chest was heaving with exertion and fear, and I had to force myself not to cry, for I felt so like it at that moment. I couldn't stand on one leg, so I had to sit on the floor in order to remove my boots. People pushed forward and strained against the rope to obtain the best view and when I stood there were gasps of revulsion and fear from those who could see all my injuries.

Father used to say that if his ship was attacked at sea he often won the fight by doing the very thing that his enemy least expected. So I turned my back on the sheriff, raised my arms high in the air and addressed the crowd with as much confidence as I could find within me.

'There ... Hands and feet burned in a fire and nothing to do with ponies, evil deeds or the Devil practising his skill at the forge.' Earlier on I had spotted the imposing figure of the Dornoch blacksmith, an honest and respected man in the community, and one not easily intimidated. Many considered the art of working metal to be bordering on magic and I knew this might make him more reluctant to speak.

'Hugh Robertson,' I said loudly, 'long before we moved to the area your boy's leg was badly hurt in a fire. Do his injuries not look similar to mine?'

'Quiet, witch!'

McNeil was behind me and I simply ignored him. At that moment people were more interested in whether the blacksmith would be brave enough to reply.

'They do indeed, Mistress Horne,' he said, addressing me respectfully. 'And in my work I've seen many such injuries to both limb and body. I myself managed to burn my own hand not so long ago.' He held it up, the white linen bandage clearly visible. 'And I should know better.'

This resulted in a few laughs and I sensed some sympathy from many in the crowd. 'And who else here has not seen burns before?' I shouted. 'Fire is ever the thing we fear, and with good reason.' Several heads nodded in agreement. 'An accident is just that, but to deliberately burn a person is a wickedness that has no place in Dornoch amongst decent people.'

'Officer—'

I turned and could see that Sheriff Ross was about to get Campbell to silence me so I made a big show of sitting down and putting on my boots. No one tried to prevent me, but as soon as I stood I was manhandled back to my place beside Mother. She took my hand in hers. By this point the clerk was standing near the bench in conversation with the sheriff and shortly afterwards he walked into the centre to make an announcement.

'This court will break for one hour. During this time no person shall approach the assize or attempt to communicate with its members in any way. Take the accused back to their cell.'

24

Dornoch, 19 June 1727

PEOPLE HAD BEEN DRINKING AS if celebrating, and it seemed that even more of them were crammed into the Town House when Mother and I were brought back from the tolbooth. During the break our jailer had tormented us with news that every possible space to sleep in town that night had been taken, as our expected execution was an event that couldn't be missed. Who wouldn't want to be able to say in years to come that they were there the day they burned the witches at Dornoch?

The first witness in the afternoon was a man we had employed as a builder. The fault was ours, as we had accepted a recommendation from a local woman who we later discovered was his sister and we hadn't checked his reputation further.

'Alasdair Strachan, I understand you were taken on by the accused to build a barn for a horse and cow?' asked the sheriff.

'I was sir, and I rue the day I ever met those witches. The older one soon turned out to be vicious and quarrelsome. I always felt uncomfortable when she was around, watching like a hawk above a mouse hole, just waiting to get me.'

'And did you build this barn?'

'I did not, for I hadn't been allowed to do more than a small part of it when she told me to leave and not come back. She gave me the evil eye, sir, and I've been suffering from it ever since with poor health and not enough work to keep an honest man alive. Will the curse be lifted when they're burned, sir?'

'You can be sure of it,' replied McNeil, when Sheriff Ross hesitated at answering.

I sensed that the sheriff's patience with me was wearing out and I wasn't sure how much more I would be allowed to speak. However, the truth was that Mother and I would burn if I said nothing to challenge this 'evidence' and so it seemed I had no choice.

'You get so little work because of your reputation for poor quality. We were new to the area and tricked by your sister into employing you.'

'Please, sir, don't let them curse me again,' said Strachan stepping back, even though he was several paces from us already.

'Don't be afraid,' said McNeil. 'Their days of cursing will soon be at an end and we will all be safer for it. You can rest assured that your fortunes will improve.'

As Strachan walked back into the crowd, McNeil looked up at the sheriff and although neither spoke I guessed as to the message he was trying to convey. I was right.

'I will not permit the accused to speak again,' said Sheriff Ross, which resulted in a cheer from some of the more drunken men in the crowd. Those who hadn't been present in the morning were no doubt surprised and offended at the idea of me talking without permission. 'Take my warning seriously,' he added, staring hard. I met his gaze without flinching, for all the good it would do. 'Call the next witness.'

This was a local farmer and from the few occasions we had spoken to him after a Sunday service he had appeared to be a decent man. It was well known that he had recently fallen on hard times and many people believed that any misfortune, unless it was so obviously a natural event, had to be caused by another person. The long list of ill luck that he recounted ranged from his hens disappearing to the recent death of his wife, although she had been sick even before Mother and I arrived in the area.

Sheriff Ross had remained silent throughout this evidence. However, he was about to surprise us all. 'Mister McKenzie, have you ever quarrelled with the accused?'

'No, sir.'

'Have you exchanged harsh words or been aware of either woman perhaps muttering in your presence or appearing to threaten you in any way whatsoever?'

'They've always been very kind, sir.'

'I see. So you have no reason to believe they would wish you harm?'

'No, sir.'

It was clear that the sheriff was angry. 'Heed my warning, Reverend McNeil. I will not allow witnesses who, by their own admission, have no reason to suppose their misfortune is linked to these women.'

'But the timing—'

'Is not enough! This is a court of law and if you are to present witnesses then I advise you strongly to ensure there is some correlation between their experiences and the accused. Do not waste our time with people when there is no link!'

I wasn't sure who was more taken aback between McNeil or me. He stood without speaking while the poor farmer hopped about from foot to foot, not knowing what to do.

'Mister McKenzie, we are sorry indeed to learn of your ill fortune. You may return to your home. We have no further need of your presence.'

He left as quickly as he could, while McNeil went over to the clerk and appeared to suggest removing some of the names on his list. There were still plenty and for nearly an hour we heard about bewitched pigs and poultry, a man who had broken his leg, a calf that had died ... Our evil seemed to have no end. But we hadn't quarrelled with any of these witnesses and the most they could accuse us of was that they felt 'uneasy in our presence' or that we 'looked at them strangely'. I thought they should try wearing my boots for a day; people looked at me strangely all the time.

The sheriff still hadn't been satisfied and he reduced two women to tears before instructing the men either side of him to dismiss their statements. It was interesting to watch the friction that developed between the sheriff and the minister. Yet I suspected that more than enough damage had been done and I could see no benefit in letting this go on. Apart from Jack and Hector I doubted that anyone believed we weren't guilty.

I caught Jack's eye. He appeared so distraught and helpless that my heart went out to him as though he was the one facing the executioner. It was time to put a stop to the stream of false accusations.

I took a deep breath.

'We're guilty!' I shouted the words.

As God is my witness, the king himself could not have commanded the silence that followed. Everyone stared in disbelief and I stared back at them, determined they would damn well hear me.

'We're guilty of being women and of having no man to speak for us. We're guilty of being intelligent and educated, of speaking out when we see injustice or cruelty. We're guilty of looking and sounding different. But we are not witches and we are not guilty of witchcraft!'

The silence continued for a few moments before the entire courtroom exploded as people shouted from every corner, and whether some agreed with me or none did at all, I couldn't tell. The sheriff's cries for silence went unheeded while McNeil almost appeared to be having a fit as he screamed and pointed, for once his words going unheard. Then I became aware of a commotion near the main door and a new voice could increasingly be heard as the owner forced his way through the crowd, those nearby rapidly quietening down at his presence.

'Let me through! Make way! I will speak. Let me through I say!'

One of the officers raised his staff, but when he realised who was heading towards him he quickly lowered it. Eventually, the small, rotund figure popped out of the crush like a stopper from a bottle of over-fermented ale and stood, panting and glaring at the surrounding faces.

'Sheriff Ross. I demand to be heard!'

'Reverend MacDonald, your arrival is timely.'

'No doubt the hand of God has played its part, as it does with all things,' replied the minister, although I had spotted that Sim was now standing next to Jack and realised he had been sent on an urgent mission to bring back the only person alive who could speak on our behalf.

'Indeed,' replied the sheriff. 'Well, I don't believe anyone here can object to you speaking, Reverend, although we've heard much evidence to confirm the guilt of these two women.'

'These two women,' answered the minister, pointing at Mother and me, 'have been regular members of my congregation since they arrived in my parish more than two years ago, and I say to you Sheriff Ross, and to everyone else in this courtroom, that Janet Horne and her daughter Aila are honest, God-fearing people and if ... rumour ... has been circulated to the contrary then I tell you it is false, it is malicious, it is superstition from a bygone age that modern men of education and culture should have no dealings with.'

This last point was aimed squarely at the assize and I thought it was a clever move to try and make these pillars of our community feel they should be above taking accusations such as this seriously.

'Reverend MacDonald.'

This was the reptile. Slithering ... slithering. With just those two words I could tell that he was about to try and disarm his rival by appearing friendly and reasonable.

'Everyone knows that you're a good man, working tirelessly for your congregation. I have heard it said many times and you are a credit to the kirk. However, for many years I have travelled throughout Scotland and gathered a great knowledge about witchcraft and how the Devil carries out evil by using the huge weaknesses women have in their body, their mind and their spirit. You and I, we do God's work in different ways. I have dedicated my life to destroying the enemies of God and have learned things that you could not possibly know ... tucked away in this remote Highland area.'

'I know people,' shot back Reverend MacDonald, 'and we're not so *remote* that I don't recognise good and evil or that I don't understand the seriousness of witchcraft. Sheriff Ross, let us end this nonsense so that honest folk can get back to their work. There is a simple test that will satisfy all.'

Reverend MacDonald also knew how to play to an audience and he had the added benefit of being known and respected by many. With a flourish he pulled out his Bible, holding it high in the air for people to see before he walked over to face my mother.

'Let Janet Horne place her hand upon the Bible and confirm that she is not a witch and has not been involved in witchcraft!'

A murmur rang throughout the crowd and several heads nodded in agreement.

'Janet, please place your hand upon the Bible.'

As he spoke these words the minister gently took my mother's hand. It was done very naturally, as if merely a kindly gesture, yet it made me wonder if he suspected something of her confusion and was making sure she did what he wanted without any hesitation or delay.

McNeil suddenly shouted out, all pretence of being friendly or reasonable having completely disappeared. 'Wait! Everyone knows that a witch will lie, even with her hand on God's good book. Let her instead recite the Lord's Prayer, for it is a fact that a witch cannot say these words.'

The opinion in the courtroom was swaying one way and another like a leaf blowing in the wind, and now people seemed to be in agreement with this latest suggestion. I feared that in her confused state my mother would not recite the prayer correctly, which would condemn us both. The sheriff appeared unsure what to do. I had to act quickly.

'I accept Reverend McNeil's challenge,' I shouted, then I launched myself into the Lord's Prayer before anyone could stop me.

'Ar n-Athair a tha air nèamh, Gu naomhaichear d' ainm.'

There was a moment of almost stunned silence before McNeil cried out. 'No! Not her. Janet Horne. Make the old one do it.'

I continued, speaking over him as best I could in an effort to reach the end and prove that I had met his test successfully.

He was equally determined to prevent me. 'Stop! Shut up! Sheriff, make her stop.'

'Agus na leig ann am buaireadh sinn; ach saor sinn o olc ...'

'If she continues then strike her,' said the sheriff.

'No!' This was Reverend MacDonald, who moved closer although he couldn't actually get between me and Campbell, who had grabbed my arm and raised his fist. I hesitated at the threat and that was weak of me. 'I will not allow violence against these innocent women.'

'They're witches!' spat McNeil.

'Until proven otherwise they're innocent.'

Then the place was in an uproar, with people shouting from every corner of the room. My mother, the minister's Bible held high in her hand, was speaking and probably saying she wasn't a witch. No one was listening. McNeil was screaming, his words lost, while Reverend MacDonald argued furiously with the officer behind us. I began once more to loudly recite the Lord's Prayer as officials ran around trying to regain order. Sheriff

Ross was puce with anger. He stood and I saw that he had obtained a staff, which he slammed several times on the bench in front of him.

'SILENCE! Officers of the court! If any person speaks without my express permission, strike them down whoever they are. That is an order.'

Everyone fell silent. I had failed. I looked at Jack and he slowly moved his hand towards the hilt of his knife, but I gave him an almost imperceptible shake of my head. They may be good fighters but it would be madness to attempt an escape. Jack, Sim and Hector were hopelessly outnumbered, and even if some still believed us to be innocent I doubted that anyone would come to our aid should things turn violent.

All eyes were now on the sheriff, who remained standing and breathing heavily as he surveyed the scene of chaos before him.

'Reverend McNeil, you say that a witch cannot repeat the Lord's Prayer?'

'I do.'

'Janet Horne, I wish you to say the Lord's Prayer.'

Mother looked at him as if trying to work out where she was. In my heart I knew we were doomed. There was nothing more I could do.

'You want me to pray?'

'That is exactly what I want.'

'I've done it before.'

'I'm pleased to know it and I would hear you now.'

'In what language, sir?'

There was a muted murmur as people wondered whether my mother was being deliberately disrespectful or trying to be clever in some way, both ideas of which went against her. I knew that Mother could recite the prayer in several languages and her question was seriously put, if unfortunate.

'Gaelic will suffice. Bring her into the centre of the court.'

'Sheriff Ross, may I speak?'

'If you must, Reverend McNeil, but for all our sakes make it brief.'

'I suggest that the younger witch is turned around so that there can be less risk of some sort of secret communication between the two witches.'

I'd never wanted to kill someone before but if I had been given the opportunity at that moment I'm not sure I would have resisted the murderous hate that overwhelmed me. As Mother was led towards the open area, Campbell harshly spun me around to face the other way. In order to show off his power to the crowd he shook me violently several times so that I was flung about in his grip like a rag doll.

'Let go of me! There is no need for this!'

'Be quiet, witch, or you'll get worse.'

Now I could only hear what was said and for several moments the courtroom was hushed. Then Mother began to speak while I said my own prayer in silence.

'Ar n-Athair a tha air nèamh, Gu naomhaichear d' ainm. Thigeadh do rìoghachd ...'

Mother stopped. The frantic beating of my heart pounded in my head as fiercely as if the cathedral's great bell was being rung to herald the death of a king ... to herald the death of the Dornoch witches.

'Tabhair dhuinn an-diugh ar n-aran làitheil.'

Dear God, help us now.

Mother had missed some of the text and moments later McNeil shouted, the ecstasy in his voice clear.

'WITCH! The Bible is clear – *thou shalt not suffer a witch to live.*'

The entire courtroom erupted into a chant that drowned out anything else my mother might have said; it drowned out any chance of justice, hope or life.

'Burn the witches!'

'Burn the witches!'

'Burn the witches!'

25

Dornoch, 19 June 1727

I HAD NEVER KNOWN SUCH FEAR. Following the accident I had developed a terror of fire, and although I managed most day-to-day situations without any problems, there were occasions that I knew would be too much for me to face. Whenever there was any burning to be done around the croft Mother would send me off on Abel with food, drink and instructions not to return until it was certain that everything had sufficiently died down.

Now, as we sat once more on our two stools, my mind felt frozen, my body felt frozen, my very soul felt frozen. I was sure those convicted of witchcraft were not burned alive, but was I wrong? Might the authorities simply decide on the day? Would I watch as flames crept slowly up my legs, consuming my body inch by inch?

After Mother's mistake in saying the Lord's Prayer the assize hadn't hesitated in reaching a guilty verdict, nor had the sheriff in announcing a sentence of execution, which was to be carried out the next day.

'I didn't do well, did I?' asked Mother.

We had been silent since our return to the cell and I wasn't sure what she was thinking. To be honest, I had been too scared to consider anything beyond my own feelings, but now I took her hand, reaching out more than just physically.

'It wasn't your fault. We're not here because of anything you've done.'

'Is there any hope?'

How do I reply to such a question?

My dilemma was answered for me by the sound of raised voices in the front office and the appearance moments later of Reverend MacDonald. Mother remained sitting as I went over to the bars.

'I'm so sorry,' said the minister. He was on the verge of tears.

'You tried your best and no one could ask for more. Thank you for speaking up for us. I hope you won't be in trouble because of it.'

'Don't worry about me.'

'How's your sister?'

'Bless you child, she's finally on the right side of recovery. When we heard Sim's urgent plea she didn't hesitate to release me from my promise not to leave her side. You mustn't lose hope, Aila. I shall pray for a miracle.'

'I think that's the only thing left to try, Reverend. Your presence here is a comfort.'

'Can I do anything else?'

'Yes. I don't know what will happen to our possessions but I'm sure Butcher will search our premises at the first opportunity to see what he can take without anyone realising.'

'I suspect you're right.'

'If you go to the side wall in the horse's stall you'll find that the third plank from the bottom is loose. Behind that are four bags of coin. I couldn't bear for Butcher to find them, for nobody will benefit other than him and the Brora tavern. Please use the money for whatever good around the parish that you can. Also, our animals will need tending to.'

'I'll set off immediately. I can be sure of a meal and a bed along the way. No one else will be leaving Dornoch ...'

'... until after the execution?'

'I'm afraid so. It's been set for noon so that even more people can attend.'

* * *

'God forgive me for the life I've lived.'

I had been staring up at one of the filthy windows, so lost in my own thoughts that I barely realised it was late evening. I certainly hadn't been aware of what Mother was doing. I turned around to see her kneeling on the filthy floor, her hands clasped tightly together.

'You don't need to ask God to forgive you for your life.'

'But I must have done something wicked to be punished like this.'

'If you want to see wickedness do not search for the looking glass.'

I helped her onto a stool then began to explain my plan in a way that she would hopefully understand. 'Mother, we have to escape this dreadful place and to achieve this I must entice the jailer into our cell.'

She watched me with an expression of wonder, just as I used to watch her as a child when she recounted the adventures she had had while travelling across Europe. I had to stop myself from taking her in my arms, from crying out in despair at the situation we were in.

'I will have to say and do things, horrible things that are not in my nature but which must be done in order to get the jailer to unlock the door. I'll get him over here ... see ... with his back to you. At that point you must get up quietly with the stool and hit him on the back of the head.'

'You want me to hit him?'

'Yes, as hard as you can.'

'Won't it hurt?'

'He won't really feel anything.'

'Well, if that's what you want.'

'It is, Mother. I know it seems wrong but you must do this so that we can escape. Do you understand what has to be done?'

'I'll hit him ... for you, my beautiful daughter.'

'I love you, never forget that. Now, close your eyes and pretend to sleep and don't react in any way until the moment is right.'

She nodded and closed her eyes. The plan seemed desperate yet I could think of nothing else and was driven by a need to act. My heart raced so fiercely that I had to take a few moments to calm myself before walking over to the bars. Since being brought back after the verdict we had been given no food or water, although at some point candles had been lit without me noticing.

'Jailer ... Jailer.'

'What? What do you want?'

His voice sounded strange, echoing along the corridor, and I suspected I had woken him from his seat by the fire.

'Come here. I've something important to tell you.' There was no response and I feared that my plan would fail at the very first hurdle. 'It's to your benefit.'

I waited, holding my breath. Every inch of my skin felt as though it was crawling with insects trying to burrow their way underneath. Then I heard movement, so I took a few steps away from the door. His face was flushed with ale and anger.

'What—'

'Shh, don't wake my mother.'

He was curious enough to rein in his temper and lowered his voice. 'What can you possibly say that's important to me?'

'It's simple really.'

'Be quick. I've no time for games.'

'Well . . . I'm a young woman with only a few hours to live. I want to lie with a man for one last time. I know you can appreciate such a desire.' I paused to make sure he was following. I had seen a more intelligent expression on our cow. 'I've been admiring you since we met. You're a good-looking man. I bet women have always been attracted to you.'

'I've had plenty over the years.'

'And I'm sure they've all been grateful . . . just as I would be.'

'You can't fool me. You're trying to work some evil.'

'I promise I'm not. If it settles your mind I won't even speak once you're in here.'

'I don't trust you. I'm going back to my fire.'

I felt a surge of panic as he made to move away and it took all of my willpower not to sound as if I had lost my mind. 'Wait! Don't you think I've an appealing figure?' He stared at me in silence. 'Surely a brave man like you is not too frightened to answer a straightforward question.'

'It's comely, I'll give you that. But look at your hands and I've heard about your feet.'

His comment confirmed my suspicion that he hadn't been in court and that might yet be to my advantage. My success depended entirely on what happened over the next few seconds and I was filled with disgust at what I was about to do.

'I didn't think it was hands or feet that men were interested in, but I know they like these.'

And God forgive me, for I undid my top garments and exposed a part of my body that no man had seen except my father. The jailer grasped the bars in his excitement. I couldn't prevent bile rising into my mouth. It stung my throat and made my eyes water.

'They're beauties and that's the truth. Just how I like them. Come closer and let me feel.'

'No.'

'Take off your clothes!'

'You can do that yourself if you come in here.'

We stared at each other, the decision whether to open the door or not hung so finely in the balance that I fancied the movement of a spider crossing the ceiling would tip the scales one way or another. Shame and despair washed over me; I had to go further.

'Don't you want to see the rest of me? You won't be disappointed. Men always compliment my legs.' I ran my right hand slowly up my thigh and it seemed to me that he no longer noticed my burns. 'And they go wild about here.' I let my hand stop as it reached a part of me that was no one's business but my own.

'You're a witch right enough.'

'There are pleasures you won't believe. All you have to do is have the courage to experience them.'

There was one more brief moment of indecision, then the spider walked across the ceiling and the scales dropped in my favour. In his excitement the jailer fumbled with the key. I positioned myself so that he would have his back to my mother, who was either playing her part really well or had in fact fallen asleep. Moments later he was standing only feet away from me, breathing heavily, his body trembling with anticipation.

'Don't make too much noise or you might wake my mother.' I raised my voice while saying this but didn't notice any reaction from her.

Without any warning he grabbed one of my breasts and squeezed hard. I gasped aloud, startled at the intensity of the unexpected pain.

'Not so harsh.' I backed away, though there was little room to manoeuvre.

'Hah, women like to be treated roughly. It's what's best for them. Now, take off the rest of your clothes.'

'There's no need to remove your breeches in such haste. Don't you know it's better to do this slowly?'

I had no knowledge of these matters beyond what my mother had explained over the years and what anyone can see beasts doing in the fields. I was trying to give Mother a chance to knock him out, but she showed no signs of moving and I was gripped by a terrible fear that all I had done was make my misery worse.

'I've no time for that nonsense. Take off your clothes or you'll feel the back of my hand!'

Please God, if I am to die then let it be untouched. Don't let this filthy brute be the only man who has known me.

'Our Father, which art in heaven.'

'What's that old hag saying?'

Mother had begun to recite the Lord's Prayer in English and it was immediately obvious that the jailer only spoke Gaelic. I was too overcome to think clearly and stood rooted in mute indecision. Then, quite clearly, I heard my father, and whether his voice really was in that cell or merely in my head I will never know, but I was suddenly reminded of the game we used to play with people who had annoyed us.

'It's a powerful curse.'

'Tell her to stop or she'll get my fist.'

'For a man it's the worst sort possible.'

'SHUT UP!'

'Give us this day our daily bread,' Mother intoned in the background.

'Your balls will go black and hard as rocks, growing so huge in size that they'll drag along the ground.'

'What!'

'But the most hideous thing will happen to your cock.'

'My cock! What's going to happen to it?'

'It will shrivel and drop off.'

'I'll soon put a stop to this.'

He turned away from me, however, with his breeches around his ankles he had to shuffle across the floor like a waddling duck, his bare arse making him so ridiculous that the scene could have come straight out of a comedy on stage. I had one opportunity, yet the only potential weapon was the nearby bucket. Fortunately, it was empty, so I grabbed the handle and reached the jailer just as he raised his hand to strike my mother, still sitting on her stool and reciting the prayer.

I didn't know if I could hold the handle with sufficient strength, but there was no time to spare, so I wrapped both hands around it and swung. The bucket was heavy and the thick metal band around the base hit him behind his ear. My left hand slipped off and I barely managed to hang on as the jailer swayed. I watched in a strange, fascinated detachment as he regained his balance and slowly turned to face me. The force of the blow had not been enough and I frantically tried to take a firmer hold. He grabbed my wrist, the bucket clattering loudly on the floor, and as his eyes refocused on me they were filled with such anger I didn't believe I would live to be executed the next day.

'You—'

It was all he said before there was a thud and his face registered complete surprise as his legs buckled. Luckily, he let go or I would have been dragged to the floor. Instead, I stepped back out of the way to see Mother standing with the stool in her hands.

'Is that what you wanted, Aila?' I couldn't even nod in reply. We looked down at the unconscious figure for several moments in silence. 'He doesn't even have much of a cock to shrivel.'

I knew that my reaction was due to fear, yet I began to laugh. Then Mother started and we were soon so helpless that I had to rest with my hands on my knees. When I finally glanced up, Jack was standing in the doorway with a wooden cudgel in his hand and the most astonished expression I had ever seen. He stared between us and the semi-naked man on the floor, then he gazed at his feet, and I didn't realise at first that it was because my breasts were still exposed. I quickly covered them.

'I had to distract him.'

'Well, you must certainly have done that.' He entered the cell and I rushed into his arms. 'Are you both unhurt?'

'Yes.'

'There are two ponies at the edge of town. You and your mother can double up on one. Wait here.' Jack left, returning moments later from the office with several lengths of rope. He bound the jailer securely and roughly stuffed a cloth into his mouth. 'That'll stop him raising the alarm. We'll lock the cell and lose the key outside.'

'I'm not leaving.'

Mother had remained silent since Jack's arrival and we turned towards her in disbelief.

'Mother, you must come now so that we can escape.'

'No, I'm too old and weary to go running off into the night.'

'You're confused,' I said, moving nearer to reassure her.

'That may be, but I've wit enough to know that you've little chance of getting away as it is. With me by your side you'll never succeed.'

I wouldn't consider such an idea. We either left together or not at all. 'Mother—'

'He knows I'm right,' she said, cutting me off and pointing at Jack, before sitting on the stool as if to emphasise her determination.

'Jack?'

He didn't answer.

'He won't try to persuade you to leave me behind because he doesn't want you to blame him in years to come.'

I didn't take my eyes off his face and saw by his expression that Mother still retained the ability for flashes of extraordinary insight. I was suddenly overwhelmed by panic.

'I won't leave you. I won't! I can't lose you and Father. How can I walk out of that door knowing that we'll never see each other again?'

'Because we have no choice. Because you must live, and for that to happen I must die. Because now there are other arms to hold you tightly at night. I know death awaits me tomorrow and I cannot escape it. At least I will be with your father again.'

'No!'

I knelt at her feet and laid my head on her lap. She stroked my hair.

'My mind is everything and I know that I'm losing it. What future is there for me? I'll become more confused, more forgetful and eventually will have none of the skills and abilities that make my life what it is ... that make me who I am. I would rather my life was finished, and if McNeil kills one witch then perhaps he'll not be so bothered about trying to get another. And until it's over there won't be any spare officers to pursue you.'

I was crying too much to speak.

'You are the future, Aila. Get away from this accursed place. Promise me that what has happened here will never be forgotten.'

'I promise.'

'Perhaps, before you go, we could pray together one last time?'

I looked up at her and then at Jack. Any delay in getting away also put his life at risk, but he nodded without hesitation. Mother took my hands in hers.

'Lord, please watch over my daughter for she is in great danger and I can no longer protect her as I have all these years.

Reveal the path that she must follow in order to escape the evil that hunts her.'

Mother opened her eyes and lifted a hand to cup my cheek. We gazed silently upon each other and I knew in my heart that I must hang on to this moment of pure love for the rest of my days.

'Aila, we must go.'

'I'll not leave my mother here with that monster,' I said, glancing at the unconscious figure on the floor.

'No, I would prefer different scenery.'

Arm in arm we walked through to the jailer's area, Jack locking the cell door behind us. Mother settled herself by the fire, which Jack stoked up while I emptied the tankard and refilled it with ale from the jug nearby. She took a sip and grimaced.

'Ah, nowhere near as good as what we made. However, it will do.'

As I leaned down to kiss her goodbye she whispered in my ear, before turning to face Jack. 'I leave my daughter's future in your hands. Look after her.'

'I will,' he replied.

Then we left, and God forgive me for it, because I knew I never would.

26

Four miles west of Dornoch, 19 June 1727

'NO. NO. NO. I WON'T hear of it!'
'You don't own me, Jack,' I shouted back. 'You can't tell me what to do.'

The argument had been going on for nearly an hour, with Jack and me pacing around each other like two stags at the height of the rutting season and everyone else huddled silently by the fire as though fearful of being impaled on the point of an antler. Malie had taken refuge with Hector, who had a muscular arm protectively around her. Eventually, Sim spoke.

'I'm not brave enough to step in between a couple in love having a dispute, but it seems to me that Aila is not going to change her mind.'

I ignored the first part of the remark. 'I'm not going to change my mind. All I ask is that I can borrow a cloak with a hood to hide my face.'

'No,' said Ellen.

'You won't help me?' I felt instantly crushed that Ellen wasn't on my side.

'I won't be helping you by giving you a cloak.'

'Why not?'

'Because, Aila, you could wear the biggest hood in the kingdom and I would still recognise you half a mile away.'

'How?' I was losing the fight to hold back the utter despair that had threatened to overwhelm me since leaving the tolbooth.

'You have such a distinctive limp on your left foot that anyone who knows you would be immediately suspicious of a hooded figure. To hide successfully in a crowd you must be openly visible to everyone, but as someone else ... An old woman. In the morning I'll turn you into someone that no one will recognise.'

'Well if you're going then I'm going as well,' said Jack.

'I won't put other people's lives at risk.'

'It also seems to me, Aila,' said Sim, as if merely continuing his comments of a little earlier, 'that you have no more right to tell any of us what to do than we have to tell you.'

I crumpled slowly to the ground near Hector, and when he raised his free arm I gratefully collapsed into his embrace, great sobs eventually finding their freedom. Malie reached over to stroke my hair.

'Enough now, Jack,' said Hector.

'I'm sorry,' I said, and kept repeating the words, my face pressed so tightly into the huge chest that they were muffled. In truth, I wasn't sure what I was saying I was sorry for. There was so much ... Leaving my mother to die, putting everyone else closest to me in danger, not being reasonable like Jack said.

I was vaguely aware of Sim stoking up the fire and of Ellen tucking a blanket around me. Malie's fingers were gentle as she wiped away the tears running down my cheeks, while an enormous hand tenderly rubbed my back. Everyone was being kind, everyone except the man I loved.

* * *

I woke up in Ellen's arms, my head rising and falling gently as it lay on her chest. It was soothing, listening to the steady beat of her heart. I didn't want to move and risk waking her, so I tried to take in the surroundings as best I could, and a few moments later I realised that Malie was cuddled into the back of me. We were all covered with blankets. I imagined Hector tucking us up the way he fussed over the ponies, although in reality I had no memory of how I got there.

Dawn was near, heralding the approaching death of my mother. Had she been discovered, sitting by the fire while the jailer lay trussed up in the cell? Was she terrified, regretting her decision not to escape? It could have been her chest that my head lay on, her arms holding me close, like she had done so often in the sanctuary of our box-bed. Those days felt as though they belonged to another lifetime. She had made her decision and nothing more could be done except for me to be amongst the crowd, my presence perhaps conveying some comfort. Even though she wouldn't see me, I had to believe that my mother would know I was close by, that at the end I was there for her.

Jack had gone wild when I told him and we had argued in a way I didn't believe was possible. But I had made up my mind, and apart from tying me to a tree there was nothing anyone could do to prevent my return to Dornoch. I didn't believe I could possibly go back to sleep, such a thing seemed almost a betrayal, but I must have been more exhausted than

I realised, for when I woke again it was daylight, Ellen had gone and I was hugging the still unconscious figure of Malie.

* * *

We passed a song thrush, the beauty of its voice in total contrast to the fear and dread that clung to Jack and me as we rode to Dornoch. Despite everything that had happened, the reason we were travelling there still seemed unbelievable.

Ellen had transformed my appearance. She had begun by tying my hair into a tight bunch before fitting a wig that added about ten years to my age, then she skilfully applied make-up and gave me strict instructions not to touch my face. Malie had fetched and held items as Ellen wrapped material around my waist and made me put on other garments so that when I was eventually in my final outer clothes I looked much heavier. The last items were woollen mittens, although they were rather large.

So we rode, and the tension between Jack and me was like a rope that both bound us and pulled us apart.

'Jack, I need you to explain all you can about what will happen.'

'Aila—'

'I'm going to see with my own eyes ... I need to be as prepared as possible.'

We rode in silence for a short while longer and I knew he was trying to work out what to say.

'There'll likely be a huge crowd and many will have been drinking.'

'I can't believe people want to watch someone being executed.'

'Some will, others will be there because the kirk insists on it. The event is a show, Aila, and shows need an audience.

Congregations throughout the area will know that they have to attend and see proof of how the Devil is a liar, for he has forsaken his follower. People will be expected to watch every detail of how a person who has turned their back on God is punished. No matter how awful, someone looking away because they can't bear the sight could later be in trouble with their kirk elders.'

'It's barbaric.'

'It's an effective way of controlling people. For months you won't see anyone stray an inch from the kirk's rules.'

'What are the practical things?'

'I can only tell you what normally happens.'

'Please.'

'If the condemned person is strong enough they'll be paraded through the streets before being taken to the place of execution, a heavy wooden stake that will have been fixed firmly into the ground. They'll be tied to this . . . and wirreit.'

'Strangled?'

'It's ugly and brutal, but a quicker way to die than being burned to death.'

'Would they ever do such a thing?'

'I've never heard of it. The customary practice is to burn the dead body.'

Despite the horror of the explanations, I needed to know more. 'Go on.'

'There'll be a large pile of wood nearby. Probably no one will want to supply it for fear of attracting bad luck, so the authorities often have to pay a forester to obtain it specially. There'll probably be other fuels like peat because it takes hours to burn a body. Sometimes they'll put the condemned person into an old, cut-down barrel part-filled with tar. The executioner will be brought in from outside the area.'

'Someone who does the strangling?' I couldn't continue and stopped the pony to dismount so that I could vomit on the ground. My stomach heaved on emptiness. My very soul was empty. I felt Jack's hand tenderly rub my back.

'I'm sorry,' he said.

'You did what I asked. I must hear the rest.'

'Come here then, let's sit on this rock.'

My legs were shaking so fiercely I was glad of his support.

'I'm going to do this quickly and then you'll hear no more.' He took a deep breath. 'They'll burn the body until there's nothing but ashes, and these will be raked over the ground so there'll be no grave, nothing to indicate that the person ever lived and no risk of a physical presence coming back from the dead to haunt their accusers.

'If there's no husband then the victim's possessions will go to the authorities to help cover their costs. Executing a witch is expensive: every single item right down to the ropes will have to be paid for, as well as the services provided by many of those involved in the trial and execution. Some will make a profit.'

I stared at him in disbelief. So people would drink and cheer, they would feel good about themselves and some would even make money, all because my mother was about to be murdered.

'How do you know all this?' I asked.

Jack hesitated but didn't answer my question. 'We must leave before your mother is tied to the stake. Believe me, you don't want what happens next in your head, for those images will never leave you. This morning will be dangerous enough, promise that you won't argue and we'll slip away when I say.'

I just looked at him, unable to speak. Jack wrapped his arms around me and I cried until I was no more than a dried husk that could be blown away by the slightest wind, never to be seen again.

*　*　*

We left the ponies at the edge of town and continued on foot through the streets, busy with people making their way towards the market square as though they were simply attending a fair. I was shocked at the number of families, despite Jack's previous warnings. No one took any notice of us as we walked slowly along, my arm through his.

Jack's golden hair was hidden under a bonnet and he wore clothes I hadn't seen him in before. His hands and face were dirty and I thought he could easily pass for a farm worker, while I could be taken for an elderly relative. Earlier that morning Ellen had made me walk up and down by our camp then she showed me how to stoop, hunching my shoulders like an older person and making me appear less tall. I made sure I did this as soon as we got off our ponies.

From the square the crowds were heading south-east towards open ground, and as we approached the tolbooth I noticed the old beggar sitting in his usual place. His eyes locked onto mine with such concentration that I found myself staring back at him, unable to even blink.

He knows. He knows.

I had fooled myself into thinking I had shown respect by always speaking and calling him 'sir', by dropping pennies that I could easily afford into his bowl. But I didn't show him true respect because I had never even bothered to find out his name.

As we passed within feet of where he sat, amongst all of the other terrible feelings that beset me, I also felt shame.

We only walked a short distance beyond the last few houses before coming upon hundreds of noisy people, which brought us to a halt.

'Jack, I need to be near the front.'

'That's going to be difficult.'

'I have to be.'

'Alright. I'll go first. I'll do my best not to cause too much upset. Walk behind me and hold on to the back of my jacket. Whatever happens we mustn't get separated.'

I moved behind him and gave his jacket a tug to confirm I had a firm hold then I bowed my head and we set off.

'Sorry, my mother's almost blind. Thank you. Sorry ...'

It was only his natural charm, and partly his imposing figure, that got us through without mishap, for there was more than one man who took offence at Jack pushing his way to the front. Once we got there I stood by his side and took his arm again before trying to make sense of the scene before us.

The crowd had formed itself roughly into the shape of a horseshoe, facing a thick piece of carpentered timber that stood about seven feet high. There was a huge pile of wood nearby as well as a large mound of peat and a small heap of coal. McNeil was talking with Sheriff Ross and a few members of the assize, who were standing near a cart, positioned in a way that made me think it would be used as a platform to speak from later on.

Although my disguise was skilfully done, I was terrified someone would realise who I was, so I tried to study the surrounding figures. There were so many they were just a blurred mass and I didn't recognise anyone. People chatted and called out greetings to friends, and there were plenty holding cups of ale as if waiting for some great entertainment. A group of drunken men had gathered behind us and started shouting 'Where's the witch!' but no one else took up the chant and it quickly died out to be replaced by raucous laughter. Jack suddenly squeezed my arm.

'They're bringing her.' His extra height allowed him a view that I didn't have. 'Oh God.'

'What is it, Jack? Tell me!'

But he didn't have to, because the cart had come into clear sight and I thought my heart would break. Mother had been stripped naked and was standing in a large, wooden barrel on the back of a cart pulled by a pony. Her hands were tied behind her back and she had been covered in tar. I assumed she was also standing in it.

She looked utterly confused ... Old, frail and shrunken, as if she had somehow shrivelled physically and spiritually. It was difficult to believe this was the same person who had knocked out the jailer only the night before.

The pony was led by Duncan and there were several officers walking close by. Jack was right: it was a show, designed to instil obedience into all who saw it. When the group passed us people nearby went wild, shouting abuse and threats, yet also asking for the Lord's protection. They really did fear her.

Although we were only a few yards apart, my mother wouldn't have been aware of our presence. It had been wrong to come and I was gripped by a terrible sense of danger, as if the Devil had just laid his hand upon my shoulder. Duncan brought the pony to a halt near the stake and it was only then that I noticed

McNeil had climbed onto the other cart. He held up his arms until everyone fell silent.

'We are here today to witness the punishment of someone who has turned their back on God, to see what happens to anyone who rejects the teachings of the Bible. Heed my warning . . . The Devil doesn't seek those who are evil, because he already owns them. He seeks righteous, good people, and therefore I tell you to search your hearts and minds. Beware of how easily you can fall under his influence.

'Look about you. Who amongst your neighbours and friends have already been corrupted? Men, look to your women, your wives and daughters, sisters and mothers. Seek out the signs of witchcraft and inform the authorities. That is your God-given duty as a Christian and as a man.'

McNeil paused. People glanced nervously around. It was the same method of control he had used that first day in the Lothmore kirk, when he had so quickly spread mistrust amongst the congregation. He studied the crowd for a long while, going almost from face to face as if searching.

Then his gaze fell upon me and stopped. It felt as though he saw easily through my pathetic disguise and that his eyes were boring into my soul, his little smile mocking me with the threat of my impending death. When he carried on, my breath escaped in gasps and sobs. Jack tenderly rubbed my arm with his spare hand and I nodded to show I was alright, although it was far from being the truth. A sense of uncontrollable panic hung around the edges of my consciousness.

'Janet Horne! Do you deny entering into a vile pact with the Devil? Do you deny carrying out his evil? Do you deny being a witch?'

Mother had her back to us. I couldn't hear any answers and it seemed to me that she simply stood in the barrel, shivering in her coat of sticky, black tar, and looked about as if wondering where she was. In a small way I considered that perhaps her confusion was a blessing.

'She confesses in all but word!' shouted McNeil.

A man behind us called out 'Burn the witch!' and a few more joined in. I saw the minister glance down at Sheriff Ross and the latter give a curt nod to the officers. While three of them began to manhandle the barrel off the cart there were shouts from everywhere as the extraordinary tension amongst the crowd was suddenly released in a tidal wave of verbal hate.

Jack and I turned towards each other. He looked scared. Then we faced the way we had to go and he swore quietly. We had made a big mistake by pushing our way to the front at that particular point because many of the latecomers were crowded behind us, forming a bulge of extra people. However, it would be impossible to try to leave any other way without attracting even more unwanted attention.

'This is likely to get messy,' said Jack. 'Whatever happens, get to a pony then ride to the camp. Don't wait.'

'Jack—'

'No! Just get out. I'll be more able to easily escape later by myself.' My eyes welled up as he moved forward and I grabbed his jacket. 'I'm sorry, my mother's taken ill and we need to find a seat. Thank you. I'm sorry ...'

The first few rows of people let us through without any problem, but the crush became worse as we reached the group of drunken men. There was no way around them.

'I'm sorry, my mother's taken ill and we need to find a seat—'

'Fuck your mother!'

'I'm not fucking his mother, look at her!'

'We don't want any trouble, please just let us past.'

'You shouldn't leave before the witch is burned.'

'Aye, that's right. It's disrespectful.'

I couldn't see which men were making the comments, but they all sounded aggressive, the voices of those seeking any excuse to brawl. Jack risked continuing to push forward, as stopping and becoming trapped would be even more dangerous.

'Push me, you bastard!'

A man lashed out and I glimpsed Jack block the punch without hitting back. He was desperate not to get involved in a fight, yet moments later he was unexpectedly pulled away from me. I was wedged and lost hold of his jacket, not realising that the mitten had fallen to the ground. If the violence went on for long the sheriff would surely send in his officers. I had to get away and tried to push myself through the tightly packed bodies. Without any warning someone grabbed my arm. I turned towards the man, on the verge of shouting for him to let me go, and looked into a bloated, cruel face I knew so well.

Butcher!

He was staring at my exposed hand then studying my face and then the hand again. Butcher reached up and roughly took hold of my jaw, moving even closer until our faces were inches apart and I could smell his sweat and ale and evil. He had an expression of such puzzlement.

Nothing about me was familiar to him, yet it was obvious he recognised an injury that could belong to no one else but Aila Horne. His gaze bored into my eyes. Father had said they were emerald green, while Mother thought they were blue.

Now they would be charred black on the pyre with the rest of my body because Butcher's expression was changing. I used all my strength to try and wrench my arm from his grip.

'Let me go this instant.'

And of course that was another mistake, because he knew my voice. Slowly his face took on a look of sinister triumph. Butcher took an enormous breath in order to shout out his discovery and at that very moment Jack's fist slammed into the side of his head with such force that I was certain he must have broken some bones. Butcher staggered, letting go of me and knocking a nearby woman to the ground. The man next to her spun around in fury.

'Knock my wife down, you drunken shit!' The man punched Butcher and he fell backwards. There was mayhem, with scuffles and fights all around us.

'Now's our chance!' cried Jack.

He forced his way forwards, dragging me with him. As it turned out several people had already moved from the back of the crowd to be farther away from the violence and we quickly reached the open without anyone else trying to stop us. Jack marched off, still hanging on to me, and I couldn't prevent myself from limping as I tried to keep up.

'Don't look back,' ordered Jack.

'I'm sorry.'

'Save your breath. We're not out of danger yet.'

The town square was deserted apart from the lone figure of the beggar. The quickest route was right past him and he struggled onto his crutches as we got nearer. When we were only a few feet away, he spoke.

'Run, Aila.'

At the mention of my name Jack's hand instinctively went to the hilt of his knife, but the old man wasn't looking at us; he was staring at where we had come from. Jack and I turned around and saw that Butcher was at the back of the crowd, talking to a group of men and pointing wildly in our direction.

'RUN!'

In one swift movement Jack put me over his shoulder and ran. My vision of the world was reduced instantly to the back of his breeches as I bounced along, helpless and hindering him. I cursed the disguise because the many extra layers of clothing made me even more useless. If we were chased there was no way we would outpace men filled with such feelings of rightful vengeance, ale and a determination to see another witch burn on this bright June day. I could just make out that we were about halfway along the street when there were angry shouts behind us. With every step I could tell that our pursuers were closing in fast.

God hear my prayer, for my folly has condemned us both.

Jack halted so abruptly that my nose bashed painfully into the hard muscles of his back, and for a few heart-stopping seconds I thought we had already been caught.

'Sim and I decided to come along to make sure you got away safely,' said Hector.

'Am I glad to see you two,' said Jack.

'It's a good job we did,' said Sim. 'Looks like we've got our work cut out, big man.'

'Go,' said Hector. I couldn't see what was happening but there was no mistaking the urgency in his voice. 'We'll gain you enough time to escape.'

'Get back safely,' I called, but we were already moving again and I doubted that anyone had heard.

Jack almost threw me onto one of the ponies. I was still trying to settle myself when we heard a scream of such agony that it didn't sound human.

Dear God, no, they're burning her alive.

'MOTHER!'

I turned and saw a pall of black smoke rise slowly into the air, a cloud of such shame and injustice that no Highland gale would ever be strong enough to disperse it.

'Oh Mother, I'm sorry. Forgive me. Please forgive me.'

'Aila, we have to leave. Your mother's free now. She's with your father and no one can hurt her anymore. She gave her life that you might live, but we must go or her huge sacrifice will be in vain.'

Jack was a blurred figure by my side. I couldn't speak. As we rode away from the evil that had been carried out against the wisest, most noble and honourable of women, I knew that whatever the future held for me, the life that I had always known was over.

27

One mile west of Dornoch, 20 June 1727

AFTER RETRIEVING THE MONEY FROM Abel's stall, Reverend MacDonald had headed back to Dornoch, yet he had skirted widely around the town without entering and had since been meandering aimlessly on his old Highland pony. Now he was on a track that led to Dornoch from the west, but was still uncertain as to whether to continue or turn away.

The truth was the minister had been unable to endure seeing two of his parishioners executed. He felt he had failed them totally, in court the day before and now too weak to offer even the slimmest glimmer of comfort by being present at the end of their lives. He bitterly blamed McNeil, the kirk, God and most of all himself, fearing that he had lost his faith along with two regular members of his congregation.

How could he return to the Lothmore kirk where McNeil must surely have contaminated the very wood of his pulpit, spitting vicious and vile hate? And how could the Almighty let two innocent women be so cruelly murdered? How could He!

The pony shied nervously and Reverend MacDonald wailed as the breeze brought to them a scent that was like nothing neither man nor beast had ever known, yet it filled them with an unspeakable dread. The minister broke down weeping and was so engrossed in his own misery that he didn't see the two figures approaching until they were upon him; a huge man with a much smaller one over his shoulder. He stared in silence as if they were some sort of biblical apparition.

'I'm Hector. You tried to help our friends in court.'

'I couldn't have failed them more,' the minister replied bitterly. 'I'm a despicable coward ... Too wretched a creature to be present when I was most needed. I openly say to you that I'm ashamed and not worthy to hold this position.'

'You're being too harsh on yourself, Reverend, and, didn't you know, only Janet was executed.'

'What?'

'Aila escaped from the tolbooth last night.'

'She escaped! Praise the Lord. Aila got away?'

'Well, she could have done. You probably know her better than me. She insisted on returning to Dornoch so that she could be there ...'

'The stupid ... foolish ... brave, loyal girl.'

'Just as Aila and Jack were leaving someone recognised her. It's a good thing that Sim and I went along to make sure they got away.' Hector explained where they were hiding and that he was trying to get there with his injured friend. Reverend MacDonald immediately dismounted.

'Quickly, get Sim on here. Just tether the pony in the area you've described and I'll find him tomorrow.'

'You're a good man, Reverend,' said Hector, gently laying the unconscious Sim over the back of the animal.

'No, I've realised today that I'm just an ordinary man trying to do good. Tell Aila she needs to get far away.'

'From the Highlands?'

'From Scotland. Heaven knows I don't like to speak ill of a fellow minister but McNeil belongs in the past. As long as he can get the authorities to listen to him he won't give up pursuing her, and the reality is that Aila's injuries make her too easy to identify. I never thought I could say such a thing, but I don't believe Aila will be safe until she's out of reach of the Church of Scotland.'

'I'll tell her, and thank you.'

'It's little enough I've done but there's one other thing. My pony is carrying four bags of coin. Let Aila know. She'll understand. Now, get going. I'll head back as far as the crossroads then I'll wait, and if anyone comes after you I'll send them off in a different direction. If God doesn't forgive that one little lie then I'll not be forgiving Him for what's happened today.'

* * *

Ellen and Malie rushed towards us as we entered our hiding place in the woods. 'Did you see the others?' asked Ellen, her face a mask of concern.

'We wouldn't have escaped without them,' said Jack, carrying me over to lay me down near one of the sledges. 'We were recognised.'

'It's all my fault,' I said feebly.

'What's done is done,' said Jack. 'Everyone made their own decisions and no one else can take the blame for the consequences.'

'What happened?' asked Malie.

'We hadn't got far from the town square when our pursuers started closing in on us. Hector and Sim appeared just in time to let us reach the ponies, but I must go back.'

'Go back?' I was horrified at the thought yet I knew in my heart that it was the only option he had.

'Yes, I'll take all three ponies. Hopefully I'll meet them on their way here and we'll simply return more quickly, but if they're in trouble I can't leave them.'

He bent down to kiss me and then immediately set about preparing the third animal. Ellen got down on the ground to take me in her arms.

'Malie, fetch blankets.'

'My mother . . .'

'I know, love, I know. We need to get you warmed.'

I hadn't realised until then that I was shaking uncontrollably and that the strange whimpering sounds I had vaguely been aware of were coming from me. I was suddenly gripped by such a violent spasm that Ellen had to hold tightly.

'Mother!'

'Shh, you're safe now. It's over. It's over.' I was aware of Malie spreading blankets yet strangely couldn't feel them landing on my body. 'Get underneath with Aila. We need to give her our heat.'

I remember feeling loved and safe, then nothing but blankness and blackness.

* * *

Later that afternoon we sat together, trying to reassure ourselves that the men would return safely, like the wives of those who had gone to war or sea had been forced to do for generations. We were like those women left behind and our tiny glimpse of that life showed what an unbelievable burden it was.

We stood suddenly at the sound of movement nearby and moments later Jack appeared leading the three ponies. Behind these Hector led Sim, who was sitting on an animal that I knew belonged to Reverend MacDonald. In three strides I was in Jack's arms.

'Thank God you're safe. We've all been so worried.'

'Sim's taken a bad knock to the head.'

I looked over to see Hector lifting his friend down and carry him to the spot where I had been laid earlier. We gathered around. Sim groaned and slowly raised a hand to his face.

'Oh, my head.'

'It's good to hear your sweet, angelic voice again,' said Hector, grinning.

'The worst thing is I can see two of you. One big ugly bastard is more than enough.'

'How about a drink?'

'Sim needs rest, not alcohol,' said Ellen, breaking into the two men's conversation. 'And he needs to be kept warm.'

'Don't risk a fire,' said Sim.

'The smoke could bring them to us,' agreed Jack. 'We're well hidden, so once it's dusk it should be safe.'

'Let me see this wound,' said Ellen, gently moving Sim so that she could examine it.

'What happened?' I asked Hector.

'There were seven of them. Sim and I were carrying a couple of unlit torches which made handy cudgels and there's a huge difference between a man simply looking for a brawl and one fighting to save his life. Once we'd knocked a few of them to the ground the others lost their enthusiasm. I thought we were going to escape unmarked, but as we backed away someone threw a rock. The first I knew of the danger was seeing Sim lying on the ground.'

Hector explained how they had come across Reverend MacDonald and the warning he gave about leaving Scotland. He was just telling me about the money when our attention was drawn back to Ellen, who had finished her examination.

'There's an impressive lump. I don't know what to do for now except keep you warm.'

For the second time that day Ellen got down on the ground and took someone in her arms. Malie didn't need to be told and she laid blankets over Sim before getting under them to cuddle into him. Hector went to take care of the ponies so Jack and I moved away to sit together on a log in order that we could speak privately.

'What am I going to do?' In my whole life, apart from my father, I had never asked a man what I should do.

'We have to take Reverend MacDonald's warning seriously, perhaps move to England?'

'You would take me there?'

'For someone so clever you can be surprisingly slow at times. I'm going to be with you wherever you end up.'

'Do you mean it, Jack? I had hoped, but never expected you would want to be with me.'

'Yes, I mean it, although you might not want me when I've told you what I'm about to say.'

'You can't—'

He held up his hand. 'Please listen and then you must decide.' We fell silent, me waiting to hear whatever wicked deed he imagined had been committed – for I couldn't believe he would have been involved in anything truly bad – and Jack preparing to speak of something that was obviously difficult to recount.

'My father was a brutal man. I didn't know at the time but when I was nine he began to spread rumours about my mother. She was a gentle woman, no match for his cunning. He spent months whispering stories into the ears of those he knew would pass them on. One morning – I had turned ten by then – we received a visit from the local minister. His name was McNeil.'

'No Jack! Not the same man?'

'He was as keen then to see women executed as he is today.'

'I never thought to mention the name of our temporary minister.'

'And I never thought to ask. It didn't take long for my poor mother to end up facing wild accusations at the kirk session, after which she was locked up in the local tolbooth. The kirk elders took it in turn to stay with her and prevent her from sleeping. Day, night, day, night . . . My mother was eventually so confused that she agreed to every increasingly mad accusation made to her, casting harmful spells on people and animals, giving her naked body to the Devil and even kissing his bloody arse.

'Everything was done very correctly, so that all those involved could feel proud and good about themselves. With a confession it was easy for the local authorities to push for a trial, and from that point her fate was almost a foregone conclusion because there was little doubt in anyone's mind that she was a witch. I simply didn't understand what was happening.'

'You were only a boy.'

'Despite her punishment she never implicated anyone else, even though they constantly pressured her to reveal the names of other witches.'

'Your mother was incredibly brave.'

Jack paused. I sensed he was about to speak of something that was so painful to him that he could hardly say the words.

'My father forced me to watch and when, later, they set fire to her dead body I found that I wasn't able to tear away my gaze. Her beautiful, sweet face blackened and distorted until it was like some hideous gargoyle. Then the wind blew about pieces of charred matter. One of them landed on my cheek. I was so horrified that I couldn't move my hand to brush it away, no matter how desperately I wanted to remove it.

'I still see that image . . . Still hear the crackle of flames and jeers of the crowd. Sometimes I wake at night and the sharp stench of burning flesh is so strong upon my skin that I can taste it. And that charred piece is always on my cheek. God help me, Aila, for I can't get rid of it. No matter how hard I scrub, I can't get rid of it!'

Jack collapsed into my arms. I had never heard anyone cry as he did. The sound came from somewhere beyond grief, a place where no person should ever have to go. No words of comfort would have helped, so I just held him as tightly as I had the strength to do. Eventually, he calmed down sufficiently to sit up again.

'I can't believe we've lost our mothers to the same evil man,' I said.

'I knew my mother was innocent yet nothing made sense to me, even when my father took in another woman. Oh he was patient, for the kirk considers fornication to be a serious crime and he was very careful never to be found out while my mother was alive.'

'Is that why he lied, because he wanted another woman?'

'My mother was from a wealthy family and quite stunning in her youth. He had apparently once been considered handsome. He charmed his way into her life, then drank away the money and beat away her beauty until he came to despise what was left.'

'You don't have to go on.'

'Hear me out, Aila. One night, when I was fifteen, he was more drunk than usual and started to boast about what he'd done. For the first time everything made sense. He goaded me with his taunts, laughing about how easy it had been. I'd never stood up to him before and picked up a knife lying on the table nearby. He mocked the idea that I would try to use it. I don't remember what happened next, only later on when I was looking down on his body and knew I had to get away that night.'

'You've been moving around ever since.'

'I developed an obsession to find out everything I could about witch trials. I hadn't done anything to help my mother, but I felt that if I could understand more about the legal process ... Well, in truth I don't know how I thought I could use such knowledge, yet the desire consumed me. Wherever we went I would hunt out local information about events connected to witches and their punishment.

'Hector and the others knew I had this need and never asked why or tried to stop me, even when I made the troupe travel to an area simply because I had heard there was a trial. Of course, I never attended the executions. We always left the area before that.'

'And then fate brought you to Dornoch.' I was about to speak further when Malie appeared.

'Ellen says you must come quickly.'

When we got back Ellen and Hector were kneeling either side of Sim, who was greatly agitated and seemed unaware of his surroundings.

'Bess! Bess, where are you!'

'I'm here, my love, right by your side.' Ellen, ever an accomplished actress, imitated her dead friend's voice.

'It's getting so dark.'

'Don't be frightened of the dark, my darling. It's a path to the light. I'll go with you and afterwards we'll always be together.'

'Promise?'

'I promise.'

'You'll say goodbye to the others?'

'Yes.'

'I'll miss them.'

Sim didn't speak for several minutes and his breathing appeared so stilled that I feared he had died. It seemed to me that all of the animals and birds nearby had fallen silent. There was no wind; not a single leaf stirred nor tree branch moved. In heaven they must have heard our tears falling, for I swear they were the only sounds.

'Bess?'

'I'm here.'

'I love you.'

'I love you too. Now sleep, my darling. When you wake everything will be well.'

Ellen bent down and tenderly kissed his lips, and in that moment Sim died.

28

Four miles west of Dornoch, 20 June 1727

GRIEF LAY UPON US AS if we were blanketed in snow and every flake had been a pinprick to our hearts. We knelt around Sim's body; Malie at his head, stroking his hair while her tears fell gently upon his face, Jack and I holding one hand between us, Ellen and Hector the other. No one had spoken for so long that the shadows of the trees had crept steadily along the ground for several yards.

'We need to bury him,' said Ellen.

'Yes, we should,' replied Hector eventually, before falling silent again.

It was me who put everyone in danger. I was a convicted witch, condemned to be executed and I had escaped from custody. The sheriff would almost certainly send out search parties in the morning. We had been fortunate that day, the drunken crowds and confusion following the burning, perhaps Reverend MacDonald sending pursuers in the wrong direction. Whatever had happened we couldn't rely on such luck again.

When Jack finally stood, he appeared to have aged about ten years. 'Let's find somewhere suitable.'

We chose an area that would be in sunshine on bright days and where the earth could be removed. It turned out that

Hector and Jack could only dig down for about three feet. It was enough. The rest of us gathered rocks and when our tasks were done we stood once more around the body. Jack bent down and began to remove the many knives that were hidden about his friend's clothing.

'I won't have him buried with weapons. That part of his life belonged to a distant past.'

When Sim was as tidy and prepared as possible, we wrapped his body in one of the curtains from the stage then Hector carried him to the grave and lowered him into it. There is something incredibly moving about seeing such a strong man cry. His sobs tore through the woods as we looked upon the bundle. It seemed so small, as if somehow death had shrunk the person within.

'How many times did he step out from behind that curtain,' said Ellen quietly. 'I keep expecting him to suddenly pull it to one side and laugh at how he's fooled us all.'

'He gave his life to save mine,' I said, speaking aloud the accusations that must surely have been going through everyone's mind.

'And mine,' said Jack.

'He saved me from something terrible,' said Malie. 'I will never forget Sim, but he would want us to get away as safely as possible.'

'He would,' agreed Hector. 'Let's finish this then, as far as God allows it, we need to decide our futures.'

* * *

Dusk had fallen by the time Sim's resting place was completed, so we made a fire. I noticed that Ellen and Hector were deep in conversation as they prepared the cooking pot. We forced ourselves to eat because, whatever we did the next day, there would be no time for food before we left our hiding place. Jack and I sorted out possessions from one of the sledges, although in truth we were after some privacy.

'We didn't finish our conversation,' he said.

I fell in love with him that first meeting at the Dornoch market, not because he was so beautiful but because he took my hand in his and revealed a secret part of himself that I could not help but love.

'Jack, you've carried this burden for long enough. Let your parents rest now ... both of them. You must know that I love you and if you really want me, even with these,' I said, holding up my hands, 'then I am yours for as long as you wish.'

'I seem to recall saying something about how someone as clever as you can be so slow at times. You think these would stop me loving you?' He took hold of my hands and kissed them.

I didn't flinch.

'I love you, Aila, and if you've been injured trying to save your father then I love you even more for your bravery. If your courage stretches far enough then marry me.'

* * *

We lit Sim's torches and positioned them to provide a circle of extra light as if we all feared that some evil would otherwise sneak upon us. The fire was kept alive with wood from the stage. It felt appropriate, symbolic of what was happening to those of us who were left. The troupe no longer existed and I could never return to the croft.

Everything that was a connection to my mother and father, to the memories of my past, was gone. I would never again brush my beautiful horse Abel nor wrap my arms around his neck, never sleep safely next to Mother in our box-bed or sit by the fire and read the family Bible while the clock ticked in the corner.

Each of us was so preoccupied by a myriad thoughts and emotions that even when our meal was finished we continued to sit in silence for some while. It was Hector who spoke first.

'I have a brother who owns a large farm near the border with England. When our father died Angus wanted me to run the farm with him. We were close, but I was filled with a desire to see what lay beyond the next few villages and so set on leaving that no offer he made could dissuade me. Now I've had my fill of travelling and I know he'll willingly take me back. Ellen and I will be married as we journey south—'

'Not just handfast,' stressed Ellen. 'It'll all be done properly.'

'It will, and as far as anyone is concerned Malie is our daughter.'

She was sitting near to him and when he put his arm out Malie nestled into his chest.

'That's the second best news I've heard today,' said Jack. 'The first is that I've asked Aila to marry me and she's said yes.'

I didn't know who was the most surprised by any of this news or, indeed, if anyone was surprised at all. It had been clear to me that Ellen loved Hector, although I couldn't work out his feelings beyond being fond of her and his natural instinct to take care of people. As for Jack and me ... It had been obvious from the start to everyone.

The two men reached over and clasped hands, hanging on to each other with tears in their eyes. No one thought less of them for that. It was only a matter of hours before we would go our separate ways.

'We'll take the bay and one sledge,' said Hector getting down to the practicalities. 'You need to take a pony each.'

'We'll travel light and across country,' agreed Jack. 'Sheriff officers are likely to be sent from Dornoch on the same track as you.'

'Yes. We won't be able to outrun them and it's well known in the town that the troupe was friendly with Janet and Aila. However, Ellen has some ideas that we believe will see us through the danger.'

'Where will you head for?' asked Ellen.

'England,' replied Jack.

'No,' I said, remembering something my father once told me and realising in that moment where our future lay. 'Ireland.'

'Ireland? Why?'

'Because, Jack, the Irish love a storyteller, and that's what you're born to be.'

He looked at me in the flickering light and nodded. I think if I had said China, Jack would have agreed.

The rest of the evening was spent organising what should be taken and what left behind. I was still disguised as a much older woman and I got Malie to help me remove the various garments wrapped about me. I would travel to my freedom, or my death, as Aila Horne. Later on, I carefully chose a moment when I could speak to Ellen alone.

'Ellen, I want you to take these,' I said, handing over two bags of coin.

'That's half of your money, Aila. I can't take this.'

'I wouldn't be here if Hector hadn't risked his life this morning. He's a proud man and wouldn't take this from me. Please, hide it on your sledge and tell him when you're far away from here, maybe on your wedding day.'

We said no more and instead hugged each other for a long time, yet we both knew it could never be long enough.

29

Four miles west of Dornoch, 21 June 1727

THAT NIGHT, FOR THE FIRST time, I lay wrapped in Jack's arms. It was still dark amongst the trees when we got up, so we lit the two usable torches to be able to load blankets and the few items that weren't already in the pack harnesses. Jack and I had already split up the money bags into smaller, and much safer, amounts.

There were two items he didn't know about and I felt they were simply too unimportant to mention when there had been so many vital things to be done. Earlier I had retrieved the hand puppets that I had used to entertain the children in Dornoch. I wanted to fulfil Bess's request and to have something to remember her by.

Our ponies would carry enough food for us to survive the next three days without relying on a tavern or remote dwelling. There were always streams to obtain water from and there would be plenty of rough pasture for the animals. Our plan was to leave no trace as to the direction in which we were heading.

Hector, Ellen and Malie were frantically busy by one of the sledges being left behind, so Jack and I watered the ponies and tethered the one belonging to Reverend MacDonald on a long rope. There was enough for it to graze on until the minister came. We were completing our final preparations as Hector came towards us. Jack held up his torch and I gasped. It wasn't just the large black beard and hair that had appeared overnight and which, in the flickering torchlight, certainly looked real . . . He seemed so different, smaller somehow than the man I had known.

'My family used to call me Ralph. It's my name from now on.'

He spoke in a broad accent that was nothing like the one I was used to hearing and I assumed this was what he had grown up with as a boy. Jack and I didn't have the chance to react before a rotund, rather nervous-looking woman hesitantly approached. She stared at us as if not sure what to do, before curtseying rather awkwardly.

'This is my wife, Florie. She doesn't say much but she's a good woman.'

Ellen bobbed and grinned as if she was almost a little simple in the head. Then a figure dressed as a boy walked into the circle of light.

'Our Hamish. He's a bit like his mother and not very talkative, but he's a hard worker. Don't forget your manners, lad.'

The 'boy' removed his cap and this time I couldn't prevent my cry of surprise. 'Malie! Your hair!'

It was gone. All that was left was a covering like the stubble of a harvested field of barley, turned red by the last rays of the setting sun. I reached over and gently stroked the prickly ends. Malie smiled, and for a few brief moments the world didn't seem such an evil place.

'Father says that when we get to our new home I can grow my hair as long as I want. I'm going to see if it will reach my waist.'

'You'll be beautiful beyond words.'

I could say no more and she flung herself into my arms. Jack and Ellen were also holding on to each other. We swapped about, and when I hugged the man we now knew as Ralph the sheer power of his body reminded me of when I used to wrap my arms around Abel's neck. That felt like another lifetime. The two men hung on to each other as though they were sailors lost overboard, clinging to the one piece of floating debris in the entire ocean. Dawn was breaking. The end was near.

We led the ponies out of our hiding place. Two sledges were left behind plus spare clothing, props and many other items . . . and Sim. No one had spoken about him that morning. I think everyone felt that he would understand this was a time for the living.

When we reached the track we walked along it together until there was enough light for Jack and me to ride the animals safely. Despite the urgency of the situation we mounted almost reluctantly, equally torn between leaving and staying. The others stood nearby, Ralph with his arms around Ellen and Malie, the husband and father he already was in all but deed. They were a blur through my tears. I suspected that everyone else was also crying, although I couldn't see well enough to tell.

That was it. We had either lost those we loved or said our farewells to those who remained. Jack turned to me.

'Ireland?'

'Ireland.'

We pointed our ponies in the direction we needed to travel and set off as if the Devil himself was at our backs, which I guess, in a sense, he was.

30

Ireland, 1758

J ACK THROWS PEAT ON THE fire and returns to the couch where he takes me in his arms once more. We both feel the cold these days; his fingers are not so nimble on the strings of his harp, nor is my voice so strong. But we're happy. I snuggle into his chest and he strokes my hair, the jet black of my youth having long ago given gracefully over to silver.

Father was correct about the Irish: God, how they love a storyteller. After our arrival, wherever we went on our new ponies, from the poorest villages to the biggest towns, Jack was feted for his talents and his looks. Yet I was not left out, and in addition to singing I discovered a gift for composing music and songs that I hadn't realised lay within me.

We made a perfect combination, in so many ways, and had travelled for almost a year when the head of a powerful family offered us his patronage, which included a cottage on his huge estate. It seemed the right time to settle down. When our firstborn came we named him Sim in honour of the man who gave his life for ours. Our second child was called Janet in honour of the wisest, kindest woman I've ever known.

We discovered almost immediately upon setting foot in Ireland that the Irish have a completely different attitude towards witchcraft and all things associated with magic. No one tried to link my injuries to anything other than what they were, the result of a tragic fire. People were far more interested in hearing me sing or asking me to compose a song or tune for them.

Our patron was an intelligent man, and when I suggested that he invest in equipment and workers to make ale he accepted my word that I could successfully oversee the entire production. I pushed my luck further by suggesting that he employ the wives of some of the men on his estate and that was how I ended up in charge of an all-female group that became a second family.

One rainy day, when Sim and Janet were young, I entertained them using the hand puppets that had once belonged to Bess. Stories seemed to flow as if coming from somewhere outside of me, and I soon needed to invent new characters in order to tell them. Several of the local women were skilled at making items and, like the real folk around us, my family of puppets grew. Jack paid the local carpenter to make a tiny theatre, and this make-believe world claimed a very real place in our lives.

It didn't stop there because word about these events quickly spread, and within months I was performing in front of dozens of children. After a few years my reputation wasn't so far behind that of Jack's. I began to wonder then if Father's comment about the Irish loving a storyteller was perhaps meant for me, that he suspected a talent that I was not to discover until much later in life.

I remember him once saying that stories tell us where we have come from. Without them we don't truly know who we are and it is only with that knowledge we can understand where our future lies, what paths we must take in order to find our destiny.

Well, I guess there are some questions that can never be answered.

Sim has gone. Even as a boy he always wanted to know what lay beyond the horizon. He reminded me so much of Father that at times I wept in secret ... The tears of a daughter's loss and of a mother's impending yet inevitable sorrow. When the time is right, you have to let go.

As accurately as we could, we told him where we thought Ralph and Ellen had moved to. We never heard from them again but, who knows, perhaps Sim will find them; and Malie, of course, now a grown woman and no doubt with a family of her own. Sim was so determined to trace his roots, to travel around Scotland and visit the Highlands. They are beautiful, for all that happened to Mother and me. I still miss the dramatic mountains and the hidden lochs, my secret rock on the edge of Loch Brora where I spent so many hours just sitting and reflecting.

Sim knows, of course. I told him the tale of what had happened when we judged him old enough to hear such a terrible story.

Poor Mother. We learned that not many years after her death the law was changed by the British parliament so that it was no longer legal to execute someone for witchcraft. Jack and I sometimes discuss our mothers, their lives not their deaths, and we wonder about the other unfortunate people who were accused on little more than rumour and ignorance; lives that were still ruined if not actually taken.

He at last found peace of mind in Ireland and his nightmares stopped, while having my own children allowed me to finally forgive myself for leaving my mother in the Dornoch tolbooth. It was only in experiencing a mother's love that I came to terms with her decision to remain, if not gladly made then certainly willingly.

I shudder, despite the warmth of the fire and Jack's body.

'Are you cold? Shall I fetch a blanket?'

'No, just hold me.'

'What are you thinking?'

'I was thinking that little Aila is going to be a storyteller just as soon as she can string more than two words together.'

'And she's going to be a beauty like her grandmother.'

'And her grandfather.' I pause, for such moments together are not to be rushed. 'I wonder how Sim is.'

'Sim can look after himself.'

'I hope he eventually comes home.'

'One day he will. The desire to constantly travel fades with the passing of the years until it becomes too dim a light to follow.'

I pray that Jack is right. We're silent for a while, watching the tendrils of smoke rise lazily from the peat, just as Mother and I used to do sitting by the hearth in Kintradwell. I wonder who lives in the cottage now, whose hand winds Father's beautiful clock, whose fingers turn the pages of our old family Bible. Did everyone ever again hug Abel and tell him their secrets? I hope his new owner was kind.

'You once promised me something that you've never yet fulfilled,' said Jack.

'What did I promise?'

'That you would tell me the words your mother whispered that last night.'

I pull away so that I can look into his face, lined and aged yet still strikingly handsome, his hair not perhaps so golden though thick and long, tied at the back in a red ribbon just as it was that first day we met.

'Have you puzzled on this all these years?'

'Well, not all the time.'

I smile. I've probably thought of those words every day since they were uttered.

'Her words were: *Jack's a man worth his salt.*'

'A man worth his salt? And have I been?'

I cup his cheek in my hand.

'Yes, my love ... Oh yes.'

Epilogue

Dornoch, present day

THE TWO WOMEN PARK THEIR car near the bookshop behind the cathedral, the older of them trying to maintain a cheery mood and not reveal her nervousness. She's been fighting this battle for several hours and increasingly losing.

'Later on we must look around the bookshop, and the cathedral's beautiful, so we have to visit that. Also, in the graveyard you can see the town's plaiden ell.'

'Mam, what on earth is a plaiden ell?'

'It's a measurement on a stone slab which was used to prove the length of cloth hundreds of years ago. It's one of only a handful of examples remaining in the whole of Scotland. Isn't that amazing? And it's right next to the market cross.'

The girl raises her eyes to the sky before answering. 'This trip is becoming worse by the minute.'

'Well, it's good to learn something about history.'

'Mam, you've dragged me across half of Scotland to somewhere I don't want to be and you still haven't told me why we're here. It's not funny.'

'Hardly dragged. I thought it was a pleasant journey. The weather's been glorious. And we've almost arrived. It's only ten minutes away.'

'Yes, but what's ten minutes away?'

They set off on foot, passing the top of the town square, and head south-east along Church Street. After a few hundred yards they turn up a side road and stop by a private garden.

'There,' says the mother, pointing.

'What . . . A stone? We've come all this way for you to show me a stone!'

'Come on.'

'This is stupid.'

They enter the garden and stand near the grey stone.

'The date says seventeen twenty-two but it should really be seventeen twenty-seven.'

'At least we've cleared that up. That's made today really worthwhile.'

'It marks the spot where the last person in Britain was executed for witchcraft. If she hadn't existed then neither of us would be here.'

'What? She's our ancestor? You're kidding! Wow.'

The younger woman takes out her mobile.

'You're not taking a selfie.'

'But Mam—'

'No. Put it away and listen. This poor woman and her daughter were both arrested and charged with witchcraft, and they were sentenced to be executed the following day. However, the daughter escaped. Now, kneel with me.'

'What!'

'Come on.'

'Someone might see.'

'Down.'

'I can't believe I'm doing this.'

'I want you to do something for me without questioning it.'
'What?'
'Place your hand on the stone.'
'Mam—'
'And close your eyes.'
'This is so weird.' The young woman does as requested. 'If my friends hear of this—'
'Shh.'
They kneel in silence for several minutes. When the younger woman speaks she sounds confused. 'Mam?'
'Keep your hand on the stone and your eyes closed. Whatever happens, I promise you won't be hurt.'
The mother studies her daughter's face and sees her expression change to one of fear. Her lips part and she moans softly.
'Keep it there!'
A few more moments pass. The expression of fear is replaced by terror before the daughter screams and pulls away her hand, immediately bursting into tears.
'It's alright, baby, it's alright. You're not hurt. Look, your hand's perfectly fine.'
'But I felt such heat and there was a terrible scream. And the smell . . .'
'I know, but it's over now and you're quite safe, I promise. See, the stone's cold. It's just an old stone with an incorrect date.'
'What's just happened to me?'
'The same thing that happened when my mother brought me here shortly after I turned eighteen. And the same thing that has happened to each female in the direct Horne line over the generations. I'm so sorry, darling. I know it was horrible,

329

but it's only by experiencing this that you can truly understand. Otherwise, the whole story sounds like some long-ago myth, which has no significance to our lives today.'

'It really was witchcraft then?'

'No, not witchcraft ... An injustice so great, it cries out to us from the past so that we should never forget.'

'What is it that I have to understand?'

'Now that's definitely not something I can explain while we're kneeling in someone's garden. Come on, dry your eyes, Aila. Let's find a nice quiet Dornoch café. You have a long story to hear, one you'll need to tell your own daughter someday ... When the time is right.'

On 8 March 2022 (International Women's Day), Nicola Sturgeon, the First Minister of Scotland, acknowledged an 'egregious historic injustice' and issued a formal, posthumous apology to the people accused of witchcraft in Scotland between the sixteenth and eighteenth centuries. On 24 May 2022, the General Assembly of the Church of Scotland issued its own apology: they 'acknowledge and regret the terrible harm caused to all those who suffered from accusations and prosecutions under Scotland's historic witchcraft laws, the majority of whom were women, and apologise for the role of the Church of Scotland and the General Assembly in such historical persecution.'

Author's Notes

The Last Witch of Scotland was inspired by the true story of a woman known as Janet Horne, the last person in Britain to be executed for witchcraft. The case is extraordinary and an anomaly, being both famous yet extremely poorly documented. Today, what are generally regarded as 'facts' are these:

In 1727, in the Sutherland parish of Loth, about twenty miles north of Dornoch in the Highlands of Scotland, a mother and daughter were accused of witchcraft and arrested. The daughter is said to have had a disfigurement of her hands and feet, and it was rumoured that Janet had turned her into a pony in order to ride around (witches transforming themselves into animals being a common belief). The Devil himself had shod her feet, hence the deformities. Janet appears to have been suffering from the early stages of dementia.

The case was heard by Captain David Ross, the sheriff depute of Sutherland. There is some doubt that the Dornoch court would have had the legal authority to try such a case. Despite this, the couple were found guilty and sentenced to be executed the following day. The daughter escaped that night from the Dornoch tolbooth. Poor Janet was not so fortunate. There appears to be no concrete evidence as to whether she was burned alive or strangled first.

By the 1720s attitudes were changing amongst people of influence and power in Scotland. They were increasingly looking to science; the Age of Enlightenment was beckoning even more greatly. After 1727, there are no other reported cases of execution for witchcraft in Britain and in 1736 the British government repealed the Witchcraft Act of 1563, making it no longer legal for someone to be executed for witchcraft.

One of the problems facing anyone trying to research the events surrounding the Dornoch case is that there are no surviving kirk session records for the parish of Loth for that part of the 1720s and no court records regarding the case itself. Many people had thought that the execution occurred in 1722 and, indeed, the stone that can be seen in Dornoch and which is claimed marks the site of the execution, is engraved '1722'. (This is in someone's private garden.)

However, most academics involved in this subject now believe that the real date was June 1727. Part of the evidence for this is a letter written by Edmund Burt, a well-known contractor for the government, who travelled extensively throughout the Highlands during this period. His letter was subsequently published in 1754 in a volume now entitled 'Burt's Letters from the North of Scotland.'

In the beginning of the year 1727, two poor Highland women (mother and daughter), in the shire of Sutherland, were accused of witchcraft, tried, and condemned to be burned. This proceeding was in a court held by the deputy-sheriff. The young one made her escape out of prison, but the old woman suffered that cruel death in a pitch barrel, in June following, at Dornoch, the head borough of that county.

334

Many of the stories that are attributed to this case were written a long time after the events and one has to wonder where the information came from. This includes Janet being asked in court to recite the Lord's Prayer in Gaelic, although this was a recognised test. If someone made a mistake it was taken as a sign of witchcraft. It has also been said that earlier in her life she travelled to Europe, in particular Italy, accompanying a lady from a wealthy Highland family.

There is actually a degree of uncertainty as to the name of the person who was executed. No name is given for many decades after the execution until 'Janet Horne' is suddenly mentioned and this has become the reference that has been used ever since. However, 'Jenny Horne' was apparently a generic term for a witch in early eighteenth-century Scotland so this does seem rather a coincidence.

On the other hand, there are people alive today with the surname Horne who claim to be descendants of the women executed in Dornoch, so the debate rumbles on regarding many points surrounding this case. Perhaps some documentary evidence may yet come to light that has so far been hidden.

I hope that Janet and her daughter will forgive me for the 'lives' I have created for them. I have not found any information regarding the husband, so the character of William is completely fictitious, as is Jack and his troupe. The various ministers in the novel also came from my imagination.

There is a reference in some records to the son of the surviving daughter being seen in the area of Sutherland decades after the execution and that he had a similar affliction of his hands to that of his mother. This would obviously imply a hereditary condition or other illness, rather than the dramatic fire that ends the first chapter.

When I started my research into the world of witchcraft trials I had no idea of the scale of this dark period in European history. The subject is huge and complex. The most comprehensive and recent study into the events in Scotland – The Survey of Scottish Witchcraft – was published by the University of Edinburgh in 2003. This identified 3,837 people who were accused of witchcraft between 1563 and 1736 when witchcraft was a capital offence.

The problem of missing records means that the figure is almost certainly higher. It is thought that roughly two-thirds of those identified were subsequently executed following a trial, although the lack of comprehensive documentary evidence makes the proportion difficult to ascertain with precision.

According to the survey, eighty-four per cent of those accused of witchcraft in Scotland were women (who were often denounced by other women). Despite a commonly held modern belief, midwives appear not to have been singled out, at least no more than women from other backgrounds. It was not unknown for someone to have had a reputation within the local community for being a witch for many years before a specific incident brought this to the attention of the authorities and any action was taken.

The customary practice in Scotland for executing someone sentenced to death for witchcraft was that they were strangled – 'wirreit at the stake' (garrotted is probably a more accurate description). It was the dead body that was burned, the aim being to leave nothing but ashes. In England, witchcraft was regarded as a felony and those convicted were normally hung then the body buried in unconsecrated ground.

Witchcraft and the associated trials have been studied by academics throughout Europe and much research has been carried out recently that provides new information and insights concerning events in individual countries. Most specialists in this field believe that the total figure for people executed for witchcraft in Europe throughout the whole of the era of persecutions was around 60,000, not millions as is sometimes quoted.

The authorities in some countries were more vigorous than others, although it is difficult to simply compare Scotland with them because the background, culture, religion and time period of each country are so different. According to The Survey of Scottish Witchcraft the gender split of those accused of witchcraft – roughly eighty-five per cent women and fifteen per cent men – was repeated in most parts of Europe. However, in areas such as Estonia, Russia and Finland the percentage of males was as high or even higher than that of women. In Iceland the percentage of males executed was as much as ninety per cent.

Tragically, there remain places in the world today where people (adults and children) with no connection to witchcraft are still accused and punished for this 'crime'.

Acknowledgements

The phrase 'the kindness of strangers' certainly comes to mind in regards to the people who have helped me to ensure that the background detail in *The Last Witch of Scotland* is as authentic and accurate as possible. Experts ranging from law to the breeding of Highland cattle and from theology to brewing ale in early eighteenth-century Scotland have been extremely generous in giving their time and knowledge, and in answering my many, often bizarre, questions. Any errors remaining are mine alone.

Meg Bateman, Dr Sandra Cardarelli, Abby Cox, Alexandra Dold, Professor John Finlay, Professor Julian Goodare, Dr Jamie Grant, Dr Lizanne Henderson, Dr Ciaran Jones, Don Jones, David McAllister, Caroline MacLeod, Alison MacWilliam, Kenneth A Matheson, Susan Millar, Anistatia Miller, Dr Tim Palmer, Dr Elizabeth Ritchie, The Revd Nigel J Robb, Maureen Shaw, Simon Urry.

A special thanks must go to Philip Ward as well as to David and Heather McAllister for proofreading the manuscript.

As ever, my love and grateful thanks to my wife Catherine for her constant support, wise guidance and love.

Also by Philip Paris

Historical Fiction
The Italian Chapel
Effie's War

Contemporary Fiction
Men Cry Alone
Casting Off (written as P. I. Paris)

Non-Fiction
Orkney's Italian Chapel: The True Story of an Icon
Nylon Kid of the North
Trouble Shooting For Printers